24/7

THE **SUBS** CLUB
BOOK IV

J.A. ROCK

Riptide Publishing
PO Box 1537
Burnsville, NC 28714
www.riptidepublishing.com

24/7

Cover art: Kanaxa, kanaxa.com
Editor: Delphine Dryden, delphinedryden.com/editing
Layout: L.C. Chase, lcchase.com/design.htm

ISBN: 978-1-62649-350-6

First edition
June, 2016

Also available in ebook:
ISBN: 978-1-62649-349-0

24/7

THE **SUBS** CLUB
BOOK IV

J.A. ROCK

RIPTIDE
PUBLISHING

TABLE OF CONTENTS

CHAPTER
ONE

I stood naked in the kitchen and reached into the cloth bag that used to hold Scrabble tiles. I scooped a handful of marbles then let most of them fall. Used my thumb to roll the remaining two against my palm until one dropped. I made a fist around the winner and drew it out of the bag. Slowly uncurled my fingers.

Black.

Well, fuck.

Eight white marbles in the bag. Two black. The odds had been in my favor, so why—

It doesn't do any good to think like that.

I stared at the marble.

You can handle it, whatever it is. As long as it's for her.

My breathing slowed, and the knot in my gut loosened.

I gazed around the kitchen. At the dishes Kel and Greg had told me to leave in the sink after supper. I had an overwhelming urge to wash them and put them away. Instead I got a glass from the cupboard and filled it with ice and water.

I could swap out the marbles. That occurred to me on the rare occasions I drew a black one. I could just put it back in the bag and grab a white one. They'd have no way of knowing. But I never did it.

They trusted me.

Stop earning black marbles if you never want to draw one.

I closed my hand around the marble again and took a deep breath, then walked to the living room. The mint-colored walls were covered in artsy, black-and-white photographs: Kel in Caracas, pointing at the National Pantheon, one leg kicked up behind her like a pinup girl. Greg photoshopped on the back of a buffalo in Yellowstone, his eyes wide, his mouth open in an *O*. A boudoir photo of Kel on a white wooden chair, wearing skintight leather shorts, a chest harness with star-shaped studs, and motorcycle boots. Her large breasts hung between the harness straps, and her dark hair fell in loose curls past her shoulders. That picture got taken down when they had company, a print of Dal Lake put up in its place. Another photo, this one of their courthouse wedding here in the city—both of them in jeans and T-shirts. There was one photo on the side table, stuck by a corner into a four-by-six frame overtop of Kel's cousin's senior portrait, of the three of us downtown last fall, outside some sushi place.

Kel was sprawled in the faded red armchair, and Greg was straddling her, kissing her neck. I felt just a second's envy. She glanced up as I entered, and smiled at me. That smile did what it always did—made my legs go numb, my skin turn warm, and my brain forget how words worked. She was one of those people who drew attention without demanding it. When I'd first met her, I'd had the stupid thought that she was like Waldo in a *Where's Waldo?* book—she looked at home in any surrounding, to the point where you might not notice her at first glance. But once you spotted her, you felt like you'd found what you'd been searching for. Like in a sea of shopkeepers or gladiators or vampires, *this* was the person who mattered.

She pushed Greg gently off, and he stood beside her chair while she straightened, tugging her black top down over the exposed skin of her stomach. I dropped my gaze to the carpet and knelt carefully in front of Kel's chair, holding out the glass of water. She took it and set it aside, then placed her hand on the top of my head in a wordless thank-you.

I spread my knees, because yeah, the spread knees, the lowered gaze, the hands clasped behind the back or the fingers laced behind the head . . . I liked this ritual, even though it felt kind of ridiculous. I wasn't always sure I saw much difference between ritual and cliché. My parents held fast to a couple of random Jewish customs and holidays. But even those traditions had seemed hollow to me in recent years. Echoes of what they'd once signified. *"We're not super Jewish,"* I'd heard my mother say once. *"But we'd never want to abandon our heritage."*

News flash: You can't abandon or change—*really* change, I mean—the things you inherit. Your nose or your laugh or your anxiety disorder. Your family's choices, from your great-grandmother getting on a boat to your grandmother going to *that* college—the one where all the girls "went Sapphic"—to your mother running away with *that* man. You can try to ignore your inheritance or else sculpt over top of it—a sort of cultural plastic surgery. *I'm agnostic now. I got my hair rebonded. I no longer have a separate sponge for scrubbing meat pans.* But everyone can tell you've had work done.

I placed my arms behind my back, clasped my left wrist in my right hand, and bowed my head. My hair brushed the knees of her pants. I could smell the environmentally friendly fabric softener she used. She leaned down and held her cupped hand where I could see it, and I unclasped briefly to drop the marble into her palm. Reclasped.

She gave a low whistle. Her legs shifted slightly. "Greg. Look here."

"Uh-oh." He sounded like he was trying not to laugh. He'd been doing better lately at not making fun of me when I was in trouble, and I'd been doing better at not taking it so hard when he did. He touched the back of my neck, and my skin prickled there. "That had to be the only black one in there, right? And, like, a thousand white ones." I stayed quiet but answered in my head: *There were two black marbles. One for forgetting to bring the strap. Saturday the twentieth. One for missing the signal to get the gear bag. Friday the twelfth.*

Kel stroked my hair gently. "What's the tally, Gould?"

"Two black, eight white, Ma'am."

"So you've been good this month?"

I made a face at the carpet. I hated questions like this. It was like being asked to "give your paper the grade you think it deserves" in freshmen comp class. "I've tried to be. But I could still improve, Ma'am."

I waited for a snort from Greg, but there was nothing. When I'd started playing with them a year ago, Greg had teased me about being a brownnoser. He hadn't meant it, really, but it had annoyed me. Submitting came a lot more naturally to me than it did to him, and I couldn't help my desperate—and okay, probably obnoxious—*need* to obey.

I'd never told him how much it bothered me. Rationally I knew it was no big deal. The teasing, the way he tried sometimes to get me in trouble. It just fucked with my headspace to want so bad to please Kel, and yet always be anticipating Greg's derision if I was too eager.

Maybe, deep down, he was afraid Kel wished he were more like me when he subbed. Which wasn't true at all. She loved her husband in a way I could only dream about being loved. Loved the way he challenged her, loved watching him learn to please her. And she loved using me to humiliate him. When I stayed balanced on one foot during a rope scene while he struggled and hopped around: *"Gould's doing what I told him to. Why can't you?"* Or, if she pegged him, and he grunted and *ow*-ed through it: *"Gould can take my cock up his ass without whining. What's your problem?"*

It had made me uncomfortable at first, because I assumed it hurt Greg's feelings, made him resent me. But then I saw how much he loved being taunted that way. He got off on the humiliation of not being able to obey the way I did, of being told he wasn't performing adequately. It creeped me out how well I understood that need. That desire to be found wanting, no matter how hard I tried to please. To be humiliated in spite of my goodness. Or maybe *because* of it.

Kel took her hand off my head and reached for one of the two cookie tins on the table beside her. Each was filled with slips of paper. The slips in the red tin all had rewards written on them. The slips in the purple tin were all punishments. We kept a jar of black and white marbles in the kitchen, and when I fucked up, I had to put a black marble in the bag. When I went above and beyond, I put a white marble in. At the start of each of our weekends together, Kel made me draw a marble to determine whether I'd be punished or rewarded. At the end of the month, she emptied the bag and we started again.

"You've been very good," she said quietly. "But I have to say, I'm excited for the chance to punish you. I almost never get to."

I didn't answer. When she held the purple tin out to me, I rummaged in it and pulled out a slip of paper. Handed it to her without looking. My heart was thudding.

Relax. It'll please her to do this to you. Whatever it is.

In my fantasies, I let her do anything to me. I let her hate me, let her terrify me, let her make me feel subhuman. She used me any way she wanted, with absolutely no regard for my feelings, and I took it all until I broke, until I really was *nothing*.

In reality, I started pissing myself over a fucking black marble.

I studied the shadows in the pile of the carpet while I waited for her to unfold the paper. Tried not to think about floor germs. My OCD was a halfhearted variety, Dave always said. I didn't like watching odd-numbered TV channels, but odd numbers in general didn't bother me. I had to pull the loops of bootlaces until they were perfectly even, but the laces on sneakers weren't an issue. I'd massage or lick Kel's feet no problem, despite the fact that feet were objectively filthy, but then get weird sometimes about sitting on the floor.

I could see Greg's shoe and khaki pant leg off to the side, and I wanted, for a second, to press closer to him. I remembered the night they'd had me sit at their kitchen table and write out the list of rewards and the list of punishments. Remembered Kel checking my work, praising my ideas for punishments even though they were nothing like what I really wanted to write. I kept all my worst ideas to myself and instead wrote down things that sounded safe. It had been Greg who'd helped me come up with rewards when I'd been too embarrassed to ask for anything beyond "Getting to come."

"Oh, look at *this*," Kel said, like she was unwrapping a gift. "We've got the ol' T & D." She nudged my chin up with her knee. "How long, babe?"

"All weekend, Ma'am." As if I could have made myself give any other answer.

Greg touched the back of my neck again. "Aw, you're torturing her. She loves seeing you come."

Kel didn't break eye contact with me. She smiled. I couldn't think of anything clever to say. When I was playing, my sense of humor went the fuck out the door. I saw the way Greg and Kel joked with each other during scenes, but for whatever reason, submission was still Super Serious Business for me.

Because I genuinely just fucking loved doing what I was told. Without protest, without jokes, without anything more than a *Yes, Sir* or *Yes, Ma'am*.

"I do like seeing him come." Kel leaned back. "But I also like seeing him struggling not to." She raised one bare foot and pressed her toes against my rising dick.

I wanted to look down—I still had trouble keeping eye contact when something felt good—but forced myself to hold her gaze. She bounced my balls up and down on her big toe. I didn't make a sound, but my breathing started to quicken. "We're going to Riddle tonight. So it'll be fun to torture him there."

I checked out for a moment, until the initial wave of nerves had passed. The club meant people watching me. Whispering about me— the old-timers getting the newbies up to speed. *Yeah, Gould used to date that guy who got killed here. He's the one who beat the shit out of Bill Henson. Then he helped run that review blog that pissed everyone off. Now he's GK and Kel's new toy.* The gossip had died down over the past year, but it hadn't gone away completely. I was pretty sure even my friends still talked behind my back.

Once, I'd been part of a group of five. My friends and I had met in our early twenties and started doing almost everything together. I mean, we just *worked*. There was Dave, our ringleader: charming but completely without a filter. Miles was slightly older than the rest of us—uptight, intellectual, almost aggressive in his maturity. Kamen was our resident dude-bro—incredibly sweet, not super bright, but open-minded almost to a fault.

Then there was me, and I didn't know what the fuck I was.

And there'd been Hal, who was all the things others said he was: reckless, hilarious, immature, a jackass. Hal and I had dated for a year, and I'd seen just how reckless he could be. How hilarious, and how much of a jackass. I'd fallen in love with him, and eventually, unable to handle his unreliability—among other things—I'd broken up with him. Just over a year later, he'd done a bondage scene in one of Riddle's playrooms with Bill Henson, a dom who'd left him tied up, alone, with a loose rope around his neck. The rope had—allegedly—caught on a section of the bench they were using and had pulled tight, strangling Hal. The DM had been in another room at the time. No one had noticed until it was too late.

It had been three years, and I couldn't even . . . *Still*. Still, I couldn't think about it without something coming loose inside my brain. The idea that Bill could have been that careless was inexcusable to me. He'd been tried for second-degree murder—no alternative charges like manslaughter or negligent homicide—and had been acquitted. And then last year, Kel and Greg had made the controversial choice to reinstate his membership to Riddle after supervising him through months of kink education and safety workshops. It had made me fucking *furious*. No legal consequences for Bill, and apparently not much in the way of social consequences either.

My friends and I had protested Bill's reinstatement at Riddle by starting the Subs Club, an organization dedicated to improving safety in our community. Except we'd—*I'd*—gotten a little carried away in suggesting we set up a blog to review local doms. After that all blew up in our faces, we'd let the Subs Club evolve into a discussion group instead. Which felt about as effective as when my grandpa used to let me sit on his lap in the driver's seat of his stationary sports car and pretend to drive. I sat behind my computer and blogged, and for what? To bring Hal back? To change the world? Bullshit.

And even the blog seemed to have fizzled out over the past couple of months. Sometimes I wasn't sure my friends remembered that the club had originally been an attempt to revolutionize the community, to get justice for Hal. On the rare occasions we still assembled, we were no more revolutionary than a book club meeting.

Honestly, the best I'd felt about the whole thing was when I'd gone to Bill's house shortly after the trial and landed a few good punches. That, at least, had been *active*.

"But you would never do anything like that," Dave had repeated the day he'd picked me up from the police station. *"You wouldn't. I know you wouldn't."*

My knuckles had been covered in dried blood, and I'd wanted to shake him and say, *But I did.*

It *was* almost like it had happened to someone else. Except that the consequences had been very real. Having my friends look at me like I couldn't be trusted. Being served a protective order three weeks later: I wasn't allowed within five hundred feet of Bill. Which was fucking fine by me, since I never wanted to see him again. But it was the only legal trouble I'd ever been in, and it had scared me.

"What time are we going?" Greg's voice jerked me back to the present.

Kel glanced at the clock on the mantle. "In about an hour. I want to have some fun here first." She refocused on me. "Eyes down," she ordered softly.

I dropped my gaze immediately.

"On the rug, please, and lie on your back."

I got on all fours and crawled to the braided rug in front of the fireplace. I stretched out, spreading my arms and legs. Kel snapped her fingers twice, which was Greg's signal, not mine, so I relaxed. Greg walked over to her and bent so she could whisper in his ear.

"Yes, Ma'am," he said quietly when she was done. He straightened and walked out of the room.

Once he was gone, Kel rose from the chair and stepped toward the rug. She knelt and leaned over me, and the ends of her hair brushed my stomach. I shivered. I wasn't sure where to look, so I just kept looking at her, because it was difficult not to. I had no fucking idea why someone as beautiful as Kel was interested in someone like me.

She traced a line down my chest with one finger. "I've been waiting all week to see you like this."

I flexed my feet. Tease and denial was an easier punishment for me to handle than physical pain. Except she'd barely touched me, and I was already hard. And if I kept looking at her eyes—hazel, deep-set, lined in black—I was a goner.

She ran her finger up my dick. I tensed, my knees bending slightly before I caught myself.

"Gonna blue-ball you all weekend." She leaned down to kiss me.

It was like I forgot, between kisses, how good they could be. My stomach dipped as her lips touched mine, and I almost raised one hand to run it through her hair. *You don't touch her without permission.* Her mouth was citrusy from lemon breath mints, and I could taste vanilla lip balm for a second before her tongue slid over mine and stopped all thoughts beyond *Don't come, don't come.*

Greg returned then, but Kel didn't break the kiss. I closed my eyes, tipped my head back, and let her explore my mouth. When she finally did lift her head, I was panting.

Greg knelt beside her. "Oh boy." He was looking at my swollen dick and shaking his head like it was a busted pipe or something. "It's gonna be a long weekend, huh?" He glanced at Kel. "You're not even gonna help him out with a cock cage or anything?"

"Nope." She held out a hand to him without turning away from me.

Greg handed her a coil of soft rope, a pair of yellow shorts. A collar, a leash. And a feather.

FML.

He set a pair of emergency shears on the end table and knelt beside us to watch.

Kel pulled me up and sat a few inches behind me, putting her legs out on either side of mine.

She picked up the rope, pulled it through her hand, and then started rigging a harness. Simple and not too tight—just a series of diamonds that wound around my torso but didn't trap my arms, didn't really bind me. As she worked, her nails scraped my skin, sending tiny jolts of pleasure through me. I concentrated on the smoothness of the rope, the pattern she was making. I tried not to look down at my body. Just wanted to pretend I looked as hot as I felt.

Eventually she urged my hips up and brought the end of the rope between my legs, then made a knot that rested just behind my balls. Shit. She'd done this one to me before—made me walk around with that knot rubbing the skin there, not quite touching my asshole or my balls. She tied the end to the back of the harness and helped me lie faceup again.

The harness relaxed me, made me feel held. She'd positioned the knots in the back so they dug in just below my shoulder blades and on either side of my lower spine. It actually felt good.

She tugged the front of the harness. "Who do you belong to, Gould?"

I opened my mouth to say, *You, Ma'am*, but hesitated.

For a year, our relationship had been just what I needed. The two of them had mentored me, helping me explore my obsession with obedience, sharing their experience and knowledge with me. I submitted to Kel and alternated between submitting to Greg too, and helping Kel top him. I'd learned a lot, and there was no pressure to commit, or to support them on some deep, emotional level. They had each other for that.

But something had happened over the past couple of months. This small but persistent voice in my head had started asking for *more*. Deeper submission. An opportunity to serve them for longer periods of time. She said things like "my boy" and "you belong to me"—phrases that were absolutely loaded for me—but she didn't mean them. I was hers for a few hours on a Friday night. A long weekend here and there. But I didn't *belong* to her.

"Gould?" Kel prompted. "Are you paying attention?"

I flinched, embarrassed. "I belong to you, Ma'am," I said, with an edge I hadn't intended.

She paused and gave me a look. Not angry or confused. Just thoughtful. She didn't comment further.

She picked up the feather first. Dragged it over my left nipple. My breath caught, and it was a few seconds before I could let it out. My skin was super fucking sensitive to begin with—I'd once had an allergy test come up positive for everything but dogs and tomatoes—and between the cool air of the room, the heat in my balls, and that feather lighting up every nerve it touched, I was in serious danger of losing control. I focused on her face. The slight curve of her mouth as her gaze followed the feather's trail. She ran the tip of the feather around my navel, then up and over my right nipple. I stayed silent. Watched her smile grow, partially hidden by the curtain of dark hair.

She turned to Greg. "You can play with him too. Since you've been a good boy today."

Greg looked down at me. Picked up the leash and stroked the leather loop down my inner thigh. I curled my toes. Kel continued with the feather, zigzagging it down my chest, bumping over the rope. It was all I could do to keep my hands and legs against the carpet, to keep my hips from rocking as Greg touched the loop to my balls. He flipped it lightly against the underside of my shaft. I arched off the rug, just for a second. He grinned and bumped Kel with his shoulder. "You ought to punish him for breaking position."

I gave him a very subtle middle finger.

He did a mock jaw-drop. "*Oh*. Definitely punish him."

She turned to him. "And to think I just said you were being a good boy. Here you are telling me how to top."

"No way!" he protested. "Did you see what he just did?"

"Did you hear what I just said?"

He ducked his head, still grinning. "Sorry, Ma'am." He shook his head at me, and I offered him the slightest of shrugs.

Kel snapped her fingers twice at him. "You can go stand in the corner. Pull your pants and shorts down."

He rose slowly. "Which corner, Ma'am?"

She nodded at one by the fireplace. "You can stand there on display until you're ready to behave."

"Yes, Ma'am." He headed to the corner, undoing his belt as he went. There was a time he would have argued, tried to slick-talk his way out of it, like I'd seen Dave do when he was in trouble. When I'd started playing with them, she was working with him on recognizing the subtle ways he sometimes undermined her authority. He didn't do it to be a dick, exactly—he just knew her soft spots and seemed as compelled to take advantage of them as I was compelled to obey her.

Kel flipped the feather around. She placed the almost-sharp quill on the tip of my left nipple and pressed slowly. I grunted and tried to keep breathing.

"And you," she said quietly to me. "Stay in position."

"Sorry," I whispered. She kept pressing until I made a stifled choking sound, and then she withdrew and circled the quill around the base of my nipple. I shook with the effort of holding still. Her breasts hung close to my face, and for a moment all I could think was *ZOMG tits tits tits tits . . .*

"Where are my eyes, Gould?" She didn't raise her voice, and I could hear the amusement as well as the firmness.

I met her gaze quickly.

She took my hand and pulled it toward her. Slid it under her shirt until I was cupping one heavy breast. *Fuck yes. Please.*

She closed her eyes as I worked two fingers under the wire of her bra and stroked the soft, slightly damp undercurve of her breast.

I pushed my other fingers under the wire, pushing the bra up, grazing her nipple with my thumb. Her breathing grew harsher, and she arched her back. She reached under her shirt and caught my wrist. Placed my arm back on the floor.

"Greg. Come here," she murmured.

Greg came to kneel again, beside and a bit behind her. His pants were still down, and his dick stuck out, hard and dark. His black hair, which had been combed back for work, had started to fall forward in little gelled waves. He was half Kashmiri and a quarter Cherokee, and was damn proud of being "both kinds of Indian." And he definitely knew how handsome he was.

"Touch me," she whispered to him.

He looked at her with so much love that a pang went through me—longing and confusion. I'd never counted on feeling so much affection for either of them. For both of them.

"How, Ma'am?" Greg asked.

She placed one of his hands on her breast the way she had with me. Then she lifted her hips and guided the other between her legs. While I watched, he massaged her breast, and she rubbed against the hand between her legs, her hips pumping in a slow, even rhythm. He kissed the side of her neck, and she turned toward him, smiling, her hair disheveled against his cheek. She reached behind her, found his dick, and began stroking it gently.

They knew each other's bodies so well. They were inelegant, almost, but it made them all the more entrancing. Like young performers whose rawness made up for a lack of polish. I sometimes felt as though I could see segments of their history intersecting like a Venn diagram, creating a center where youth and uncertainty were overlaid with a clamoring adoration of each other's bodies that masqueraded as confidence, and finally overlaid by a very sure and grown-up love.

I wanted to learn that kind of love.

She let go of his cock. Brought one arm up and bent the elbow so her palm cupped the back of his head as she rocked against him. He made small circles with his fingers on the front of her black pants. Kissed the side of her neck again as he pushed her breast up.

She winced. "Easy on the boobs. My nephew's been punching them."

Greg laughed. "You need to tell him that's no longer appropriate at his age."

"How old is he?" I asked.

Kel glanced at me. "Fifteen."

"*What?*"

She snickered as Greg nuzzled her cheek. "Kidding. He's four."

Greg set his chin on her shoulder. "Still, too old for boob-punching."

"Or not old enough." Kel rolled her eyes. "I let him do it once when he was, like, two, because it was kind of cute. And my boobs *are* huge—I could totally see why a toddler would find them fascinating. But now . . . ugh."

I don't even know your nephew's name. The thought hit me hard. I wanted to believe I'd do just about anything for her, and yet . . .

Can you really care about her when you hardly know her?

Greg went back to stroking her breasts, more gently. I watched her eyes fall shut, watched little furrows appear between her brows. I made a soft noise—didn't mean to, but they both looked at me. Her eyes flashed, dark and lovely.

"You wanna watch me come?" she whispered.

I nodded. *So fucking much.*

I just wished I could be the one to make it happen.

She sped up the motion of her hips while Greg continued to touch her. Suddenly her chin dipped, and her hair brushed my chest again. Her soft cries rose in pitch, and she ducked her head lower. Her hips stopped moving. With one final half pant, half whimper, she went still.

My balls ached, and all it would have taken to get me off was a hand on my dick. Luckily, neither of them tried it. Kel took a moment to recover, then sat up, her focus on me. I tried to look at the ceiling.

Kel ran a hand down my chest, almost to my groin, and I tensed until my thighs shook with the effort of not coming. She gripped the rope between my legs and pulled the knot hard against my taint. An ache started low in my gut, then spread, and a strange sensation, half faintness and half pleasure, took over my body. She pulled more firmly, and I choked back a gasp.

I closed my eyes. She ran her fingertips up and down my chest until I relaxed. Forgot about the room, forgot about my dick, and just focused on her touch. She let go of the rope.

"You liked watching that?" she asked. "Open your eyes and answer me."

I opened my eyes, my mind hazy, my head pounding. "Yes, Ma'am. I liked it."

She didn't take her gaze off me. "Greg, would you get us some water, please?"

Greg rose. "Yes, Ma'am. May I pull my pants up?"

"No. And stay gone awhile."

"Yes, Ma'am." He left the room.

Supporting my head, Kel used the harness to haul me up so I was kneeling, facing her. She stroked my hair, and I stared back at her, my thoughts so hopelessly jumbled for a moment that I was terrified of being asked a question and literally not being able to respond.

But she waited. Pushed her fingers into my white-boy 'fro so she could rub my scalp. Pleasure unwound through me, individual threads of it that seemed connected to the movement of her fingers. I could disappear into subspace faster than anyone I knew. Could lose myself in any kind of repetition—a voice, a touch, an action. My mom used to put on classical music in the nursery and come in later to find me lying in the crib, staring up at the ceiling like I was in a trance. Said she'd hear me on the baby monitor, babbling along softly to Bach. Unfortunately, it hadn't given way to any real musical talent—except for a brief stint playing the police sergeant in *The Pirates of Penzance* in Hebrew school.

"Gould?"

I didn't answer.

She tugged firmly on a handful of hair, and that helped me focus. "What was that about?"

"What, Ma'am?"

"'Who do you belong to?' You gave me the weirdest look."

I'd never played with anyone as perceptive as Kel. I'd played mostly with guys until two years ago, and they'd rarely made an effort to read into the things I *didn't* say. Plenty of doms, male and female, had gotten irritated with me for not communicating very well. Kel didn't get annoyed. But she did call me out when she thought I was holding back.

I looked at the carpet. In a pool of lamplight, I could make out uneven vacuum tracks.

"No," she said.

I glanced up again. "I don't know. I got distracted."

I'd rather take a correction for not focusing than try to explain, and she knew that. "We're not through talking," she whispered, tugging my hair again.

I nodded. I'd spent so much time searching for a kind of dominance that fit me, that I almost hadn't recognized it once I'd found it. Kel was gentle, but she didn't put up with bullshit. And I needed that. Too often, I fooled people. They assumed that since I wanted to obey and *appeared* to obey, they didn't have to push me. But if they didn't get after me, I'd feed them all kinds of crap. Tell them whatever I had to in order to get them to leave me alone, let me sink into the privacy of my mind.

Sometimes my life felt like it was divided between seeking that privacy, and feeling incredibly lonely because so many people were quick to grant it to me.

Greg entered the room again with clothes tucked under his arm and a glass of water in his hand. He stopped at the end table to grab the still-full glass I'd brought Kel earlier. Gave that to Kel, dropped the clothes on the back of the couch, then stepped toward me. I reached for the second glass, but he surprised me by cupping the back of my head and holding the glass to my lips so I could drink. Kel had assigned Greg and me goals over the past few months. I was supposed to open up more—to Greg, not just Kel. Greg was supposed to be less hesitant about touching me. He did a pretty good job in general, but he still gave off a bit of a *But I'm a straight guy* vibe when he was asked to handle me. Which in turn made me super uncomfortable, and yeah . . . Sometimes I just wished he could leave the touching to Kel.

Kel handed her empty glass to Greg and picked up the yellow shorts. "All right. I say we head to Riddle."

The shorts were Spandex and assless—exactly what you wanted to be wearing in public when you felt about as sexy naked as a Nick Nolte mug shot. I knew Kel understood—she was overweight too; we'd talked about it. My friends fancied themselves social justice warriors. So yes, I got that I was supposed to look in the mirror and love what I saw. That I set a bad example when I allowed myself to be ashamed of my body. But I couldn't fucking help it.

And my friends could pretend to sympathize, but they *didn't* know. They were all thin and in good shape. Kamen had the kind of abs that could sell you a gym membership. Dave would stand shirtless in the bathroom of our apartment, staring into the mirror and complaining about, like, a *mole*, or a single hair sprouting from his shoulder, and I'd want to punch him just a little bit. They didn't feel their stomachs paunch up every time they bent over to get fucked, or have to worry about what they looked like in assless shorts. Kamen's body hair looked badass; mine looked like someone had covered my chest in Elmer's glue and thrown a fistful of pubes at it.

You could pretend whatever you wanted, but aesthetics *did* matter in kink. The community was full of people of all shapes and ages and sizes, but it was just like every other arena of life—the young, pretty people seemed to see the most action. And the people like me got offers from doms to "put you on a treadmill."

Okay, that had only happened once. On the internet. Dave said I was paranoid. *"Look how many people at Riddle are overweight. No one cares."* What the fuck ever. I'd never bothered telling Dave that when a ripped guy approached me at the club, it was usually to ask, "Who's your friend?" and see if I'd introduce him to Dave.

I lifted my hips so Kel could finish pulling my shorts on. She tugged the front pouch, adjusting my dick and balls. "Very nice. Get on all fours."

I did. My ass felt god-awfully naked, framed by the tight nylon. The shorts fit awkwardly over the rope, and made the knot between my legs dig harder into the skin. I tried for a second to suck my stomach in, then gave up.

She stroked both cheeks. "Gorgeous."

The way she said it—every fucking time she said it—I sort of believed her.

She left me there while she changed into the clothes Greg had brought her—dark jeans and a leather vest with columns of steel rings down the panels. She talked while she dressed. "Just like we've been practicing. Serve Greg and me in any way we require. Keep alert for nonverbal cues. Have at least one conversation with someone who's not us." She grinned.

I snorted. "Yes, Ma'am."

She shrugged out of her bra and then pulled the vest on, zipping it over her breasts. "Greg. Collar him, please."

Greg knelt and buckled the collar around my neck. A flimsy, faux-leather thing they'd gotten me a few months ago. I liked it, because it was from them, and it was cute if you were into cute shit— the cheap plastic padlock had an angry cat etched on it. But I wished sometimes that I had a real collar. One that *meant* something.

Greg finished fastening the collar and stood. Handed me a pair of sweatpants. I looked at Kel, who nodded. I stood, wincing as the knot dug in again, and put the pants on. She clipped the leash to the collar and led me to the laundry room, where she put a large overcoat on me. She only fastened two of the buttons. We headed out to the garage.

CHAPTER 2
TWO

U sually at eleven on a Friday night, Riddle was packed. But it was February and the weather was lousy, and the main lounge was fairly clear when we arrived. The music was quiet, even in Chaos, the largest playroom. Part of me was grateful for the emptiness—the fewer people watching me walk around in assless shorts, the better. But there was a certain anonymity in a crowd that I missed.

"GK!"

I turned as a woman approached Greg. Everyone at Riddle called Greg "GK." It had taken me some time to get used to using his first name. Greg and Kel stopped to talk for a few minutes. I stood there, my gaze tracing the slack leash between Kel and me, trying to remember who the woman was. While I'd been a member of Riddle almost since it opened, Kel and Greg and I had run in different circles before we'd started playing together. I was getting better at learning their friends' names, but there were a *lot* of names to keep track of. Fewer, I supposed, since Hal. Riddle had lost a good chunk of its membership over the past two and a half years, including a handful of people who'd claimed to be Kel and Greg's close friends.

BellaSade was leaning in the doorway to Chaos. Bella wasn't known for her enthusiasm, but we'd always gotten along well. She gave me what passed for a smile. I checked the club, as I always did, for any sign of Bill. Kel and Greg swore he never came here anymore, but what if he decided to make an exception? I noticed that despite the sparseness of the crowd, there was a DM stationed at each playroom. Before Hal, one DM, maybe two, would circulate through the whole club. Now three of them stood like museum guards in the doorways, silently watching the mostly empty rooms.

My friends and I used to come here together a lot. They could all stroll in and find play partners within minutes, despite the purported heterosexuality of ninety percent of Riddle's clientele. We'd enter as a group, sit at the dry bar, and have a soda together. Then they'd go off with their chosen partners, leaving me to talk to Regina or whoever was bartending. Regina, who loved to play matchmaker, would try to introduce me to potential doms, but I usually bolted before they could ask me to do a scene.

Eventually I'd head over to the bookshelf in the lounge and read the dust jackets I already knew by heart. Or I'd hide in the coatroom under the pretext of checking my phone. Or I'd play this game I'd been playing with myself since high school. I started with one image: a wasteland or a jungle or a beach. A room in a fortress. An opulent dinner party. I placed myself there, and then started walking. It was kind of like a first-person video game. I'd hack through the jungle vines or crawl across the desert or make my way up a massive staircase. Occasionally I'd encounter people—feral children or zombies or hostile royalty—but the most important thing about the game was that I never let myself stop and think. Whatever appeared in my mind, I just had to go with it, just had to keep telling the story. Buildings crumbled, forests went up in flames. I fell through the ice and ended up in some sea monster's underwater lair. And I kept going.

It had been an awesome distraction when I was a teenager, carrying me away from algebra lectures or the cacophony in the halls between classes. Now that I was an adult, it seemed pathetic. I saw how I used it to deflect human interaction. To space out during conversations or work meetings or scenes. Or sex.

The woman whose name I didn't know walked away. Kel left Greg to put our gear suitcase on the racks while she led me to the coatroom. She unclipped the leash. Unbuttoned my overcoat and slid it off, helped me out of my sweats, then hung everything up. Stepped back and looked me over. "How are you feeling?"

"Okay."

She smiled slightly. "Is that much of an answer?"

I snorted. "Sorry. Uh . . . I'll be all right in a few minutes." I couldn't get my shoulders to relax.

She reached out and traced the rope diamonds over my chest. "Does this help?"

"Yes, Ma'am." The harness did help. So did the collar. What would have been really fucking awesome right about then was a blindfold.

She gazed at me a moment. If I were less of a coward, I'd have asked if I could kiss her. If I could run my fingers over the soft skin of her cheek and smooth her hair over her shoulder. But I never made the first move.

Behind Kel, the curtain parted and a rope top named Rachel ducked in. She was completely naked and holding a silk robe. "Sorry," she whispered. She grabbed a hanger and hung up the robe. It immediately slid off the hanger. "Shit." She picked it up off the floor and tried again, twisting sections of it around the hanger to keep it up. She rushed out again.

How did people do it? Walk around naked like it was nothing?

Kel was still watching me. She hooked a finger in my collar and tugged until I looked at her. "Come here."

I stepped forward, and she put her arms around me. I hesitated a second, then hugged her back. She smelled fucking amazing—not flowery like a lot of women, but like a combination of coconut and leather and metal and mint. I was in love with the softness of her body, the way her breasts pushed against my chest, the chill of her vest's steel rings against my skin. I was a few inches taller than she was, but she still had a presence that made me feel like she was physically larger, stronger, and I appreciated that. She rubbed my back, sliding her fingers under a section of rope.

"You tell me if you're having trouble."

I stiffened. I always had a hard time with shit like this. I hated being so needy, and yet her reassurance meant a lot to me. It was like the old days when Dave would come find me in the club and make sure I was doing all right. I didn't *need* anyone checking up on me. But I was secretly glad when he did. We'd had a term—PDF, for "perfect dungeon friend." Someone who wouldn't cock or vag block you, but who had your back. Dave had always been my PDF.

I tightened my arms around her, and I felt this soul-deep *pull*, like I couldn't stand to lose this contact. And it wasn't just me—something about the way she held me was more intense, more sexually charged than a typical mentor hug. We let go, and she stared at me with an expression I couldn't read. She placed a hand on my chest. I looked down at her purple nails and swallowed.

You could tell her now. Tell her you'll do anything for her. Tell her she doesn't have to treat you like you'll break. That you'll dance on the bar in these fucking shorts if she tells you to. That she can use you as a footstool in front of all her friends.

"Okay?" she asked.

"Okay," I whispered.

She led me out of the coatroom and into the lounge. I kept my gaze down until we reached the bar. Greg was sitting between two empty stools, and had placed a towel over the stool to his left. I went to the stool to Greg's right and pulled it out for her. Waited until she was sitting before I went to the stool with the towel and took a seat. Regina came over to me, smiling. "Let me guess—a root beer, a Diet Coke, and a water."

Greg grinned at her. "Making it easy for him."

She laughed and put her hands over her face, shaking her head. "I know, I'm sorry. It's just slow tonight."

Regina had caught on quickly to the fact that I was expected to order for Greg and Kel when we were at the bar, and she often came right to me to take the order. Except part of what I was supposed to be working on when we were out in public was speaking up. Flagging down a server at a restaurant if we needed more ketchup or wanted to order dessert. Finding an employee in a store and asking if we didn't know where something was. Things I'd avoided doing most of my adult life.

Regina started pouring the sodas. I wondered if she counted as someone I could have a conversation with who was not Greg or Kel. Probably not. I glanced around, looking for contenders. Gang Spank was crossing from Chaos to Tranquility, wearing a bright-green T-shirt and purple briefs. Kid was so skinny it hurt to look at him. I felt bad for him, since there were barely enough people in the club tonight to get his usual spank circle going. Like, literal spanking, not jerking off. His thing was to get passed from lap to lap until his ass was so bruised it looked like it was covered in charcoal dust.

I'd never really talked to him. Maybe tonight was the night to change that.

He disappeared into Tranquility, the room where Hal had died. I turned away.

A couple down at the other end of the bar was talking softly. "He looks like a starving Ethiopian," the guy said.

"He's trans," the woman replied.

The guy shrugged. "What does that have to do with anything?"

Points for thinking being trans was no big deal. But points off for the starving-Ethiopian comment.

I'd never planned on joining the PC police. But being part of the Subs Club meant endless discussions about othering and microaggressions and off-color comments. So in my imagination, I spoke up. I told the guy that using Africa's starvation epidemic as a way to make derogatory comments about someone's appearance was not cool. *That* was the conversation I had tonight. And in an even more potent fantasy, I didn't give a shit, because the world was an unjust and impolite place, and there was nothing I could do about that.

Regina brought the drinks to me, and I distributed them—root beer for Kel, Diet Coke for Greg.

"I love your collar," Regina said to me. "That little kitty on the lock is cute."

I laughed self-consciously. "Thanks." And immediately my thoughts were on collars. Not cheap novelty collars, but *slave* collars. With padlocks you couldn't break, that had to be unlocked by your Master. Thick, wide leather collars. Thin steel bands. Elegant chains.

I wasn't sure why I'd been thinking about this stuff so much lately. I'd been content through most of my twenties to move through the kink scene without any particular MO. I didn't have specific kinks like Dave, who wanted discipline, or Miles, who wanted pain, or Kamen who wanted . . . Okay, I didn't know what Kamen wanted. From what I could tell, his dom Ryan liked dressing him up in panties and horse gear, and that did it for both of them.

And I still didn't understand exactly what I wanted. I wasn't a huge fan of pain, but I liked taking it because someone told me I had to. Being disciplined embarrassed the hell out of me, but sometimes

I needed to be embarrassed. I liked sexual and domestic service. But I guess what I was most interested in was just . . . *submission*.

The word meant different things depending on who I was with. Submission was something I could give or take away without a dom even noticing. Some of them, they made me want to give it—and so I did. Let go and just fucking disappeared into the illusion of powerlessness. Others I obeyed because I liked obeying, but in my mind, I wasn't *theirs*. Not even temporarily. I stayed in my own world, one they'd never see or know about. I was allowing, but I wasn't submitting.

Occasionally those doms noticed something was up. *"You're so quiet."* Or *"I can't read you." "I don't know if you're enjoying this." "Are you paying attention?"* Sometimes they got nervous, or frustrated, or both. Sometimes they gave me increasingly complex orders to try to engage me. Some of them hit me harder, like I was challenging them and inflicting pain was the only way to rise to the challenge. Some of them stopped the scene and tried to talk to me. But they couldn't make me come out of my head if I didn't want to. Unless the other person was someone I truly respected and wanted to obey, compliance was like scratching all around an itch without ever hitting the right spot.

"Gould?" Greg asked.

I snapped around to look at him. "Yes, sir?"

"Kel's been trying to get your attention for a while." He kept his voice quiet, and he didn't sound impatient, but my stomach dropped as I looked over at Kel and saw her empty cup.

We'd been working on silent cues—she or Greg would signal to me if they needed something rather than telling me what they wanted. But keeping her drink filled was such a basic thing that I should have been on it even without a signal. And definitely without Greg having to prompt me.

Heat spread down my neck and chest. I forced myself to meet her gaze. "Sorry, Ma'am."

Christ, it's not the end of the world. She wouldn't be mad. She'd correct me—hopefully not here—but she wouldn't be angry. But my embarrassment was out of all proportion to the situation.

I tried to signal to Regina, but she was busy with the couple at the other end of the bar. I made myself take a breath. *Calm down.*

Regina turned and saw me. Left the other couple with a little wave and came back toward me. Leaned on the counter on her elbows. "What's up?"

I made myself smile. "Could I get another root beer, please?"

"Of course." She grabbed Kel's cup and refilled it. Handed it to me. I passed it down to Kel, my throat tight.

She nodded a thank-you and took a sip of her drink.

Greg nudged me, grinning. "What do we pay you the big bucks for, huh? Don't space out on us."

I smiled back, but I couldn't get rid of the shame. And it *was* shame—my whole body was hot and my head pounded, and I was as pissed at myself for overreacting as I was about making a mistake in the first place.

I watched them both for a moment without making eye contact. Greg's cup was still almost full. There was a ring of condensation on the table, and I took my napkin and quickly wiped it up.

Kel leaned over and whispered to Greg, then stood. Passed my stool and tapped my shoulder lightly, then continued walking.

I rose, almost relieved, and followed her to Chaos.

Chaos was a room for people who liked their scenes loud and heavily accessorized. There was a padded bondage table, a dentist's chair, a huge chain spiderweb attached to the floor and the ceiling. Various cages, the infamous dildo iron maiden, and a wide, floor-to-ceiling ladder that people used for all kinds of things. There was a smaller room next door called Refinement, which was quieter and less tricked out. Then across the lounge was Tranquility, tiny and private, with just some wall hooks, a bondage frame, and the bench where Hal had died. I hadn't been in there since Hal. Not even once.

I expected Kel to go to the rack that held our suitcase. She only ever used two implements to correct me. One was a leather slapper, which was more noise than pain. It worked well, because the noise, especially if it was used in public, caused me plenty of embarrassment without actually doing more than stinging a little. The other was an evil stick—a very thin, flexible carbon rod attached to a handle. It didn't look like much, but all she had to do was bend the carbon part back, then let it fly, and it was like being branded. She'd never given me more than one stroke with that—anything more would have been overkill, and we both knew it.

But if she told me I had to take a hundred with it, I would.

Instead of going for the bag, she led me over to the dog kennel in one corner. It was my favorite part of Chaos—black wire, with a thick fleece pad inside and a blanket draped over top. The blanket could be folded down over the door to make it completely dark inside.

She placed a hand on my shoulder, and I jumped.

"Easy," she whispered.

I waited, not sure if I should speak.

She moved her hand up to the back of my neck, and I bowed my head. "If you can't focus out there, why don't you spend some time in here until you're ready to serve attentively." There was no anger in the words at all, but my throat tightened again.

"I'm sorry, Ma'am." I wanted to ask for another chance. Tell her I was ready to serve, to pay attention. Wanted to beg her, on my knees, and then have her kick me aside, force me into the cage.

"I know you are." She rubbed my neck. "And you understand what this is about, don't you?"

I nodded.

"Tell me."

"It's about focus. About staying out of my head. Not about the drink." We'd been over and over this. Early on in our time together, it had been harder for me to understand. If I got corrected after failing to get her a drink, I assumed that Kel's lack of drink was the *reason* for the correction. Which was ridiculous. Kel could get her own drink any time she wanted. The issue was that I was supposed to be attuned to her needs—anticipate them. I wasn't expected to read her mind, but I was expected to pay attention. And I couldn't do that if I was focusing inward.

"Good." She kissed my temple, then leaned down and opened the kennel. Grabbed a towel from the nearby shelf and spread it over the fleece pad inside the cage. "I'll ask Bella to keep an eye on you. Call out if you need her."

I crawled into the cage. She shut the door and latched it, but didn't pull the blanket down over the door. It would have been more of a mind-fuck if she'd left me completely alone in the dark. But Kel and Greg never left me unsupervised, even in a situation like this where I could easily have let myself out.

I watched Kel approach Bella and say something to her. Bella glanced at me and nodded. Kel returned to the lounge. I sat on the towel, focusing on the pressure of the knot between my legs, my knees against my chest.

Normally I loved confinement. It was a chance to unwind and reflect. Kel rarely used it as punishment, but in this case it was effective. I couldn't disappear inside my head, because I was too aware of why I was here. I'd lost my chance to serve. I'd lost the right to be close to Kel and Greg.

God, it was silly. Everything we did was a little silly—from the kneeling to the honorifics to the talk of "correcting," like I was a toddler whose behavior needed to be adjusted. But it all did something to my brain that was anything but laughable.

"Your whole fucking image of yourself is based on how other people see you," Hal had said once.

Maybe so, asshole, I thought to him, wherever he was. *Sometimes. Sometimes I care way too much about what people think of me. And other times I only care about what I want.*

Two people walked by the cage, talking. Their voices were familiar—the couple from the bar. The woman's high heels clicked on the tile floor. They stopped at a bench just to the right of the cage. I could see the hem of the woman's floral dress, and the guy's black pants. He was holding a bunch of colorful nylon rope at his side.

"So what are you thinking?" he asked.

"I dunno," the woman said. "Surprise me."

I shifted, trying to get into a more comfortable position.

The guy whapped the rope coil against his leg. "You want to try Bill Henson-ing?"

I froze. *What the fuck?*

"What's that?" The woman sounded suspicious.

The guy laughed. "You know. It's that thing people are doing now. Remember that guy, Bill Henson? Who killed that sub here a few years ago?"

"Ew, yeah."

"Well, it's like a thing now. You tie a rope around your partner's neck and pretend to choke them—you don't really do it, obviously. But you twist the rope until it's tight enough to scare them a little. It's called Bill Henson-ing."

The woman gave a shocked huff of laughter. "Oh my God. That is so wrong I don't even want to talk about it."

I couldn't move. Couldn't form a coherent thought.

The guy rocked back on his heels, the coils of rope swinging. "There was all kinds of creepy shit about it online. People would write about their Bill Henson-ing experiences. Probably ninety percent of them were made up. But someone posted a video on Fet and got in huge trouble."

"Isn't Bill Henson still a member here?" The woman sounded like she knew the answer already and was secretly enjoying this.

"Yeah, they did let him back in. Which, like, are you fucking kidding me? But I heard he got so much shit that he never comes here now."

"Good. Who would want to play with a guy who'd *killed* someone?"

"Uhhh, a ton of people," the man said. "Do you have any idea how many offers he got after that? I heard people actually wrote to him asking him to kill them. People were trying to make him into some kind of edge-play Jesus."

My stomach lurched violently.

The woman groaned. "People are fucked up. *You're* fucked up."

The guy laughed again. "Hey. *I'm* just kidding. Some people aren't."

The woman lifted one high-heeled foot to rub the opposite calf. "Well, I absolutely do not want to try Bill Henson-ing."

"Fine," he said. I heard them kiss. "If you change your mind . . ."

They walked on past the bench, her voice carrying. "That is *not* something to joke about!"

I couldn't tell if I needed to get the fuck out of this cage, or if I wanted to hide in here forever. I leaned against the bars and stared out the cage door at the empty iron maiden.

So this was where we were now. People were still talking about Hal's death, except they'd turned it into some kind of joke. Hashtag

BillHensoning. People hadn't *forgotten*—they'd just forgotten it was a tragedy. Bill was both a legend and a punch line. And Hal—Hal could have been anyone. A sacrifice, like the blond cheerleader in a slasher movie. You were never supposed to care about her—her favorite color or her college plans or her views on socialized medicine. She was just there to die so you could feel a momentary thrill. So you could laugh with your friends later about the way her blood-covered tits had bounced as she tried to run away.

I could have been anyone too. The victim's ex-boyfriend. A fine prop for a tragedy, but no one of any real importance.

I closed my eyes and tried to lose myself. I started with one image: A bombed-out, four-story industrial ruin under a smoggy night sky. I walked up a wrecked wooden staircase. All around me, graffiti curled like worms around the giant gouges in the walls, and occasionally streetlight caught a rat's fur as it scuttled through the rubble. I kept climbing, and on the third staircase, a board gave out, and I fell back down to the first floor, landing hard on a pile of broken concrete and wood. A rope appeared from a ragged hole in the ceiling above me, a wide loop in it, and I wasn't sure whether I was supposed to hang myself with it or slip it around my waist like a vaudeville performer to be hoisted up.

I grabbed the rope, wrapped it around my bloodied arm, and immediately I was being pulled up through the hole in the ceiling, up through a matching hole in the third floor, and through broken windows and wall gashes, I could see the dirty city, the moon, streetlights, and then I was hauled through the hole in the fourth floor, broken planks scraping my back like claws. I was standing on the top floor, looking around. Expecting to see the person who'd been holding the rope.

But the rope was gone, and the fourth floor was empty, and that was how it was supposed to be. I was searching for someone just out of reach, someone I wanted to make suffer. And yet somehow I was always the one who ended up bleeding.

CHAPTER

THREE

I woke in the night facing Kel, Greg's warmth at my back. Yellowish streetlight poured in through the open curtains. I wasn't sure why I'd woken, but then I rolled to look up at the ceiling and saw, out of the corner of my eye, the glow of Greg's phone as he tapped away on it.

The night came back to me in fragments. Kel and Greg had come to get me from the cage. I'd stayed focused on them the rest of the night, ordering drink refills, making small talk with whoever they introduced me to, even as the term "Bill Henson-ing" chewed a hole in my brain. They'd thought I was upset about being corrected. Kel clearly felt guilty about it, and had assured me it was over and forgotten. Greg had socked me lightly on the shoulder and said, *"It's not a big deal."*

Back home, Greg had treated us to Freddie Mercury impressions. Freddie was Greg's ultimate man crush and "the best Indian since Gandhi." Greg actually had a decent voice, and he'd kept Kel laughing until she finally shushed him. *"Are you thirty-five or twelve? The neighbors are gonna call the cops."*

I'd stayed quiet. I hadn't known how to talk to them about Bill Henson-ing. The three of us didn't discuss Bill when we were together. Pretended like Dumbo wasn't blundering around the room, shitting on the furniture. And suddenly, I'd been completely not okay with that. How *could* I want to serve these two? When they'd given Bill a second chance he didn't deserve, when they couldn't even say his fucking name in front of me? When Hal had died on their watch? What was *wrong* with me?

That happened sometimes: I'd get these flashes of anger toward them. I just had to wait this one out, and it would go away.

In bed, Kel had played with my dick, trying to tease me to the edge without letting me come. But I couldn't stay hard. Finally she'd taken me aside and tried to find out what was wrong, and I'd remained silent in that stubborn, frozen-smiled way that had worked my whole life to get people to leave me alone. Eventually, it had worked on her, and she'd suggested we all go to sleep.

I was hard now, though. And horny as fuck. I just kept repeating *Bill Henson-ing* in my head, and my anger and frustration translated to a painful level of arousal. I groaned softly.

Greg looked over, face blue from the light of the screen. "Hey."

"Hey," I mumbled.

He glanced back at his phone and tapped the screen. "I wake you up?"

I shook my head, yawning. Under the blankets, I moved my hand to my groin. I wasn't planning to touch myself, exactly. I just wanted to . . .

He set his phone on the night table, then rolled to face me. "You okay?"

I turned my head toward him. His eyes, even in the dimness of the room, were something else. Huge and dark. Thick lashes. *"Everyone tells me my eyes make me look 'nice,'"* he'd told me once. *"I'm like, 'How do you know I'm not a killer? Ted Bundy, he had nice eyes.'"*

I felt him. A lot of people said I had a "sweet" face. That I looked "kind." Sweet and kind weren't bad things to be, they just . . . the occasional "badass" would have been cool. "Chiseled." "Rugged." "Too much man to handle."

Riddle had only been open a year and a half when Hal died. I'd known Greg and Kel vaguely before the incident. They'd always said hi if they were at Riddle when my friends and I came in. Greg used to joke that my group was "trouble."

A couple of months after Hal's death, Riddle had hosted a support group. Brought in a kink-friendly grief counselor and made it free for anyone who wanted to attend, even nonmembers.

I was sure it would be stupid, but my friends and I weren't talking much, and I couldn't explain to my family what I was going through. They read the news articles and kept making comments about Hal's "proclivities." Pressed me for information about whether I'd known Hal was "into that stuff." So I'd gone to the support group.

Halfway through the session, I'd started shaking and couldn't stop. The participants on either side of me turned to stare, and the woman to my left tried to put her hand on my shoulder, and I'd jumped back so fast I'd knocked my chair over. The counselor, who had skin that sort of hung on either side of her chin dimple like miniature jowls, said something I didn't hear. I headed for the front, ignoring the voices around me. But at the exit, I apparently forgot how doors worked. I stared at it for a moment, like it was a dead end in some complicated maze, and then I heard Greg's voice.

"You okay?"

The answer was no, and it was a stupid question, but it had cut through my panic. I looked at him, and he seemed kind of . . . *ready*, like he thought I might attack or something, but his eyes were so— sorry, Greg—nice. I'd told him he had nice eyes, because I would rather have given him anything other than an honest answer to his question. Then I'd started laughing. Hard.

To his credit, he hadn't called the white coats. He'd just smiled and said, "My mom calls them pretty. Which is, like, exactly what a guy wants to hear, right?"

The part of me that was, at the time, finding political correctness increasingly fashionable wanted to argue that men could be pretty too. And the rest of me knew *exactly* what he was talking about. I didn't want to be *sweet* or *gentle* or *kind*. I'd laughed harder.

Greg had stuck his hands in his pockets. "You want me to get you a cab or something? Or you want to try to finish the session?"

I'd stopped laughing. "I want to leave."

"Do me a favor? Tell me you're going to a friend's? Or your family's? You don't look like you should be alone."

"I'm going to a friend's." I'd wanted him to stop talking. Wanted him to let me disappear. But I'd also liked his voice in that moment. It was different from his "Heeeeyyy, here comes trouble!" voice when my friends and I came into the club together.

"You're bullshitting me, right?"

"Yeah."

"Okay. What if you hung out with me for a few minutes? Until you calm down some? We don't have to go back to the circle jerk of sadness."

I couldn't tell if he was being an asshole or my fucking hero. I'd kind of liked that he was both.

"Do I have to talk about my feelings with you?"

He grinned and shook his head. "Nah. Unless you want."

"Fuck off." In my mind, it was unforgivable, saying that to someone who was being nice to me. Someone I hardly knew. But he just smiled again. Took me into Chaos, and we sat on the giant padded table.

"Why'd you have it here?" I'd demanded.

"Huh?"

"This grief circle jerk. Why have it in the building where he died?"

He'd shrugged. "Because it's the only public space we have. And Kel thought it would be cathartic."

I tried to shake the memory off.

Greg's arm snaked under the covers until his hand rested on my thigh. Then he slid it higher, his fingers brushing my dick. "Mmm. No wonder you can't sleep."

I didn't speak. Didn't ask. Didn't beg. He made a loose fist around my cock. It hurt a little when he started jerking me off dry. But tonight I liked it. I lifted my hips slightly, wanting to push into his hand. I whimpered, barely a sound at all, but he heard it and laughed softly.

"Shh. Don't wake her."

I knew then that he wasn't gonna stop until I came, and I didn't care. I wanted the release.

"Shh," he repeated, and I realized I was panting.

Usually, nobody had to remind me to be quiet. But something about this—the secrecy of it, the thrill, made me want to moan, or maybe laugh. I clamped my legs together, then spread them again when he whispered fiercely in my ear, "Open up."

It was probably fucked up to think this way, but being ordered around by a straight guy just fucking *did* it for me. I always felt a power imbalance when I interacted with straight men. They had this privilege, this institutionalized authority they couldn't even see. Part of me was always waiting for them to make me feel inferior in some way. Part of me *wanted* them to, even though I hated that they could. I hadn't even been bullied that much as a kid—not more than anyone else—but where Dave and Kamen and even Miles seemed to have no trouble being buddy-buddy with straight guys, I was always wary around them. And somehow that wariness became *Fuck me, now* when I was with Greg.

He clapped his other hand over my mouth. I closed my eyes, breathing hard against his palm. He kept working me, hooking one leg over mine to keep me in place.

"Hold still," he whispered. I tried to obey. I opened my eyes and tilted my head toward Kel. Focused on her sleeping face, the streetlight making her hair shine, casting a glow on her cheek. I thought we might actually get away with it, and I didn't *want* to get away with it. But as his hand moved faster, her eyes opened. I hummed against Greg's hand.

He took his hand away, and I figured by the way his rhythm faltered that he knew she was awake.

She watched me as I lay there, pumping my hips in time with Greg's hand, the pressure in my balls building.

Then she leaned over and kissed me.

I came hard. Greg ran his hand down the front of my left thigh, wiping cum into the hair on my legs.

Kel groped my softening dick. I flinched, but let her do it. She jerked her hand roughly up and down around the shaft. I tensed at the overstimulation, my pleasure turning to something almost like nausea.

For just a moment, I was lost, reeling. *You can put a rope around your partner's neck and scare them, and it's called Bill Henson-ing.*

People have written to him, asking him to kill them.

I forced myself to focus on where I was and what was happening.

I'd failed at my fucking black marble punishment, but who the fuck *cared* about marbles anyway, when—

Greg started chuckling. Then Kel joined in, her laugh so good-natured and sleepy that it relaxed me for a moment. She closed her eyes and groaned, punching the pillow lightly with one fist. "Gould. Get the stick and beat Greg's ass, please."

I thought she was kidding, but she nudged me with her leg.

"You really want me to?" I asked.

She smiled with her eyes still closed. "Yes. Five with the stick. Make 'em count."

"But Ma'am—" Greg started.

"Take what you've got coming."

"I didn't do anything."

"You made Gould come, and you knew exactly what you were doing."

"Technically *you* made him come."

"Technically *I* came," I put in.

She pushed her face into the pillow and said, voice muffled, "Ohhh, Greg, if you can look me in the eye and tell me you weren't trying to get Gould in trouble, I'll let you off."

"Get me off?"

She raised her head. "*Let* you off. Just try."

He leaned over me and put his face inches from hers. Silence, while I shook with laughter underneath Greg.

"I cannot tell a lie," Greg admitted after a moment. He kissed her. "I just wanted to give you a good show."

"That I wasn't awake for?"

"The end was the only part that mattered. The rest was just a lot of fapping."

She hit him with her pillow. "Gould. Five."

Greg climbed out of bed. I followed groggily, my legs weak. Stumbled to the closet. A long, flat, walnut stick hung on a nail behind Greg's dress shirts. It was heavier than it looked, and had the word *BAD* on it.

I shut the closet door. Greg was standing in the center of the room. I gave him an awkward smile he probably didn't see. I was terrible at administering punishment. I always ended up both jealous of and embarrassed for Greg. "All fours," I told him. "Ass up."

He knelt slowly in the center of the room, then put his arms out in front of him and bent forward until his ass was in the air.

"This is unjust," he announced.

I waved the stick. "You should stop trying to get me in trouble. It never goes well for you."

He and Kel both laughed.

I took a moment to stroke his ass, since I liked when they did that for me before a correction. Even in the near dark, I could see how tense he was. I lined up the stick, then drew back and struck him.

"Harder," Kel called from the bed.

"That actually was pretty weak, man," Greg agreed.

I whacked him considerably harder. He hissed.

Another, almost on his thighs. He made a strangled sound. "I regret nothing!"

I hit him again in the same place, the stick making a satisfying *thwack*. He gave a muffled protest and reached back with one hand.

"Is he rubbing?" Kel asked from the bed.

"Uh . . ." I said, watching him rub.

"Two extra," Kel ordered.

I delivered the final three strokes fast and hard. Greg yelped at each one, shifting his weight back and forth on his knees.

Kel gave a pleased sigh. "Very nice."

Greg snorted. "Yeah, for *you*."

"Come back to bed."

Greg hesitated. "Wait. Aren't you going to punish *him*?"

I went still, waiting for the answer.

"That's none of your business," Kel murmured.

"But—"

"But if you'd like ten more, by all means, keep arguing."

Greg shook his head at me. "You get away with murder." He said it affectionately, but there was an edge to his tone. Or maybe I imagined it. Listened for it because I thought it *should* be there.

I returned the stick to the closet. When I turned around, Greg was still watching me.

"It was worth it," he whispered.

"I heard that," Kel said.

He squeezed my shoulder, then wandered back to the bed. I watched the silhouette of his dick and balls swaying as he put one knee up on the mattress. He curled beside Kel. "You can't blame me, Ma'am. Can you? He's fucking hot when he comes."

"I think you're getting gayer by the minute."

"My heteroflexibility is increasing. It's all the yoga." He tugged the covers over her shoulder.

I tried to shake off my unease—disappointment?—at not being corrected. I needed Kel to be harder on me. I *didn't* want to get away with murder.

Kel mumbled and swatted at Greg as he tried to stroke her back. "I need to sleep."

"*I'm* the one who has to get up in the morning. And I'm the only one who hasn't come today."

"Oh, my whittled-down nub of a heart is breaking. Go to sleep."

I stayed at the edge of the bed, wanting to get back in the middle, but that didn't look like it was gonna happen. In that moment, I felt so fucking far from them. I watched as Greg spooned her and she sank against him with a soft sigh. *I used to have this. I had someone who'd annoy the shit out of me in the middle of the night. Someone I could banter with even while I was half-asleep.*

He was taken away from me, and you called it an accident. You said we all needed to move on. You made it sound like forgiveness is a choice, and it's not. You have to feel it, believe it, mean it.

For a second, I hated them both.

I'd tried to move on. I'd read a ton of shit online about grief and forgiveness. I'd turned to my mostly discarded faith. I knew I wasn't the only one who felt the loss: my friends, the community, Kel and Greg . . . lots of people had suffered. But sometimes I thought I was the only one who wasn't healing with time. My friends struggled with their grief occasionally, but for the most part, they'd moved on. Found relationships. Started families or new careers. And I was still stuck on one night, one thought: *Bill shouldn't have gotten away with it. He shouldn't have fucking gotten away with it.*

I crawled onto the edge of the bed and lay facing the wall. Listened to the bed creak as they shifted, the light pop of their lips as they kissed.

He shouldn't have fucking gotten away with it.

The kept kissing, and with every kiss, I repeated the words:

He shouldn't have gotten away with it.

He shouldn't have gotten away with it.

I closed my eyes.

He shouldn't have.

But he did.

CHAPTER
FOUR

I woke again to sunlight on the comforter. Greg was gone—he had an off-site meeting today, which meant a Saturday morning alone with Kel. I couldn't remember this happening before. I was suddenly nervous and excited.

Kel was facing away from me, her shoulder rising and falling gently under the sheet. I wanted to touch her. Wanted to curl against her and feel her arms around me. Wanted her to fuck me until I couldn't move. Wanted her to correct me for coming last night.

You could ask.

Fucking whatever. My brain was like some machine where you put in insignificant events and it spat them out as multi-act melodramas. Complete with *O I am slain*s and soap opera eye-darts and grief-stricken wails.

My groin was still sticky, the sheet under me a little stiff, and I felt another flash of guilt. I started to get up, inching my way down the bed. Kel made a sleepy noise but didn't wake.

I crawled out from under the covers and slipped out of the room. Went downstairs and tackled the dishes in the sink. Chopped some fruit, scrambled some eggs. Loaded up a plate for Kel. The strawberries in the fridge were kind of old, and I stared at them a moment, smiling.

Hal and I had bought out-of-season strawberries one night years ago, when we'd gone to the store to buy wine. We'd paid five bucks or whatever for a carton, because for some reason lumpy, wilted strawberries had seemed like the best idea in the world. Once we were home, we'd gotten distracted by wine and had left the strawberries out. By the time we finally remembered them the next day, they were already growing mold, which Hal said looked like gray beards.

So he'd taken a Sharpie and drawn faces on the moldy strawberries, until we had all these little bearded strawberry men. We'd forced them into different tableaus and taken pictures.

A couple of years later, I'd gotten a new laptop and lost those photos.

Oh fucking well.

That had been toward the end of our relationship. One of those increasingly rare evenings where we didn't fight. Where whatever had drawn us together in the first place came alive again, and I could almost convince myself I didn't need to break up with him. That we could work through this.

I slipped quietly upstairs and into the bedroom. Kel stirred and rolled over. Smiled, eyes half shut, eyeliner smudges under them. "Where'd you go?"

"Breakfast." I put the plate on the nightstand and sat on the bed.

"You are a miracle. I was just thinking how—" yawn "—hungry I was."

"I'm like the Dead Men of Dunharrow. Just when you think all hope is lost . . ."

"Are all your friends this obsessed with *Lord of the Rings*? Because Kamen recently compared the chili cook-off to the battle of the Pelennor Fields."

"He helped with the chili thing?" Riddle had recently entered a local chili cook-off and won, beating out Sullivan's Pub, the three-time champion. Kel had declared it proof that the club had found its footing again after a rough few years.

I wasn't sure why I was surprised Kamen had helped. He worked as a cook at the Green Kitchen, and he made damn good chili. I just hadn't heard him mention anything about the cook-off.

She scratched her scalp, tousling her hair. Put the back of her fist over her mouth as she yawned again. "Yeah, he was a lifesaver. I was gonna use my mom's old recipe, but I couldn't find it." She shrugged, as though it were no big deal, but I could see how much it bothered her.

At sixteen, Kel had lost her mom to lung cancer. It was one of the first things we'd really bonded over. I'd been skittish around her at first, convinced she couldn't possibly understand what I was going through with Hal. And then one night at Riddle she'd told me about her mom—about the funeral, where the hearse had gotten a flat tire. About how she and her mom used to fight all the time, even after her mom got sick, but how Kel had always gone to her with every problem, every curveball life threw. And I'd started to feel like maybe Kel was someone I could talk to.

"Anyway," she said. "This dom named Olympio had a good base recipe. Kamen stepped in, did this fantastic seasoning, and then added some secret ingredient at the end."

"Okay, his secret ingredient is crushed tortilla chips, and it's not a secret."

"Yeah, he did tell us what it was pretty much immediately." She reached for the plate and grabbed a strawberry. "You are literally the greatest."

I hovered by the bed. "I didn't even hear Greg leave."

She took a bite, holding a cupped hand underneath to catch the juice. "Oh my God, he woke me up at six thirty to try to get me to let him come. Or more specifically, let him come inside me. He's like a little kid on Christmas morning. Except he wants very adult things."

"You didn't let him?"

"Nerp. Sent him to his meeting with blue balls." Glanced at the plate, then at me. Furrowed her brow. "Can I feed you?"

"Uh, sure."

"Come kneel over here." She pointed to the floor beside the bed.

I stepped forward and knelt.

Kel pulled a grape off the stem and held it out to me. I leaned forward and took it in my mouth, trying not to feel weird.

She dropped the tiny piece of stem back on the plate.

"You don't have to ask," I said, as she picked up a strawberry.

She paused. "Hmm?"

"If you ever want to do something to me. You can just tell me what to do. If it's not something I can handle, I'll say so."

She nodded, not looking at me. "I just want you to have a good time."

"I always do." It was true, for the most part.

She pulled the top off a strawberry. "Last night, at the club. I didn't mean to make you feel—"

"It wasn't you," I said immediately. "I liked what you did last night. I want you to call me out when I screw up." *Aaaaaand keep going . . .*

I didn't keep going.

She shook her head. "You don't screw up. You're ridiculously *good.*"

No. No, Jesus, quit saying that. "Not always. Last night, I came when I wasn't s—"

"Oh please. Greg'll take any opportunity to stir up trouble."

"I could've said no."

"Hey, Gould?" She spoke softly. "I made my decision."

Okay. All right. Then that was that. Or that should have been that.

I nodded slowly. *But why is your decision always to believe the best of me?*

She fed me the strawberry. Dropped the top on the plate and leaned back, hands laced over her belly. "So what are we gonna do today?"

"What time does Greg get back?"

"Noon-ish." She patted the bed.

I stretched out beside her. She put a hand on my ass, and I tensed for a second, then pushed up gently against her palm.

The first time I'd slept in a bed with the two of them had been about nine months ago. I'd lain awake almost the whole night, not moving. As though I were somewhere I wasn't supposed to be, and if they woke, they'd want to know what the hell I was doing there. They'd both been very professional mentors for the first few months—they'd kept the guest room ready for me, and after we played, I'd turn in there, and they'd go back to their room. Sometimes I'd hear them having sex, or hear Kel whipping Greg. I'd sort of liked the isolation, the sense of banishment. The idea that I existed to entertain them, and when they were done with me, they would put me away. But it had also been incredibly fucking lonely.

Kel wound an arm around me and pulled me against her. Her hair smelled like coconut shampoo and drifted, thick and heavy, across my face. Her breasts were warm, the skin slightly damp, her nipples hardening as she kissed my jaw. I swallowed.

She ran her hand up my back. I went still as my dick nudged her thigh. She paused too, her breath tickling my ear. Then she shifted her hips until my dick was between her legs and I could feel the wetness there.

I closed my eyes. *Don't. Fucking. Come.*

"Go get the glass cock," she whispered. "And my harness."

I stumbled out of bed, grateful for the chance to recover. I dragged the suitcase out from under the bed and found a bottle of toy cleaner and the box that contained the glass dildo. I was about to zip the case again when I spotted a silicone ring gag. I hesitated for a second, then grabbed it too and went to the bathroom.

I set the stuff on the counter and removed the dildo from the box. It was beautiful—six inches long, clear glass with ridges on the shaft and blue and silver helixes inside. It had a circular base so it could be used as a strap-on, and a flared head. I held the glass in my hand, feeling it warm under my skin. Ran my thumb over the ridges. I turned on the faucet. Splashed some cold water on my dick, then washed the dildo and set it on a hand towel. I washed the ring gag too, a couple of times. I'd seen her use it on Greg before, and I felt a little weird about taking their toy without talking to Kel about it. But I wanted to try this.

I thought for a moment, then picked up the dildo again. Turned the water on as hot as it would go and held the glass under it for a few moments. I shook it dry, then placed it on the towel again next to the gag, took the towel by the edges, and returned to the bedroom. Kel was sitting on the edge of the bed.

I grabbed her harness and the lube from the suitcase, added those to the bundle, then pushed the bag back under the bed. Spread the towel beside her and arranged the items in a row. Then I knelt in front of her.

She touched my cheek with the back of her hand. Glanced over at the towel, and I saw her notice the ring gag.

She looked back at me, raising her eyebrows. I didn't say anything.

We'd never used gags before. There'd never been a reason to. I didn't talk if I was told to be quiet, didn't close my mouth if I was told to keep it open, didn't resist pain if someone wanted to give it to me. But I still liked restraints of any kind—liked to imagine needing them. About being so emotionally wrecked or in so much physical agony that I couldn't control myself, couldn't stop crying or struggling.

I held my breath as she picked up the gag. She didn't speak, just held my jaw and placed the silicone ring in my mouth. It felt bigger than it had looked—I couldn't figure out how my teeth were supposed to fit around it. She buckled the strap around my head, and then stroked my cheek again. "Very nice."

I tried swallowing. I felt like a blow-up doll, my mouth stuck in a permanent *O*. The straps dug into my cheeks, and I moved my tongue, trying to find a place for it to rest comfortably.

She stood and nodded at the harness and dildo. I picked them up, untwisted the straps, and put the dildo through the steel ring on the front of the harness. Held the harness open so she could step into it. She steadied herself with a hand on my shoulder. I adjusted the strap around her waist, trying to ignore how close my face was to her crotch, how much I wanted to be forced to go down on her for as long as she wanted . . .

Spit was starting to run down my chin and neck, and I wiped it with the back of my hand.

"Signal?" she asked.

I held up the non–spit-covered hand, palm facing her.

"Good."

I put my hand down. Sat back on my heels until my mouth was level with the dildo.

She cupped my cheek gently and guided the dildo into my mouth. The ridges in the glass made a soft rasping noise against the silicone ring. She only put a couple of inches in at first, giving me time to get used to it. I ran my tongue around the tip, exploring the different textures of the head and the shaft. She pushed in deeper, and I tried to swallow. It was a strange feeling—I wanted to wrap my lips around the dildo, but I couldn't because of the gag. I didn't even have that small illusion of control.

She threaded her fingers through my hair. The glass was heavy and warm on my tongue. I licked across the ridges, gagging slightly as she forced it all the way in. She started to thrust. I flinched through the first few seconds. Listened to her breathing get faster, fighting the urge to use my tongue to push back against the dildo, to try to control the speed and angle. After a moment, I relaxed and opened up, let her fill my mouth.

She moaned softly, tugging my hair. I kept my wrists crossed behind my back and tried to stay balanced while she fucked my throat.

Her fingers twisted, wrenching a fistful of hair, and my dick jerked. The glass head skimmed along the roof of my mouth as she pumped faster. She stroked my cheek with her other hand, the movement gentle and easy. I'd never met a top who could do that quite like she could—maintain different rhythms simultaneously.

She pulled out and bent me over the bed. I could hear her lubing the dildo and tried not to tense up. Ass play was far from my favorite thing in the world, and I'd been semi-fasting since last night to prepare for the possibility that she'd want to fuck me.

She was careful—she always was. The glass was still slightly warm underneath the coating of lube, and I was surprised by how easily the head went in. She stopped with the dildo halfway inside me and waited for my nod. Then she shoved the rest of the way in.

A cry caught in the back of my wide-open throat. I closed my eyes, trying to bite down on the ring as the burn spread through my body.

I was drooling all over the comforter. Her thrusts were slow but firm, each one lifting my hips slightly. Once the initial pain faded, I started getting hard again. She sped up, and the friction between my dick and the bed put me back in the danger zone.

OhfuckshitnononofuckfuckingyesGodshitno . . .

I moved my hips back to meet her on her next thrust. She gave a low whimper, and then she just went at it—short, sharp strokes that knocked the breath out of my lungs. I gripped the covers and took it, in love with the feeling of being hers. Her fuck toy, her property. She reached between my legs and took hold of my dick, and I flexed my thighs, shuddering as I tried not to come. She started stroking me. Ran her thumb in circles on my balls until I choked on a groan.

Bill Henson-ing.

I tried to push the thought aside, but it just got louder in my mind. *Bill Henson-ing. I heard people actually wrote to him asking him to kill them . . .*

My back dipped, and my head snapped up.

Kel stroked my dick harder. I started to lose myself in the pleasure again.

Was he sorry? I'd heard people say that Bill's life had been ruined. That he'd never forgive himself. But how did I know if he was truly sorry?

Kel's quick, harsh whimpers sounded in my ear. Her cock rubbed my prostate over and over, and I clenched, which made things worse. I took a sharp breath, sending a burst of cold air into my throat, and with a massive effort, forced Bill out of my mind. I wanted to let Kel know everything—how good she made me feel, how fucking . . . safe. She got me out of my head, made me want to come back to a world I'd abandoned for the past couple of years.

I grunted as she pulled me suddenly to my feet, her arms locked around me. The rigidness of the glass actually hurt in this position, but I didn't struggle. She rocked onto her toes, driving up into me while she held me in place. She kept one hand on my dick, stroking with an ease that didn't match the speed with which she was fucking me. Pressure built in my balls until my knees were shaking.

She cried out and stopped moving. Three more hard thrusts, and the dildo slid out of me. She let go of my dick.

Fuck, that was close.

Panting, she pushed me back over the bed. I lay there, bent at the waist, trying to get my breathing under control. She unbuckled the gag and eased it out. I worked my mouth for a few seconds, swallowing rapidly. Swiped at my wet chin with my fist.

I heard her go into the bathroom and wash up. Took that time to wipe my face on the comforter. A few minutes later, she was back, sans strap-on. She climbed onto the bed and stretched out on her side. Grabbed one of the pillows to put under her breasts. She'd explained to me once that with boobs that big, she needed a pillow under them when she lay on her side. It had been early on in our mentorship, and I'd had no idea what I was allowed to say about or think about or do with her breasts, so I'd just stammered an, *"Oh, interesting."*

She patted the space beside her. I crawled up next to her, waiting for my heart to slow.

She ran her hand down my chest and over my stomach. I jerked as her fingertips brushed the base of my dick, and she smiled. I looked down at where her skin met mine. At the goose bumps that had followed her touch. Then I lifted my gaze to meet hers. She was beautiful in a way that, over the past few months, I'd stopped being able to ignore. Not that I'd ever ignored it. I'd just shoved those feelings aside so that I didn't get in the habit of wanting anything more from her than mentorship.

She had these very light freckles under her eyes, freckles you could only see up close. I loved watching the way that skin creased when she smiled. Loved the slightly upturned corners of her mouth, the way she kept tucking her hair behind her ears even though it was too thick to stay there. I moved my hand just a little, wanting to trace the line of her cleavage, trail my fingers along the tops of her breasts.

And then something happened. I could feel the moment she detached. She took her hand away and rolled onto her back, staring at the ceiling. She did this sometimes, and I could never figure out what triggered it. Though I'd be lying if I said I hadn't noticed that it often happened right after we did a scene, and was especially likely to happen if Greg wasn't there.

"You like the gag?" she asked.

"Mm-hmm."

"Gould. What kind of answer is that?"

"Legit."

She laughed. "Legit, huh?" She rubbed her eye with the heel of her hand, then let her arm fall on her pillow. "We could go to the grocery store. I need to get enemas for later."

"Right. Eggs, milk, and enemas."

She tipped her face toward me. "I want you and Greg to have a contest. Dave's dom gave me the idea."

"D's giving you advice now?" Dave's partner, D—also a David—was an interesting guy, to say the least. Burly, stoic, and bemused by things like technology and veganism, he did have occasional bursts of creativity where punishment was concerned.

"He was saying how he makes subs hold an enema for a certain amount of time. If they make it past that time, they can expel in the toilet. If they have to go sooner, they have to shit in some kid's plastic potty thing. So I was like, ooh, I could modify that. Give you and Greg enemas at the same time—"

"Oh God."

She grinned. "Loser has to go in a bucket. I think I have one somewhere."

"You need to stop talking to D."

She laughed. "I almost never see him. I have to take advantage of his wisdom when I can." She paused. "I even talked to David recently."

"Really? When?"

"A couple of weeks ago."

"He didn't tell me."

She went back to studying the ceiling. "He's still pretending he hates Greg and me. But we were all very civil."

"He *is* just pretending." I wasn't totally sure about that. Dave had clashed pretty hard with Greg and Kel during the early incarnation of the Subs Club. And with decent reason—Kel and Greg had really been touting the *Bill made a mistake* party line. They'd told the Subs Club to stop making waves. It had been infuriating to hear that kind of bullshit from two people who'd put themselves in charge of keeping players safe. But even though I'd known I should be as angry with them as Dave was, I'd sort of . . . I don't know. I'd been drawn to them. *The enemy*, Dave had said. *Masters of incompetence.* Yet for some reason, I could never make myself hate them.

Dave had declared a brief truce with them last winter, but in the spring, Kel and Greg had made modifications to Riddle's privacy policy that had set Dave off again. He and I had fought for days about my choice to keep playing with them. And I hadn't even been able to defend myself, because it didn't make sense to me either. But his hostility toward Kel and Greg had become almost affectionate lately. As though he were making an effort to get along with them for my sake.

I shifted. My ass and jaw still ached. "What'd you guys talk about?"

"The kink fair. Dave wants to offer us a booth."

Interesting. Dave had mentioned to me he was going to extend the invite, but I wasn't sure he'd do it.

Kel didn't say anything for a while.

"So grocery shopping," I said finally. "What else?" Personally, I would have been glad to lie here with her until Greg got back.

"We could go to lunch. Get Greg to meet us." She rolled toward the night table to get her phone. "I'll text him. Anywhere in particular you want to go?"

I don't care where we go. I want you to decide.

She swiped her screen to unlock it.

I like you so much, but I'm worried I'm never gonna stop thinking about Bill. I need you to be harder on me. I need you to force me out of this mess inside my head.

Please.

I watched her type her message to Greg. "Anywhere you want is fine."

She kept typing.

It was like I could hear a nonexistent clock ticking. "Ma'am?"

She looked at me. "Yes?"

We weren't strangers. I might not know her as well as Greg did, but I knew how to make her laugh. Knew what music she liked, her favorite movies, the things she hated about her job. I didn't know her nephew's name, but I could find out. *So why is it so scary to ask for what I want?* "I should be corrected. For last night."

I thought I saw a brief smile before she rolled over to set the phone on the night table. "Why is that?"

This was even more nerve-racking when she wasn't looking at me. "I wasn't supposed to come, and I did. When Greg started, um— started that, I let him. I wanted it. And so I went against what you wanted."

She turned back to me. Didn't say anything.

"You should have punished me too," I told her.

She touched my temple, and I held eye contact. Her expression wasn't at all unkind, but her voice was firm. "I decided that you didn't need to be corrected."

"I know, but . . ."

But nothing. It's her decision. You claim you want her to take charge, and when she does, you question her?

But I needed this.

It's not about you.

She raised her eyebrows. "Go on."

I shook my head. Sighed. "Sorry. Shit. It was your choice. I shouldn't have . . ."

She ran her fingers through my hair. Waited.

I tried to laugh. "I just keep fucking things up this weekend."

"Okay, hey. Hey. Come here." She slid an arm under me. Pulled me a little closer.

I should never have opened my mouth. Now we'd have to have some goddamn conversation about my feelings. All I wanted was to be quiet, the way I'd been when she and I had first started playing together. Quiet and stoic, needing nothing from her but simple instructions to follow. When had that stopped being enough?

"Why so hard on yourself?" she asked. "Have I been too hard on you?"

"No," I said, still frustrated. *Not hard enough. I think. I don't know.*

She was gonna wait for me to explain. I could let her wait. There were places I could go. Start with one image—a land covered in volcanic ash. Burnt-out craters. Tiny, yellow-eyed creatures skittering across the wasteland. She took my hand, and I couldn't stay in the wasteland. I had to look at her.

"I want more," I said finally.

Surprisingly, my honesty didn't send the world up in flames.

She ran her thumb along my knuckles. "More?"

"More than you want to . . . to do, probably." *Fuck.*

She watched me. "What do I want to do?"

Downstairs, the garage door opened, and a moment later, a car door slammed. Of course Greg would get home right fucking now.

She sat up, and so did I. "Hold that thought," she said.

"Anyone home?" Greg called.

"Up here!" Kel called back.

There were footsteps on the stairs, and a moment later, Greg entered the room.

"Hey." He was carrying two foam containers. "I made off with a bunch of doughnuts from the meeting, and . . ." He looked back and forth between us. "Everything okay?"

Kel kept her hand in mine. "Gould and I are talking about what he wants."

"Oh." Greg set the containers on the nightstand, then came to sit on the edge of the bed—on my side, not Kel's. I sort of wanted him to go away, but that wasn't right. He needed to hear this too. He folded his hands between his knees. "What's wanted?"

"I don't know." My heart felt too high in my chest, and it was pounding too hard. "Forget it."

"Oh no," Kel said sharply. "Enough of that. Tell me what's going on."

For some reason those words, her tone, filled me with relief. "Sometimes I just want . . . I want to see what things would be like if you had more control over me."

"All right."

"All right?"

"Keep going."

"I like what we do. But I . . . Sometimes you're too polite with me. You can *use* me. Like, anytime, anywhere, for anything."

She squeezed my hand.

"I *do* want to belong to you. It's just hard when we only see each other for a few hours at a time. Because I can't—I can't say stuff like that and not mean it."

"Mean what?"

I sounded so stupid. "I can't say 'I belong to you' anymore, because I—I don't know if I do. I know I do when I'm here, but then I go home, and I . . ." Greg was watching me. I didn't want to keep going.

"I want to serve you," I said after a while. "Even when we're not together. I'm not asking to move in or anything. But would you consider seeing me for longer than a weekend? Or just . . . I mean, some people have online arrangements, and—"

"How much longer?" she asked quietly.

Here goes nothing. "A week? Maybe? To try an actual . . . 24/7 . . . thing?"

She let go of my hand and ran her thumb and forefinger toward each other along the base of my throat. Where a collar would rest. She was good at that—using the smallest gestures to say something important. "What do you want to do for me, babe?"

"Anything," I said immediately, embarrassed by the thickness in my voice. "Really. All the stuff I do now, just . . . more. I want to bring you your drinks and, I don't know, clean your whole house with a fucking toothbrush. Run your errands. Make you come." I glanced at Greg, who was sitting perfectly still, watching us, and then I turned back to her. "Make *him* come. Just tell me what you want. I can handle that. I can handle being treated like—like property."

"Easy." Her fingertips grazed my shoulder again, and I stopped talking. "You want more of a service-oriented agreement?"

More like I want to be your slave and sign a fucking contract and never be allowed to say no to you again.

I looked at her, not sure how to respond. I finally nodded. "Something like that."

"Be honest."

I sighed. "I look up stuff about master/slave relationships, sometimes." I could feel her jolt, and so I added quickly, "I know that's too intense for, like, where we are right now. And I'm not asking for *that*, but . . ."

She traced a circle around the bone at the base of my neck.

Keep going. "But what if it was sort of like that?"

It was stupid. You had to be tough as fuck to be a slave. And I was anything but tough. You had to know, deeply, the person you were offering to serve.

Greg was staring at Kel with an expression I couldn't read, and suddenly I was sorry I'd brought any of this up. They were *married*. They loved each other. They mentored me because it only took a few hours out of their week. Now I was asking to horn in on their life, their marriage. What I had with my friends—*that* was deep, that was permanent. What did I have with Kel except a tendency to treat her like a celebrity whose autograph I was afraid to ask for?

"It could be mostly online." I attempted damage control. "If you don't want to be around me that much."

"Oh my God, Gould." She laughed, but it sounded a little forced. "I want to be around you as much as possible."

Seriously?

She exchanged another glance with Greg. Something was going on between them that I couldn't figure out. He gave her the barest hint of a smile, and nodded. She refocused on me. "But you're right, an arrangement like that is intense."

"I know. I shouldn't have—"

Greg cleared his throat. "Well, Kel's not exactly a stranger to that sort of thing."

I looked at him again. Was he talking about their D/s relationship? He looked like he was trying not to smile.

"Oh please." Kel was half-smiling too.

I shifted. "Am I missing something?"

Now he grinned openly. "What do you think, Master K? You gonna come out of retirement for one last heist?"

"What are you guys talking about?" I asked.

Kel swung her legs over the bed. Stood and walked to the closet to grab her robe. "He's talking about my dark past."

"You have a dark past?"

Greg started to laugh.

She shrugged the robe on and turned back to us, tying it shut. She gave a little shrug, and a private smile. "I may have dabbled in M/s. In my twenties."

I stared at her. "Seriously?" I thought back to everything they'd told me about their histories in the lifestyle. Kel had never mentioned being a master.

She walked back to the bed. "Uh-huh." She climbed up on the mattress on her hands and knees and kissed Greg, then me. "It feels like forever ago."

"Why'd you stop?"

"Well." She patted my knee and sat back on her heels. "It's complicated."

I gave her a look that hopefully let her know I was unimpressed. "You wouldn't let me get away with an answer like that."

"Fair enough." She tugged the robe's sash tighter. "I always liked the *idea* of M/s. But it was a community where I felt a little unwelcome. Not totally, but there were issues."

"Like what?"

She placed her hands on her knees and seemed to consider her words carefully. "It's kind of cliquish. You've got the titleholder crowd. The ones who compete and go to conventions and everything. They're a good group, but they can be very bound by tradition. They're the ones who've said things to me like, master/slave isn't part of BDSM and you're doing it wrong if you think it is. Or, dead seriously, one guy told me I couldn't run a BDSM dungeon and be a real master, because the two lifestyles required very different skills."

"Yeah," I said. "I mean, I know it's supposed to be different from, like, D/s."

"M/s is very much a lifestyle, in a way that D/s doesn't have to be."
I nodded.

"A slave signs away the right to say no."

That sounded incredible. Terrifying and incredible. Right now, I could safeword out of any task I didn't want to perform, any correction I didn't feel like taking, any sex act I didn't enjoy. I never did, but still—the option was always there. What if that power was taken away from me? What if my only choices were to take what I was given, or break my contract?

She went on. "I think a lot of people use the terms 'master' and 'slave' as a role-play thing, but real M/s is definitely not an arrangement you enter into for kicks."

"Yeah," I agreed.

"And I guess that's why I gave it up. Being a master isn't something you dabble in. You're either cut out for it, or you're not."

We were all quiet. Even Greg. He finally muttered something I didn't catch.

Kel turned to him. "What's that?"

"I said you were cut out for it."

She gazed at him evenly, and once again I had the sense that there was some history here I wasn't privy to. "I'm not so sure I was."

I ran my finger along the edge of the comforter. "I don't know exactly what I want," I admitted. "I just . . . I like being told what to do. I really, really do. And I'd give you so much more than you've been taking. If you wanted."

"Can I make a suggestion?" Greg asked.

We both turned to him.

He scrubbed a hand over his gelled hair. "What if we try a week, like Gould said? We could start next Sunday, or something." He turned to Kel. "You use Gould however you want each day, but you set aside some time every night to talk to him about your, uh, 'dark past.' Help him figure out if M/s is what he's looking for, or if he'd be just as happy with a more intense submission."

Kel was silent a moment. "I don't have any expertise."

"You trained with Master Tan," Greg said.

Who's Master Tan?

"But I never..." Kel looked nervous, which surprised me. "I never went that far. I never owned a slave. I don't know why we're talking about this when it's a big leap from mentorship to—"

Greg shifted. "We don't have to treat it like we're signing a contract in blood. Let's just spend a week together, kick things up a notch, and see what happens."

Kel studied the comforter for a few seconds, then lifted her head again and faced me. "Gould?"

Hell fucking yes. "If you want to, then yeah. I mean, definitely. I'll try not to be in the way. If I am, you can just tell me t—"

"You know," Kel interrupted, casting another smile at Greg. "Greg and I have been discussing lately whether to ask if you want to spend more time with us."

I stared at her. "Really?"

She nodded. "We were thinking about kinky destinations. I have a friend who's opening a dungeon-themed B&B in Indiana. Or there are weeklong retreats, camps. Conferences. We just weren't sure you wanted to go on vacation with a boring old married couple."

"You're not old. Or boring."

"We've started watching *Wheel of Fortune* regularly," Greg warned.

I grinned. "Well, hey. Don't forget, I'm thirty now." I was only twenty-eight, but last fall, my friends had thrown me a thirtieth birthday party, since I knew that my actual thirtieth birthday was going to be miserable. My parents were already planning a party—I was pretty sure just so they could bemoan the fact that I was unmarried and childless.

They both laughed. "Well," Greg said. "The point is, a week is not too long to have you around."

Kel looked from me to Greg. "We could draw up a temporary contract, just for the week. If we start next Sunday, that gives us the next few days to figure out what we want the contract to say."

Greg pulled his legs up onto the bed. Crossed his ankles. "And here's my question: if it *does* turn out, Gould, that you're looking for a master—and Kel, if it turns out you want to be one—what then?"

"I don't think we have to worry about that yet," Kel said quickly. "That would take more than a week to determine."

We've had a year.

Greg's mouth twisted to the side. "But if you take things to that level, even for a week, there's an emotional investment that you can't . . . You know what I mean? You can't just say, 'Okay, that was fun. See you around.' when the contract is up."

He had consistently surprised me throughout the time I'd known him. Half the time I convinced myself he was a man-child who didn't really take submission seriously. But then he'd come out with these insights, this very obvious passion for his lifestyle. I'd never felt the attraction to him that I did toward Kel. Had never felt as comfortable with him, as interested in serving him. But I *did* care about him. And I did need him to be part of this.

"I know," Kel said. "But what we're talking about now is another step in our mentorship. Not a binding arrangement. We're just experimenting."

"Oo-kay." Greg held up his hands in an exaggerated *you're the boss* gesture.

"Greg." Her voice sharpened.

He hesitated. "I'm sorry."

"Why?" Her tone was still hard.

"Because I shouldn't have said it like that." He sounded sincere, and I thought back to all the times when we'd first gotten together that I'd heard him challenge her, and seen her let it slide. Just in the year I'd been with them, I'd seen them grow more serious. Seen her come into her own as a dom.

I was there for that.

Maybe I did belong here, in a way. Not permanently. Not the way they belonged to each other. But maybe it wasn't so crazy to be asking for this.

She rubbed his back. "And what about you? You're not just gonna stay on the sidelines. You have to be part of the process."

"I know." He reached out with one arm. She leaned forward and caught his hand, swung it gently. He smiled at her. "I'll help you with whatever you need."

That part made me kind of nervous. Would I have any control over how Greg interacted with me? Right now, I rarely took orders from him. But if my submission was going to be more intense, if I asked for more rules and a greater degree of humiliation, did that mean I'd have to answer to him the same way I did to her?

She turned to me again. "So we'll spend this week talking protocol."

I nodded. "Okay." We had some protocol in place already—I usually addressed her as "Ma'am" and was almost always naked when I was in their house. We'd just never been consistent. If we were entering a scenario where I was expected to follow certain rules, we discussed it beforehand. What we'd never had was several days together during which I had to follow all the rules all the time. Where the rules weren't a kind of obstacle course for me to complete, but a part of my daily existence. "So how do we figure that out?"

"We can talk more about it today and tomorrow. I'll give you some writing assignments this week. You can list some scenarios you're imagining. Tell me what you're picturing when you think about being a slave—or a full-time sub, I guess is what we're talking about. Give me some goals that you want to work on. Not just relating to your submission, but in general."

"This sounds kind of like what D and Dave do . . . but not."

"Ooh, yes. Ask Dave if you have questions. I'll bet he'd help."

Yeah, because I really wanted to ask my best friend to help me figure out what I wanted out of consensual slavery. But she was right. Dave would gladly help. His relationship with D had been complicated at first, because Dave had wanted "real" discipline—punishments that were truly punishments, not sex games. But he'd also been convinced that no dom was trustworthy enough to be given that level of control. He and D had eventually agreed to give domestic discipline a try, and it seemed to be working out for them.

"Okay," I said. "Cool."

Greg glanced over at the nightstand. "Should we celebrate with doughnuts?"

"Absolutely." Kel leaned over to grab one of the containers. "And then Gould and I were gonna go buy enemas."

Greg snorted. "Ooookay."

She popped open the container and took a doughnut. "For a contest tonight. Between you and Gould."

He groaned. Grabbed a sprinkled doughnut, then nodded at me.

I took a chocolate frosted one, still feeling kind of numb. I couldn't believe I'd just talked to them about this. I couldn't believe they'd said yes.

Greg chewed for a few seconds, then glanced at Kel. "Why don't you send Gould? Make him go buy the stuff you're gonna torture him with?"

She looked at me. Her lips curved upward.

Greg picked a sprinkle off his lap. "You could even make him tell the cashier what the stuff is for."

I went still.

Kel rolled her eyes. Reached out and pushed the doughnut into his mouth when he went to take a bite. "Shut it."

He laughed, sprinkles falling from his lips. "It was worth a shot."

She addressed me again. "Gould. Get dressed. Go downstairs, get my credit card from my bag and the grocery list from the fridge, and go to the store." She said it casually, but I caught the shift in her voice, that quiet authority. I was relieved, and so fucking ready.

"Yes, Ma'am."

She paused. "Next week, when you're staying with us, I'll expect you to familiarize yourself with what we usually keep stocked, food-wise. If you notice we're low on something, you'll get a card from one of us, and you'll go get what we need. I don't expect to have to remind you."

Again, that relief washed over me. "Yes, Ma'am."

She gave me a small, crooked smile. "Thank you."

I finished my doughnut and stood. Dressed in front of them, not even bothering to feel self-conscious. I left the room, unable to stop myself from grinning.

This was going to be fun.

CHAPTER

FIVE

I got home early Sunday evening, feeling simultaneously exhausted and like I'd never sleep again.

Kel had, as promised, given me writing assignments. My first was to email her three goals for my week of service. She, in turn, was going to email me some protocol ideas. Greg would be Kel's second-in-command when we were together—he had the right to use me for sex whenever he wanted, to assign me chores, and to correct me for protocol infractions. Greg actually seemed more excited about this whole arrangement than I'd expected, and for the first time in two and a half years, I felt a genuine hope that things were changing for me. That I was actually moving forward.

The duplex was quiet and smelled faintly of pot. Crumbs and a couple of Dave's comic books were on the kitchen table. I stood at the counter, chugging water and thinking about what I wanted my goals to be, when Dave's bedroom door creaked open.

"Hey." He wandered into the kitchen and sat at the table. Pulled the comics close and stacked them. "I thought I heard you come in. How was your weekend?"

It was a little weird that he hadn't hugged me. He usually never missed an opportunity.

"It was good. It was . . . really good, actually."

"Cool."

He didn't invite me to elaborate, and I felt kind of weird telling him how awesome my weekend had been when he was clearly upset about something. "What have you been up to?"

"Nothing." He whacked the comics against the edge of the table. "I've done literally nothing. In forever. No homework, no cooking, no . . . I don't know what else I do."

"Did you have to work yesterday?"

"Yep. And Steve was being a little fucker. Plus we got a new tea in—this monkey-picked oolong—and they're touting it as, like, the cure for all of humanity's ailments. And people are actually paying nine dollars an ounce for it, which makes me feel like humans are dumb and we'll never achieve time travel."

"Well, at least you'll be out of there soon."

"Pshh. We'll see." Dave worked at the tea store in the mall, though he was currently in styling school, pursuing his hairdresser dreams. And bringing home mannequin heads. Lots and lots of Styrofoam mannequin heads. He lowered his forehead to the table. "Ughhh, I hate commuting to school."

I tried to think what subject could possibly cheer him up. "How's the kink fair going?"

He raised his head. "The what?"

"Uh, Kinkstravaganzapalooza? That thing you've been trying to put together for almost a year?" I hadn't heard him talk about it much lately. Right up to a couple of months ago, he'd been unstoppable—scouting different venues, booking presenters, putting together panels—and then it had just kind of ground to a halt. As far as I knew, the fair was scheduled for August sixteenth, and I was down to help with decorating and promotion.

He rubbed his cheeks with his fingertips. "Fine. I spent hours painting a banner, only to find that Kamen had gotten Miles to make banners at A2A."

"That was weeks ago. You already told me about it."

He shrugged. "I've mostly delegated kink fair stuff to Maya, honestly."

Maya was our youngest Subs Club member. We'd met her when the Subs Club gave a talk at Hymland College—Hymen College, to the locals—last year. She was twenty, bright, and fiercely interested in kink. She didn't have much practical experience in the scene, but, with the help of a local all-female group called Finger Bang, she'd developed an academic understanding of it to rival Miles's.

I leaned against the counter. "I thought this was your masterpiece. Your culmination of, like, trying to take the Subs Club on the road."

"Yeah, well, I've been busy. And Maya's ravenous for leadership opportunities. It all works out. Also, Ryan. He's helping a lot too." Kamen's boyfriend and Dave had gotten off to a rocky start last year, but had become closer over the past few months.

I set my glass down. "Didn't Kamen say Ryan was done with activism?"

"I promised him free haircuts."

I got the water filter pitcher out of the fridge and poured him some water. "Is something wrong?"

Dave didn't answer right away. He placed one finger on the edge of the comic stack. "D asked me to move in with him."

I just stood there for a second, holding the glass I'd meant to give him. "Oh. Wow."

D and Dave had been a couple for over a year now. It wasn't unreasonable that they'd consider living together. And I was happy for him. Of course I was. I was just surprised.

Dave glanced out the window. "We were thinking about early summer. June. When the lease is up."

"Okay. Yeah. That's soon."

"But it doesn't have to be right then," he said quickly, looking at me. "If you have trouble finding another roommate, I can stay and, you know, I could pay rent until we find someone. Or if you want to move . . . I mean, that's up to you."

"I'll have to think about it." I took a seat. Handed him the water.

I'd known, I'd *known* this would happen someday. I just hadn't thought it would happen *now*.

The duplex. Subs Club headquarters. Dave had already been living here three years ago, and when his old roommate had moved out, Dave had invited me to move in. It had been shortly after Hal's death, and I think Dave really just wanted to keep an eye on me. I'd withdrawn from the group big time, and to be honest, I didn't remember that period very well. I'd moved in, and . . . yeah. Best choice of my life. I loved all my friends, but there was something special between Dave and me that neither of us could explain.

"I'm sorry," he said.

"Why?"

"For abandoning you."

"You're not abandoning me."

He glanced at me guiltily. "You know how much I want a giant poster of you on my wall. Or your face in a locket. You make me feel like *everything* is gonna be okay. I love you."

"I love you too."

"You're not mad, are you?"

"Of course not."

"Tell me it'll all be okay."

I tried to smile. "It'll all be okay."

I liked this role. Liked the way my friends looked to me for reassurance. Considering everything that went on in my head, it was surprising they asked me for advice a lot. My roommate in college had once explained the different types of quiet to me: hot-quiet, sullen-quiet, and wise-quiet. Hot-quiet meant you were brooding and mysterious. Sullen-quiet encompassed people who were stuck up or misanthropic. And wise-quiet meant you seemed to know the secrets of the universe, and people found you reassuring. *"You're wise-quiet,"* he'd told me.

Dave fidgeted. "The others are coming over. We're gonna show Miles his present."

I grinned. The Subs Club, minus Miles and his partner, Drix, had recently collaborated on a video project in honor of A2A. "Oh, cool."

"He's going to hate it."

"That's what's gonna make it so fun."

He hesitated. "Don't tell anybody what I just told you," he warned. "I'm not ready yet."

"Okay," I promised.

"Gould?"

"Yeah?"

"Can I seriously make a poster of your face?"

"That'd be weird."

"I know. But I need your face to hang on my ceiling when I'm living at D's."

"You can make a poster of my face."

"Thanks. I'll bet Miles would do it cheap. At the store."

"Maybe."

"Let's ask." He gave me a sort of wary, sidelong look. "Ricky's definitely gonna be at the kink fair."

I kept my voice neutral. "That's fine. I figured he would be."

"I mean, he's gonna help me present and stuff. So maybe at some point before the fair, you guys could try to talk?"

Ricky Chuy had once been the Subs Club's biggest fan. Young, enthusiastic, and so sweet and naive you thought he had to be faking it, he used to tag along with us to Riddle sometimes, trying to get the hang of the scene. A few months ago, though, we'd learned he'd been playing with Bill. That they were in a long-term partnership. I'd said some shit to Ricky that I wasn't terribly proud of, but that I wasn't about to take back. Ricky and I hadn't spoken since.

I swept some crumbs off the table. "Yeah."

Dave looked relieved. "Good. Because I've been thinking about what Kamen said—about how maybe it's not really our business what Ricky does with Bill."

I stared at him. "Oh?"

"Like, if Ricky wants to get himself killed, then hey." He paused. "Or . . . if he says Bill treats him well, then maybe . . . Bill treats him well." He shrugged awkwardly.

I shifted. "Right."

"Okay, cool." He stood. "I'm gonna put some laundry in before they get here. Like I haven't had all friggin' day to do that."

"See? If you were living with D, he'd cane your ass and you'd never put off doing laundry again."

He glared at me. "Ha-ha. I'm gonna go order sandwiches."

He went to his room to call Mel's, the shop down the street. And I sat there trying to figure out at what point Dave—the Subs Club founder, staunch anti-Bill crusader, and my best friend—had become willing to give Bill Henson the benefit of the doubt.

"Why am I so very, very afraid?" Miles took a seat on our couch. He still had a piece of lettuce on his sweater from his sandwich.

Drix sat beside him and put an arm around him. They looked, as always, hilarious together—Miles in his starched shirt and glasses and Mr. Rogers cardigan. Drix massively tall and dressed all in black, his long, dark-blond hair in a ponytail at the base of his neck. I had a habit, when he was around, of staring at his mouth, waiting to catch a glimpse of his filed vampyre teeth. They were endlessly fascinating.

Dave was sprawled on the recliner, and Maya and I were on the floor, pinching each other and then pretending to look innocent. Kamen was crouched by the TV.

"Dude, don't be." Kamen hooked his laptop to the television. "This is awesome. We made you a commercial."

Miles straightened. "What?"

Dave belched.

"A commercial," Kamen repeated. "For A2A. You said you wanted to do more advertising and stuff. So we went to A2A and did some after-hours filming."

Miles's mouth fell open slightly. "How would you have g—"

Kamen grinned. "Jason let us in. We told him you asked us to film there." Miles's perpetually anxious employee, Jason, had wanted to call Miles to confirm this, but Kamen had talked him out of it.

Drix laughed. "I love this already."

"It turned out really good," Maya told him. "We wanted to invite you to participate, but we needed to keep it top secret from Miles. And you were a security risk."

"Dude." Kamen pulled up the video. "Drix keeps, like, the ancient secrets of his coven. We totally should have put him in this." He hit Play and scrambled up onto the couch on Miles's other side. "Check this the fuck out."

The opening shot was the exterior of A2A. Dave got out of his car and walked to the entrance. Cut to inside the store. The bells on the door tinkled. Dave stepped up to the register, where Kamen was pretending to work, though the camera had caught the reflection of a Tetris game on the computer screen.

"Hi," onscreen-Dave said to Kamen. "I need to order some polo shirts for my bowling league. Do you do custom shirts?"

Kamen looked up. The camera zoomed in on his face, and he stared straight into the lens and raised an eyebrow. "Do we do custom shirts?"

Electro-rock started to play, and there was a montage of shots of the store's interior, including some footage of Miles at the register, frowning over a binder of order forms.

Miles tensed. "When the hell did you—"

"Shh," Kamen pointed at the screen. "This is the best part."

The camera cut to Kamen facing a wall of sports T-shirts. Kamen spun toward the camera and started walking casually as he spoke, hands in his pockets. The camera followed him. "A2A has the city's widest selection of custom T-shirts, tote bags, bumper stickers . . . Pretty much anything you can personalize, A2A's got it."

Dave popped into the frame as a new character, wearing a baseball cap, sunglasses, and a surfer wig. He started to unbutton his jeans. "Can you even personalize my—"

"Whoa there, valued customer," Kamen interrupted, pushing him back. "Not in front of the kids." He winked at the camera and dropped his voice to a stage whisper. "But yes, we can."

Drix guffawed. Miles groaned.

Cut to a close-up of Dave in his regular Dave-clothes again, sitting in A2A's storeroom. "I didn't think I'd be able to find anyone in this city who could do the kind of customized order I needed—and so fast!"

Cut back to Kamen in the main store. "Whether you're looking for shot glasses for your cousin's *quinceañera*, mugs for your grandpa's birthday, or T-shirts for your local wet T-shirt contest—" Cut to Dave, Kamen, and Ryan dancing aggressively to the electro-rock in matching *SLIPPERY WHEN WET* shirts. Back to Kamen addressing the camera. "—A2A will hook you up."

There was a shot of Miles behind the front desk, oblivious to the camera. Kamen continued in voice-over: "A2A offers years of business experience. Plus friendly staff." Cut to Jason standing by a T-shirt rack. He looked up and gave a small, nervous smile. "And satisfied customers." Cut to Dave, holding up a stack of polo shirts and grinning, while Ryan stood beside him with a *WORLD'S BEST MOM* mug.

Back to Kamen. "So why not support local business *and* get the custom-made swag of your dreams?"

Cut to Maya, holding two *eHarmony matched me with Captain Morgan* flasks and smiling woodenly. "Wow. Thanks, A2A." She took a swig from one of the flasks.

Miles slow-turned to Kamen. "She's *underage.*"

"Barely," Maya shot back.

Kamen waved Miles off. "It was water."

Back onscreen, I walked into A2A in a cop uniform from the Halloween store, carrying D's police baton. I looked every bit as awkward as I probably had onstage in *Pirates of Penzance.* "Excuse me," I said to the assembled crowd of satisfied customers. "I'm afraid I'm gonna have to throw you all in jail."

They turned to me.

"But *why?*" Ryan asked, shrugging theatrically.

I pointed the baton at them. "Because prices this low are *illegal.*"

We faced the camera and laughed.

"Seriously though," I said to them, "there's like a predatory pricing law you have to follow, and . . ." The dialogue faded out as the music swelled. Kamen's acoustic cover of "I Love My Shirt" by Donovan played over the credits.

We looked at Miles.

His mouth hung open. "Honestly, I have no idea what to say."

Kamen patted his shoulder. "You're welcome, man. And Ricky thinks he can get this on air at the local station."

"*No,*" Miles said immediately. He took a breath. "I mean, thank you. That commercial is . . . charming, and I'm . . . very surprised that you were able to . . . do that without my knowledge."

Ryan shrugged. "We're sneaky as fuck."

Maya leaned back against the couch. "I threatened to show Jason my piece if he didn't let us in."

"Pffff," Kamen said. "That's Maya. Packin' heat."

"I *do* have a gun," Maya insisted.

Dave turned to her. "Are you serious?"

"Uh, yeah."

Kamen was open-mouthed. "Since *when?*" He'd grown strangely protective of Maya over the past few months.

"Roxie Hart lives in my glove box. A Christmas gift from my lovely, conservative father, who took me to the range and taught me to fire it and everything. I sort of hate guns, but the parking garage at Hymen is pretty skeevy. Also I like shooting way more than I thought I would."

"It is fun," I agreed.

Dave whirled toward me. "When have you ever shot?"

"I told you. My brother used to take me hunting. And to the range." I almost never saw my two *much* older brothers. One was an NRA-obsessed doomsdayer, and the other experimented on laboratory animals. So it was all just as well.

Dave shook his head and jerked a thumb at me. "What do I always say about this guy? He's the craziest motherfucker of us all."

Kamen eyed Maya. "What the hell? You have a gun? You're 'talking' to Fucktopus—whatever that means?" Fucktopus was a cephalopod furry who made occasional appearances on the Subs Club discussion board. He and Maya had started getting friendly a few months ago. "Who even are you?"

"Aw, Dad." She grinned at him. "Don't get your panties in a bunch."

Kamen went bright red at that.

"Just be safe," he muttered.

"You loved Fucktopus when you met him," Dave pointed out.

"Yeah, that was before he started putting his tentacles all over Maya."

Maya threw her head back. "Oh, for fuck's sake."

Drix laughed. "Kamen just cares a lot."

"Seriously." Kamen looked around the room. "I just want to say that I'm really proud of all of us. "Miles has a ballin' store, Ryan and I are basically YouTube sensations from 'Snow Wanderer.' Drix is a vampyre yoga instructor. Dave is almost a hairdresser. Maya's, like, owning the fuck out of this kink fair planning." His gaze fell on me. "Gould is magical and gives everyone happiness and dangerous confidence, like cocaine made from unicorn dandruff."

"Thank you," I said.

"And dudes," Kamen went on, "think about it. Subs Club used to just be us sitting around eating sandwiches and talking about BDSM."

"And alienating our community by rating doms," Miles pointed out.

"Yeah, but look at us now."

Dave cocked his head. "You mean, look how we still sit around eating sandwiches and talking about BDSM?"

Kamen shot him a look. "We *also* do events in the community. I'm serious. We created this thing as a way to help people be able to talk. And learn. Even though a lot of people already think they know stuff and just want to argue about it on our message board."

Drix leaned forward. "I agree. I don't know that much about BDSM. But I've learned a lot from your guys' blog." Drix was a sadist, and a pretty kinky guy in his own right, but he hadn't had any formal BDSM knowledge before meeting Miles.

I sat quietly for a moment. Something was bothering me. "Well, it started as a way to get justice for Hal."

Everyone looked at me.

"I mean, yes, we wanted people to swap knowledge. But we did start it for a very specific *reason*." I had to be careful, or I was going to set everyone off worrying about me, treating me like some bomb ready to detonate at any mention of Hal. I forced my tone lighter. "We wanted to stop people from playing with doms like Bill."

Right? I couldn't be the only one who thought that. We'd wanted to show careless doms, predatory doms, that there were consequences. That even if the law failed, or never got involved, they would have to answer to someone.

That they wouldn't fucking get away with it.

"Yeah." Kamen smiled, almost like he felt sorry for me. "But it's become a lot more than that. *I* think."

Has it?

Kamen turned to Ryan. "Ry, can you get my guitar from the kitchen?"

"Yes, dear." Ryan got up and went to the kitchen.

Dave shook his head at Kamen. "You're gonna break into song now?"

"You keep telling me to write a Subs Club theme song. So I did."

"Bullshit. Did you really?"

"Just wait, David. Just wait."

Drix laughed.

Ryan came back in and handed the guitar to Kamen, who positioned it and tried a few chords.

Kamen cleared his throat. "Everyone listen." He started to sing:
"Subs Club, Subs Club

Eating lots of sandwiches and talking about stuff

There's nothing that can break the bonds

Of friendship, yeah, it's true

Our hearts and sandwiches are big enough to fill up me and you . . . "

He looked up, waiting for our reaction. Miles and Drix applauded politely. Dave nodded. "There *might* be stronger lyrics somewhere in the history of songwriting. But it's very sweet."

Kamen high-fived him. "Dude, you all. We're awesome. I love you guys. I love sandwiches. I love this house . . ." He looked around the kitchen. "Let's just kick the upstairs neighbors out and all live here together."

I glanced at Dave, who didn't meet my eye.

I walked into work on Monday convinced everyone would be able to tell I had a secret. But it was just like any other Monday. Except that I was twenty minutes late because I'd been up half the night thinking about my goals. John, Anna, and Maddy said hi to me as I walked past the lobby and toward the loan office. Des asked if I'd had a good weekend, because Des asked everyone if they'd had a good weekend. Carla, who was on the phone, waved acrylic-nailed fingers at me.

I stood near Carla's desk a moment, listening to her "Mm-hmm" and "I hear you" into the phone.

"Oh-kay," Carla said. "Okay, yes. All right, thank *you*, hon. You have a blessed morning." She hung up the phone. "Fuckin' bitch."

"Hi, Carla."

She stretched, popping her knuckles. "Oh, *man*. I just want a blunt and some food. What time—? It's only 8:22. Gould, what am I gonna do?"

"Uh . . . you could just take your lunch early, I guess. And I have some friends who could hook you up with the other thing."

She grinned. "Oh, hon. You make me smile. You do, you *do*." She held out a pink slip of paper to me. "You got a message."

"Already?" I took it from her.

"Mm-hmm. They called soon as the bank opened." She got distracted as Tom from consumer lending walked out of his office and crossed the lobby.

"Whoo." Carla leaned back in her chair, staring after Tom. "I really wanna *fuck* him."

We went through this at least once a week. "That's sexual harassment, Carla."

"Not if he doesn't hear me say it."

"No, I . . . think it still is."

She cracked her knuckles again, purple nails flashing. "You're so good, hmm? Always so good."

"I have some dark secrets."

She cackled. "I *bet*! I bet. It's always the quiet ones."

I smiled and took my message slip back into my office. Sat down, breathed out. The loan office was decent—private, quiet. I shared it with IT Joe, but IT Joe didn't talk much. I turned on the computer and logged in. Stared at the screen, trying to summon the motivation to pull up loan applications.

I glanced at the slip of paper. Who the fuck would call for me, specifically, right when the bank opened?

It took me a few seconds to decipher Carla's scrawl. *Cass*, it read. And then a familiar number.

For a second, I didn't feel anything. It was like my brain refused to fully register the information. Then I felt annoyed, mostly.

Why at work? Why not on my cell?

She'd probably deleted my contact info years ago. I hesitated for a few seconds, then picked up the phone and called the number.

A scratchy female voice answered. "Hello?"

"Cass? It's Gould."

A pause. Then a cough. I could almost smell the smoke on her clothes, the hairspray she used that smelled like citronella. "Gould. Hey."

"Hey."

"You wondering why I called?"

Uh, yes. "It's been a while." I hadn't seen Hal's parents since the funeral. Cass had hugged me, sobbing—I hadn't even been able to picture her crying until I'd seen it happen—and said we should stay in touch. But we hadn't. Not at all.

Something rattled on the other end of the phone. "Ben and I found a box. We'd gotten it from Hal's room. Said 'Do Not Open,' and we didn't for a long time. But . . ." A small clicking sound. I could picture her with her fingers at her mouth, biting her nails. She used to do that all the time—stop in mid-sentence to bite off a thumbnail or pick at her cuticles.

"Oh," I said. A Do Not Open box didn't sound like Hal. Or, it sounded like a teenage Hal—not the Hal I'd known.

"You want it?"

"Um, what's in it?"

"Video games. Books. Nothin' secret." Another pause. "We can give it to Goodwill."

"No," I said quickly. "I'll take it." *Why?* Like I didn't have enough of Hal's old stuff? But I wanted to see what video games, what books.

"You want us to ship it?"

"That'd be great."

Another cough. "You mind paying on delivery?"

I rolled my eyes. How many times had Cass and Ben called Hal, asking for money? And how many times had Hal guilted me into sending them some, since I was the one with the steady income? "Sure," I muttered.

"Okay. We'll send it tomorrow."

I sat there for a moment after we ended the call, drumming my fingers on the desk. I'd never cared much for Cass and Ben. My own parents weren't always a picnic—they'd had me nearly twenty years after my two brothers, and I got the sense that while they'd been enthusiastic parents in their early twenties, having me in their forties had been like trying to get the band back together and then discovering the magic just wasn't there anymore. But they weren't bad people.

Cass and Ben on the other hand . . . They'd done drugs Hal's entire childhood. They'd literally introduced Hal to their dealer when he was a teenager. They'd left him home alone for days at a time from age seven onward—taught him how to microwave mac 'n' cheese and frozen dinners. They'd treated me like an ATM. They'd just been general shitheads.

But fuck if talking to Cass didn't feel like a link to Hal.

Hal, who had, for a time, been *it* for me. I'd grown up shy. Hearing from my mom that the squeaky wheel got the oil, but knowing I'd rather fall off the fucking wagon than make a sound. I'd stumbled through high school and college checking off the boxes—I kissed a girl, I got drunk, I kissed a boy, I got drunker, I joined a liberal students society, I graduated summa cum laude—not because I was all that smart, but because I did whatever I was told, from turning in assignments on time to studying even on Friday nights. I got a job. I opened a Roth IRA. I'd assumed that my life would barrel on, uneventful and relatively safe, and that my only adventures would involve me starting with a single image and dreaming my way into wars or castles or avalanches.

And then Hal had come along. I'd met him at a synagogue potluck. He was talking to a girl named Rebecca and telling her about some empty house outside of town that he sometimes snuck into. His fly was down. I normally wouldn't have said anything. But he was just so . . . I don't know. Not beautiful, exactly, but captivating. Friendly and open and chill as fuck. He seemed like the kind of person who'd just laugh it off if you told him his fly was down, so I probably didn't need to feel embarrassed on his behalf. Yet I didn't want to say anything because I was enjoying the glimpse of smiley-face boxers.

I finally went up to him and told him. As predicted, he laughed and pulled his zipper up, thanking me.

"Nice boxers," I said, surprising myself.

He'd grinned again. "What are *you* wearing?"

"Um . . ." I hadn't been prepared for that. But without even thinking, I'd reached into my jeans and pulled up the waistband of my plain blue boxers and showed him. It was like the rest of the synagogue potluck didn't exist. Like there was no danger my mother would glance over at any moment and see me showing my boxers to a stranger.

Hal nodded at my underwear, stroking his chin like he was thinking. "You could get crazier." He met my gaze. "You could pull off wacky boxers. James Bond, dinosaurs, rainbows. Playing cards."

"There are playing-card boxers?"

"Hell yeah. And your ass would look good with a nine of diamonds on it. I mean, it'd look better with nothing on it at all, but if it *has* to be covered . . ."

I'd expected to be more shocked. More prudishly outraged. No one had ever hit on me that directly before, and I'd been aware, in some corner of my brain, that I was insecure about my body and therefore especially susceptible to flattery but also alert to the possibility of mockery. Yet the words that came out of my mouth weren't, *How* dare *you, sir! I said good day.* They were, "My birthday's coming up. Maybe someone ought to get me some playing-card boxers."

And he had. He'd gotten my number that night, and my address a few days later, and this sloppily wrapped package showed up at my apartment two days after my birthday. So of course, I'd had to call him and thank him. And invite him over to see how they looked on me.

I straightened my tie. The loan office suddenly felt cold. My memories of Hal worked like that sometimes—I'd feel, for a few minutes, like he was right beside me. Feel his warmth, the movements of his body. Then it would all fade suddenly, leaving the space around me so empty I almost couldn't stand it.

We'd stayed friends after we'd broken up. Dave said he'd barely felt a ripple in the group dynamic. So it was easy to forget that I'd ever hated Hal, resented him, felt trapped in that relationship and unsure how to get myself the fuck out.

Bill.

That name, always buzzing at the edge of my mind, landing on my memories of Hal and spoiling each one. That was what I hated: that I couldn't think of one without the other. That whatever page I flipped to in Hal's story, I already knew how it ended.

Bill Henson-ing.

Bill Henson, the man, the legend. Edge-play Jesus. Had people really contacted him asking him to kill them? How awful would that feel?

Don't fucking pity him.

Was he sorry?

I closed my eyes. I'd tried so fucking hard over the years to imagine how I'd feel if I—God forbid—ran someone over with my car or something. Wouldn't I want a second chance? I sure as hell wouldn't want people messaging me to ask if I'd be willing to run them over too. Wouldn't I need forgiveness?

The thing was, I wasn't sure I would. I'd always believed people *shouldn't* get away with the bad things they did. Even mistakes.

Miles and I had disagreed after Bill's arraignment. I'd been fucking thrilled with the second-degree murder charge. I didn't care if it seemed *"odd, given the circumstances,"* according to Miles. I was just like, fuck yes. Gross criminal negligence. Reckless disregard for human life. *Murder.*

But Miles insisted the charge should have been involuntary manslaughter. *"We'll definitely get a conviction that way,"* he'd said, as though we were the prosecution. *"He wasn't even in the room when Hal died. A jury might have a hard time finding him guilty of murder. Unless there's information about the case that hasn't been made available to us."*

I'd hung on to that last bit even as people in the community had started to forgive Bill, or at least express sympathy at the "excessive" charge: *"Unless there's information about the case that hasn't been made available to us."* I'd waited for someone to reveal what had really happened that evening: *Yes, Bill risked Hal's life on purpose. He was angry at Hal and so he tied him like that to hurt him, or he was a sociopath with no regard for human life. He understood the danger and left Hal there anyway.* I'd heard the bullshit about how Hal had had one hand free, how the knot had been quick release, how Bill had only left him alone for a few minutes. For some reason, that all just made it worse. I wanted there to be malice, I wanted there to be intent to harm. I didn't want to believe Hal was dead because someone was just *stupid.*

I hadn't followed the trial, but Kamen had. He'd said it had gone down as Miles had predicted—not enough evidence for a murder conviction. Said the defense had done a hatchet job on Hal's character—harping on the fact that Hal was stoned and taking poppers that night, claiming he'd lied to Bill about his sobriety and pressured Bill into the rope scene. The defense attorney's post-trial statement was the only part of that whole circus I'd watched. I remembered her pinched, wind-burned face as she'd declared that the prosecution had been *"arrogant"* and *"too ambitious"* in seeking a murder charge. *"Any other county,"* she'd said, *"would have had the sense to offer a manslaughter plea."*

But then why had the motion to reduce the charge to manslaughter been denied? Why, unless there was some reason it *had* to be murder? I'd played out dozens of scenarios in my head. Maybe Bill had a friend in the court system who'd done him a favor. Maybe there was evidence that had been suppressed. Or maybe it really was just a fucking stupid, stupid accident, and if Bill had possessed an ounce of sense, Hal would still be here.

My anger grew until my hand was shaking on the desk.

It's you, I wanted to tell Bill. *You're the reason that every time I start to get something I want, it doesn't work out. I try to think about Greg and Kel. My friends, my job, my future. And I always end up stuck with you.*

You stupid fucker. I wish I'd done more than punch you in the fucking face. I wish I'd killed you. At least that would be fair. That would be karma.

I wish I knew how to make you hurt the way I hurt.

I just hope that someday, you learn what it's like to die alone. To be afraid, and have no one fucking there.

Part of me felt guilty about the words as soon as I thought them.

And part of me was surprised by how much I meant them.

I sat in front of my laptop that night, stumped once more by my goals.

I want to learn to obey without thinking, I typed. That sounded creepy. I backspaced. *To learn to obey without hesitation.*

I already mostly did that.

To obey with full trust.

Did that make it sound like I didn't trust them already?

To experience real degradation. I didn't want to list that one until I knew how to explain it. Explain that even though I was obsessed with the idea of doing things correctly and well, I wanted to know what it was like to have that never be enough. To be treated like shit, no matter how "good" I was.

I want to be a better servant.

Too generic.

I want to know what it's like to have every minute of my life controlled by someone else.

I sighed and shut the laptop. This was hard.

Because I don't have any specific fantasies beyond just doing whatever the fuck she says. I don't want to know what those orders are going to be. I don't want to know how I'll feel when she gives them. I just want to have to deal with shit as it happens.

Sometimes I could feel it—how willing I'd be to give the right person *anything*. I didn't mean give them whatever they wanted, regardless of the cost to my health and happiness. I meant give them all that I could safely give without losing myself. I meant give them so much fucking loyalty and love. Whatever was beautiful to them, I'd try my hardest to show them that. If that meant seeing me cry, or seeing me come, or using me as a coat-tree, I'd do it.

I'd argued with Hal when we'd first met—about politics, religion, about where we were going to eat on our dates. He had the kind of personality that made debating fun—he never let it turn nasty. Once we'd officially gotten together, though, I'd mostly stopped that. I started agreeing with him as much as possible. I think because on some level, I'd hoped that if I acted submissive enough in our daily life, he'd have no choice but to pick up the reins and be dominant.

When I tried to think how Hal would feel about me being with Greg and Kel, I honestly wasn't sure. He'd acted chill about everything—like there was nothing a person could do that was completely unforgivable. But I'd known him better than almost anyone, and I knew there was plenty he got pissed about.

A memory stole over me, dark and unwelcome: Hal and me on the fairgrounds. I pushed it away.

It wasn't like I was in love with Kel and Greg. Wasn't like I'd *replaced* Hal with these two. I wasn't even totally sure how I'd ended up in this situation.

I was lonely, and they were nice to me. So I said I'd do a scene with them.

That wasn't right. Even before Hal died, I'd had trouble being around Kel without feeling, I don't know . . . tingly. Sweaty-palmed and tongue-tied, like I had a high school crush. I'd wanted to kneel at her feet the first time I'd seen her. And the way she and Greg had acted around me—like I was something special—had felt good, especially after my breakup with Hal.

After Hal was gone, I'd told my friends I never wanted to go back to Riddle. But I'd lied. I'd gone sometimes. I'd talked to Kel and Greg. They'd started inviting me to stay some nights after the club was closed—I'd help them with cleanup, and they'd drive me home.

Years before that, when I was just starting out in the local scene, Dave and I were in a bookstore, and he'd dragged me to the erotica section and pulled some BDSM book off the shelf and read aloud from it in this exaggeratedly breathy voice.

"'He locked eyes with her across the aisle, and she looked quickly away, her gaze dropping to the floor. His pulse raced. How perfect she would look kneeling before him, a collar around her neck. 'Excuse me,' he said, his voice low. She glanced up, her blue eyes meeting his brown orbs fleetingly. 'Yes?' Her tone was soft, husky. 'Do you know where the baking aisle is?' he asked. 'Aisle nine,' she whispered, staring at the floor. My God, he almost expected her to go to her knees before him. Everything about her screamed submissive.'" Dave had looked up. "What the *fuck*? Seriously, who writes this shit? They're in the bread aisle, and he can tell she's submissive because she looked at the floor? Someone needs to tell—" he glanced at the cover "—Erika Narrow that submission is a thing you do in the bedroom. Subs don't walk around averting their eyes and calling everyone 'Sir' and 'Ma'am.'"

I'd shrugged. "I'll bet some do."

It was back when Dave and I were fooling around on occasion, before I'd gotten serious with Hal. So after that, anytime he wanted us to jerk each other off, he'd ask me if I knew where the baking aisle was. It was the dumbest thing, but I'd laughed every time.

I had a feeling I *was* one of those people who was submissive outside the bedroom. And not even the badass kind of sub I was supposed to be: strong and proud and nobody's doormat. I went through my life letting people and circumstances act upon me. Secretly hoping I'd have to endure unexpected sensations at the whims of others. I'd been the same way with my faith when I was younger. I'd clung to the idea of God's will. The hope that I would be led, protected, shown a clear path. That someone was always watching, assessing me. *Correcting me.* When I built stories in my head, I almost never gave myself battles to fight. Things just *happened*—my limbs were severed or my face was charred or I was buried under rubble, and I just kept going, transformed by each event. Not necessarily braver. Not necessarily stronger. Just different.

I wanted to believe that asking Kel to own me for a week was a bold act. But maybe it was just a way to feed my own weakness. Kel and Greg were safe. They looked out for me. And even if I'd grown and toughened somewhat over the years, I was still pathetically hungry for that security. I trusted them to understand my need without taking advantage of it.

The other possibility was the one I was more afraid to consider: That I knew I'd never be in love with anyone again the way I'd been in love with Hal. That I felt guilty about losing him, and guiltier still that Bill Henson was a free man. So I'd picked one of the worst ways I could think of to punish myself. I'd made myself serve two people who were on Bill's side.

No. I didn't want to reduce my feelings about Kel and Greg to that. I wasn't punishing myself by submitting to them. But sometimes when I looked at them, I got this strange mix of panic and anger and guilt, and it became almost a struggle to kneel for them, to do what they asked. And I *loved* the way that felt. That private battle, and the way I always caved in the end.

So maybe it was fucked up, but to me that was kind of the point of kink. Not the fucked-up-ness, exactly, but the fact that you got to piss on society's idea of fucked up. And nobody could stop you. Finger-waggers couldn't storm your house and tell you it was wrong for one person to call another a kike or a cunt or a fag. Couldn't stop you from taking a shit on your partner's face. Couldn't say you were weak or crazy for wanting to be dressed like a baby or walked like a dog. With kink, you had the power to be your sickest, most secret self.

Maybe one of my goals could be to make that sickness less secret. *I want to serve more in public. I want strangers to punish me.*

Dave came home, smelling like chamomile. "What're you doing?" he asked, throwing his coat over a chair and taking a seat on my lap.

I wrapped my arms around him and eyed my laptop. Might as well tell him. "Kel and I are gonna try a whole week together. And Greg, I mean. Obviously."

He turned toward me as much as he could. "What? When?"

"Starting Sunday."

"So, what, you're gonna go live with them for a week?"

"That's the idea."

He faced forward, bony ass digging into my thigh. "You guys are getting serious, huh?" He tried to say it neutrally, which I appreciated.

"I've been kind of interested in 24/7 stuff for a while."

He tipped his head back. "Really? *You?*"

"Why not me?"

He slid off me and went to the fridge. Got out some bread and deli ham. "Because . . . I dunno. I'd have thought it would drive you crazy to have someone dominating you all the time. You're all independent and shit."

"Well, you're basically 24/7 with D, aren't you?"

He made a face. And a sandwich. "I guess. But I don't live with him yet. So he can't monitor me, thank God."

"See, I want to be, like, *controlled.*"

He raised his eyebrows at me and took a bite of sandwich. "You are just full of surprises." He nodded at the ham. "You want me to make you one?"

"Nah. I've eaten too many sandwiches lately. And we're out of my kind of bread."

He chewed contemplatively. Swallowed. "I guess I knew you liked being ordered around. But every time I ask you what you're doing with GK and Kel, you get all weird."

"I don't get weird. I told you, I help train Greg, and then I just . . . do whatever Kel tells me."

"What does she tell you to do?"

"Ummm . . . she pegs me. Does rope shit. I bring her drinks and whatever. If we're out in public and need help at, like, a store, I have to be the one to ask."

His forehead wrinkled, and then he shrugged. "Whatever floats your boat." I could tell he wanted to ask something else, but he didn't.

I looked at the laptop again. "Anyway, I have to write some, like, goals for our week together."

"They gave you homework?"

"D totally used to give you homework, so don't even judge."

He grinned. "If you want, I can give you some of my old essays to copy."

"I have a crazy feeling Kel and Greg would know the difference between my writing and yours."

"It's still weird to hear you call him Greg. He'll always be GK to me."

"Did I tell you about how I used to call Kel 'Ma'am' and him 'Greg'? Except every time I said, 'Yes, Greg,' all we could think about was *A Very Brady Sequel* where Marcia says 'Yes, Greg,' all low and sensual when they're about to kiss..."

"Ha." He brought the rest of the sandwich over and sat on me again.

"So now I call him 'sir,' if I'm subbing to him. But with a lowercase *S*."

"That's cute."

We sat in silence for a moment. I considered telling him about my conversation with Cass, but I wasn't really in the mood to get into a discussion about Hal.

He nudged my shin with his heel. "Be careful, okay?"

"With what?"

"Everything. Ever." He leaned his head back against my shoulder. Peeled a strip of ham off the end of his sandwich and dangled it near my mouth. I relented and ate it out of his hand. He mock-gasped. "Bad Jew."

As though I didn't eat pork all the fucking time. But I played along. "I should give back all my Hanukkah presents."

He laughed, and the sound vibrated pleasantly against my body. "I'm nervous about moving," he said after a while.

"It'll be fun."

"What if it's not? What if it's horrible? What if we only like each other because we don't see each other that much?"

"Only one way to find out, right?"

He burped and took another bite of sandwich. "I guess."

"I think it'll be good."

He set his crusts on top of my laptop. Brushed off his hands and leaned back again. "What if he starts punishing me all the time because he sees all the bad stuff I do that I never even tell him about?"

"You tell him what he needs to know. You're probably harder on yourself than he would be. I think, if anything, you'll get way more of the fun kind of spanking and less of the for-real caning."

"I don't know." He sounded discouraged. I would have expected him to be much more excited about this.

I waited, but he didn't say anything else. "What's wrong?" I asked, placing my chin on his shoulder.

"The DD thing. It's harder than I thought it would be," he added defensively.

I squeezed him. "I never thought it sounded easy."

He stayed like that for a few minutes, tense and still. Then he sighed dramatically. "Everything's fine if I'm the one who goes to him and is like, 'I deserve it.' And we never do it without talking about it first, without agreeing. But still. When it's his idea, it's . . . it's not as simple as, like, we do it and it's all over and forgiven. Sometimes I feel pissed off afterwards. Sometimes I don't even know I'm still pissed off until like two weeks later. I remember old punishments, and I know he does too. There's no such thing as a clean slate. 'Aw, you're forgiven and everything's fine now.' That's bullshit."

This surprised me. I'd been under the impression that DD had been working out pretty great for Dave. "Well, if you don't want to do it anymore—"

"I do, though. Don't listen to me. I like it. It's just stupid. I'm stupid. I'm not stupid. It's just difficult."

"I know."

He paused. "And then I wonder what I'm gonna do when I'm older, if I stay with him. I know I'm not supposed to be like, 'Ooh, spanking, hot,' when it's the real discipline stuff, but, like, maybe I was drawn to this kind of relationship because there's something hot about being, like, young and needing someone to keep me in line. Does that make sense?"

"You've always had kind of a daddy thing."

He snorted. "I have, haven't I?"

"Yep."

"So what's this gonna look like when I'm thirty? Forty? And I'm too old to be cute, and he's using a walker."

"D's what, ten years older than you are?"

"Twelve."

"He's not gonna be using a walker next year. Or a decade from now."

"Well, when I'm sixty, then. And he's seventy-two."

"It's gonna look perfect."

He rolled his head back again. "I just want to be clear that I love D."

"I know."

He swung his legs off me and stood. "Like, a lot."

"I know."

"I just hate hair school and the world and growing up." He disappeared into his room.

I opened the laptop again. I had an email from Kel. Subject line: *Suggested Protocol.*

She'd given me a list of ideas for rules and told me to pick my favorites. I rejected a few right off the bat, like shaving all my body hair or getting pedicured or always keeping my head below Kel's. I also decided bowing to them whenever they entered a room would be stupid, and that I didn't want to remain on my hands and knees at all times.

I went with *strip upon entering the house, always speak respectfully, be ready to serve sexually at any time, ask permission to eat, shower, and use the bathroom, complete all assigned chores within the time limits given, answer all questions promptly,* and *email an update once a day from work.* I also said yes to keeping the kitchen stocked and never coming without permission. I paused at *keep Kel and Greg apprised of all personal goals, concerns, and questions throughout the week.*

They definitely wanted me to say yes to that one. But . . . privacy.

Tell me how you feel *about this, Gould,* got exhausting. Also, I didn't want them to be concerned about my concerns.

I sighed and said yes to the apprising. Once I'd sent my list back to Kel, I returned to my Word doc and started to write.

I don't know exactly what my goals are or what I need. I want to be challenged. I want to serve in ways that aren't easy. I want to be called out for everything I do wrong. I want to be humiliated sometimes—really *humiliated, not just embarrassed a little. I want to practice serving in public and having to answer to others. I want to be asked questions I can't answer. I want to be scared once in a while.*

I made myself stop. This was supposed to be about what *she* wanted, right? I wanted whatever Kel wanted.

God, this was so fucking confusing.

I stared for a moment at a horrible elf doll Dave had placed on top of our stereo system. I remembered the satisfaction I'd taken, after Hal died, in never telling anyone how I really felt. Because people do this thing where they—they try to help when you're hurting, and it's nice of them, but they almost never get it right. I got sort of addicted to having people talk to me about grief—listening to them sympathize and offer advice—and then nodding. Saying, *You're right. I never thought about it that way. I* should *try journaling.* Something about the relief on their faces when they thought they'd reached me. The way they seemed to think grief could be contained in tidy moments like this, where I was sad and then I got a hug and some BS about a "better place" or "healing with time" and then my sadness ebbed.

What was actually inside me was so ugly. I mean *so* ugly.

I was afraid that the things I really wanted, the things I really felt, would be too ugly for Kel and Greg. But I was also afraid that I'd do the same thing to them that I'd done to the people who'd tried to help me grieve: I'd shut them out. I'd nod and I'd follow the script and make them feel like they'd done a perfect job of owning me. But inside I'd be restless, unsatisfied.

Don't shut them out.
But don't scare them away.
Be honest.
Just not too honest.
Come on, Gould. It's not that difficult. Right?

I got a reply from Kel the next morning with an informal contract, listing all the rules we'd discussed, and ending with this:

While my submissive, Gould, will not be subjected to any activities that might cause permanent physical or psychological harm, Gould agrees to serve in any way I deem fit, whether domestically or sexually. He agrees to suffer for my amusement if I wish it, to keep the house and yard tidy, to be used by others if I require it, and to anticipate my needs whenever possible. While he is required to ask permission to go anywhere outside of work and his dominants' home, he is not forbidden from taking initiative and acquiring or arranging things that will improve the comfort of his Ma'am and sir.

Should he safeword, the contract for the week is broken, and while we may renegotiate and attempt another week of service in the future, a safeword will effectively end the agreement for this week.

Gould promises to make us aware in advance of any possible emotional or physical triggers, including old injuries, current health conditions, phobias, past abuse, etc., and to keep a dialogue ongoing about his progress, concerns, and desires.

Most importantly, he will remember that as my property, he is valuable, and is to be cherished and cared for. He has more than earned this opportunity to serve, through his kindness, intelligence, and dedication.

I read that section over and over, getting a strange feeling each time I got to the last paragraph. Like I had to detach myself in order to avoid taking the full impact of the words.

I wasn't sure how to address the triggers thing. I didn't have any that I knew of. No phobias. I still had some issues regarding Hal's death, but I didn't think that would come up, like, in a scene. Aside from obsessive thoughts about Bill, which could hit me anywhere, anytime. But I was used to that. I didn't know what my concerns were. There was the wanting-privacy thing, but I wasn't about to share that with them.

Greg had included a section too:

While I am only second-in-command, I promise to be a good dominant to Gould any way I can. I request that he address me as 'sir' during our interactions and obey any orders he receives from me, except in instances where Ma'am has recruited him to help with my training. I reserve the right to use Gould, with Ma'am's permission, for my pleasure or for hers. Any refusal to obey an order will result in a correction, but also a discussion. Gould promises to be as open with me as he is with Ma'am about any problems he is having.

Then there was a space for me to write my ... requests? Promises? I stared at the doc for a moment, then started to type.

I promise to obey all orders I receive from Ma'am and sir, and to answer all questions truthfully. What was I, being sworn in before the court? I deleted the last part of the sentence ... *and to be honest with them about my experiences. I promise to serve loyally. To treat them with respect and ...*

Love? Would they interpret that the wrong way?

To treat them with respect, and care. I want them to know how grateful I am to them for everything they've taught me. For their kindness and patience.

I hesitated.

I'm ready to show them what I've learned.

CHAPTER SIX

G reg and Kel's house was a bit like a castle—a narrow stone building with a small, sort of half-assed turret. They'd gotten the place from Kel's dad when he'd moved into a condo a few years ago. They complained sometimes about feeling out of place in their "rich" neighborhood, since they weren't lawyers or surgeons. In addition to running Riddle, Greg worked for a nonprofit that collected curriculum data from universities, and Kel worked part-time at a health food store despite having very little interest in whole grains or natural shampoo.

Sunday evening at five after six, I walked up the steps and rang the bell. I'd showered just before coming here, and my hair was still damp and it was cold as fuck outside.

Kel answered, wearing tight jeans and a low-cut purple sweater. Her hair had been straightened, and she had in small, figure eight–shaped gold earrings. For a second I froze. Was I supposed to say something, do something? Greet her in some special way? I couldn't remember.

She gave me a huge smile. "Well, well."

I grinned back, hands deep in my pockets. "Well, well."

"Come on in, beautiful."

I stepped inside, trying not to let my nervousness show. Whatever was cooking in the kitchen smelled amazing.

She pulled me into a hug. "Oh, I am *so* glad you're here," she whispered. She kicked the door shut without letting me go.

I hugged her back. "I'm really glad to be here."

She leaned back, placing her hands on my shoulders. "You smell good."

"I tried some of Dave's bodywash. It has some really gay-retirement-home name, like 'Vibrant Hills.' He swears by it."

"Well, it's working for you. You can strip in the living room. Greg made dinner."

I followed her into the living room, where I struggled out of my shirt. I never could get the hang of stripping gracefully. I slid my jeans off. Then my boxers—red-and-white gingham, like a picnic tablecloth. A recent birthday present from Dave. I removed my socks, folded everything, and left it all in a stack by the wall. I turned to go to the kitchen.

Kel was blocking the doorway, leaning against the doorframe with her arms folded. I paused.

"Kneel for me," she said casually.

I knelt, the carpet prickling my knees. Clasped my left wrist in my right hand behind my back.

She stepped forward and drew the faux leather collar out of her pocket. She buckled it around my neck. My skin seemed to buzz where her fingers brushed it. She patted my head when she was done.

"Now crawl." She turned and walked away without even waiting to see if I'd obey.

I crawled after her.

In the kitchen, Greg was standing at the stove, naked except for a bright-blue apron. He gave me a sheepish smile. "Hey."

I looked up at him. "Hi, sir. Nice apron."

"Thanks."

"Is it so we don't end up with a dinner full of pubes?"

"Actually, it's to protect my jibbly bits from hot oil. But thank you for the image."

"You two." Kel took a seat at the table. "Starting already?"

"Of *course* not, Ma'am," Greg said sweetly. "So I've got gluten-free pasta—I think it's brown rice?" He checked the package. "Yep. With white wine Dijon sauce. And there's flourless brownies for dessert."

"Nice," I said.

"How's your weekend been?"

I sat back on my heels. "Oh, fine. I had to work a half day yesterday, which sucked. But now I can take a half day sometime this week."

I tried to act like it was not at all weird to be having this conversation naked on my knees.

Kel snapped her fingers. I crawled over to where she pointed under the table. She had a crop, which I hadn't noticed before. She used it to stroke my dick and balls without looking at me, while she talked to Greg about a mutual friend. I breathed out, the collar pressing against my throat, my dick slowly rising.

After a few minutes, Greg brought the food over. It smelled ridiculously good. He served Kel first, then filled his own bowl. Then he filled a third bowl and set it on the floor next to me.

Well. This was new.

My face grew warm as I took the fork he handed me. I ate quietly on the floor, accepting occasional bouts of teasing whenever Kel put down her fork and picked up the crop. At one point she ordered me to stop eating and get on my hands and knees again, facing away from her, my knees spread. She had me put my bowl in front of me and eat hands-free, while she gave my asshole a series of light, fast whacks with the crop. It stung just enough that I couldn't focus on eating and ended up with white wine Dijon sauce all over my face. She made me turn and look at her so she could see the mess, then sent me over to Greg so he could wipe my mouth.

My dick was bumping the underside of my stomach, and my skin was burning. I didn't feel ashamed, exactly—just very sure of my place. And very aware that there was no way to hide from them, no way I could use obedience to escape scrutiny.

They let me sit at the table for dessert, and we talked about work and Riddle and Greg's family. I cleared the table and loaded the dishwasher, then got permission from Kel to go wash my face. We eventually gathered on the floor of the living room for naked Scrabble. They were big on naked games. Kel was winning, and I had just played *allium*.

"Not a word," Greg said. "Spank him."

I grinned. "Uhhh, that's what onions are, chef."

Kel laughed. "Would you like to challenge, Greg?"

"Nah," he muttered, smirking. "I'll let him have it."

"Uh-huh. You know I'm right." I drew six new tiles and then looked up at Kel. "May I use the bathroom, Ma'am?"

She nodded. "Absolutely."

I got up, and she got up with me.

I was a little confused as she walked beside me to the bathroom. But I didn't think much of it until she stood to my right at the toilet and took my dick in her hand.

Um . . .

I glanced at her. She gazed back at me, her expression mildly amused. "Go on."

I didn't want to be the one who said, *You're holding my dick*, but . . .

"Now, Gould." Perfectly calm, like there was nothing unusual about this at all.

God-fucking-damn it.

I didn't want to say *I can't*. But I also didn't think I *could*.

This is exactly what you asked for. No choice. To be controlled.

I tilted my head back, willing myself to, you know. *Let it go. Let it go-o-o . . .*

I thought about waterfalls, pouring teakettles, fucking Roman fountains.

"Should I tell Greg to get the slapper?"

"No, Ma'am."

I could do this. I could so do this. I pushed, and the pressure built, but just when I thought I was gonna go, my stomach tightened and nothing happened.

She dug the heel of her hand into my abdomen, hard.

Piss trickled out of me, then turned to a stream. I closed my eyes, but she swatted my thigh sharply. I made myself look down at her hand holding my cock, at the jet of liquid coming out of me.

Being ashamed isn't an option. All you have to do is what she says.

She shook my dick dry, kissed the back of my neck, and gave me another hard slap. "Good boy. Next time, piss right away, or I'll make you hold it all night." She turned to the sink and washed her hands.

"Yes, Ma'am," I said quietly.

This. This was exactly the kind of stuff I'd wanted. These ordinary mortifications—nothing particularly sexy about them, but they humbled me so completely.

I caught a glimpse of the two of us in the mirror. I looked—not handsome, exactly. I'd never look handsome. But I didn't look as awkward as I felt. And she was . . . I mean, seriously, *how*? I wanted to run my hands down her back, kiss each bone of her spine, trace her hips and then slide my hands forward and down until I reached the coarse hair between her legs, until my fingers slipped inside her.

Ask if you can touch her.

Except how could she possibly see me as a viable sexual being when she'd just held my dick while I pissed?

When I met her gaze in the mirror again, she was staring back at me, and I swallowed nervously at what I saw in her expression. She didn't look disgusted. She looked satisfied, happy.

"Ma'am?" I whispered. "Could I—"

She was already turning to face me. She kissed me gently on the cheek, and then, after a second, on the lips. It was a deep kiss, the kind that can make you feel like you've just woken up from a hundred-year sleep to find the whole world different and stunning. It was not the way mentors and mentees kissed, and I didn't give a flying fuck. Shocks of pleasure rippled through me as I leaned into her. I teased her mouth open with my tongue, and she moaned, her nipples hard against my chest, my dick pressed against her pubic hair. I could feel the warmth between her legs, and I wanted so badly to go to my knees. To have her grab my hair and shove my face against her cunt and not let me stop until she'd come as many times as she wanted.

We broke apart, breathing hard.

"Sorry," she whispered, not sounding it at all.

"Why?" We'd done plenty more in the past, and yet something about this kiss felt stranger, more meaningful than anything else we'd shared.

She shook her head. One side of her mouth quirked up. "I'm supposed to be in control."

She turned and left with a single snap of her fingers. I stared after her a moment, then followed.

The three of us continued the game, which Kel eventually won. Greg went to make popcorn. When he came back, holding the hot bag by the very edge, Kel grinned at him.

"What?" He sat, offering her some.

She took a handful. "I was just admiring your curly butt hair."

He snorted. "You should talk."

"Oh, you did not go there."

"Didn't you get turned down for sex once because of your hairy ass?"

She threw a kernel at him.

I picked the kernel up and set it on the coffee table. "You have a hairy ass?"

Kel had pegged me several times over the past year, but we never really had the kind of sex that involved me getting up close and personal with her ass.

She finished chewing. "I have hair in my ass crack. Not an obscene amount. It's not, like, creating a fairy tale tangle of vines over my butthole. It's just normal human hair."

Greg passed the bag to me. "You're a hirsute beast."

She shoved him, laughing. "You're sooo not coming for at least a year." She took the bag when I offered it to her. "Anyway, I had this guy once, and I wanted him to rim me. You'd have thought I was asking him to lick a fucking Ugg boot. He wouldn't do it. So I started shaving any time I thought I might end up naked around anyone. You know, just in case I asked a guy to worship my body and he was like, 'No way am I gonna worship that chimpanzee ass.' And then I realized how fucking ridiculous that was. Because— Okay, Gould, I'm sure you've encountered men who have hairy cracks, right?"

"I definitely have."

"And were you like, 'Oh, I can't possibly eat this ass—it's got hair on it?'"

"That has never happened. I like hair."

"Same." She set the bag on the floor in front of Greg.

"But I shaved mine for a while," I admitted. "For that exact reason. Some doms are really weird about, like, wanting subs to be smooth."

"Well, I stopped doing it years ago. Because call me crazy, but I don't think it's gonna kill anyone to go down on a woman who has ass hair."

I shifted, crossing my legs. "Dave shaves every day. No kidding. And he got on this big kick for a while about cleaning his asshole with witch hazel."

She raised her eyebrows. "Are you serious?"

"Dead serious."

Greg pushed the bag aside. "God. All this talk of eating asses. I can't enjoy my popcorn anymore."

Kel took another big handful of popcorn and shoved it in her mouth. "Mmm. Ass corn."

"Stop!"

She laughed, trying belatedly to cover her mouth. "What's your problem with assholes? I know the one time I suggested you rim Gould, you were, like, deeply horrified."

"I'm just not that into assholes. Especially guy assholes. Sue me— it's a straight-guy thing. We can't shake all the stuff society teaches us."

"What does society teach you about assholes?"

"That that's gay-guy territory."

I felt a spark of irritation, even though it wasn't his fault that straight guys were raised to think they should never have to eat ass.

"You rimmed me once," Kel said.

"Yeah, but you kinda had to convince me."

"Was it the crack hair?"

He grinned. "Maybe."

"Shut up. So it's just asses? Because you don't seem to mind sucking Gould's dick."

"Dicks are no big deal. It's just, where the literal shit comes out . . ."

"Um—" I reached for the bag "—the first time you sucked me off, you looked like you were eating buffalo balls on a reality show."

"But I'm better with dicks now." He looked at Kel. "Aren't I better with dicks?"

She nodded. "You are better with dicks. God knows I've had you practice blowing me enough."

"But I'm, like, better with actual guys' dicks. Probably because regular dicks are small compared to your strap-on."

"Well. I haven't had you practice on anyone but Gould."

"Nuh-uh. There was that guy a couple of years ago. At Riddle? You made me blow him for like an hour."

"It was five minutes."

"Sheesh, gimme some credit."

I passed the bag to Kel again. "I don't really like rimming either. Giving, I mean." I'd only received once. And later I'd checked the guy's profile on Fet, and it was all about how much he loved eating ass. Like, he would eat anyone's ass, "you can look however," and he didn't want anything in return. It made me feel . . . insignificant, I guess. I'd had this stupid idea that being rimmed meant somebody wanted *me*, specifically. Wanted to make me feel good. That rimjob was the first time I'd realized you could still feel used by someone who was wholeheartedly dedicated to making you come.

"Really?" Greg said.

"Uh, yeah, dude. Not all queer guys like it. Just like I don't care about stuff up my ass."

"What do you mean don't care about it?"

Kel touched my shoulder, still looking at Greg. "He means he'll do anal play as part of his training. But it's not his thing. Where have you been this past year?"

"I mean, I knew he didn't *love* it. But I thought he *liked* it."

"Sometimes." I shrugged.

Kel pulled me closer to her. "So this week, we're gonna fuck him whenever we want. So he can practice."

I snorted. "Aw. Thanks, guys."

Kel glanced back and forth between both of us, smiling. "I'm really looking forward to this week. I'll just say that right now."

Greg smiled too. "You've been so much happier since we started playing with Gould."

"Have I?"

"You used to come home and the first thing you'd tell me was how stressful everything was at work. Then last year, it turned to, 'I wonder if we could get Gould to come over tonight . . .'"

Seriously?

Her cheeks flushed a little. "Well, can you blame me?"

"Of course not." Greg grinned again. "Just made me kind of jealous was all."

I studied him. "Were you really jealous?" The subject had come up before, but he always blew it off.

He shook more popcorn into his hand. "It would be hard to be jealous of you."

Kel gave a little gasp and a laugh. "Greg!"

He seemed confused for a second. "Oh, come on. I didn't mean it like . . . You *have* qualities people would be jealous of. I just mean I didn't get jealous, because I—" His shoulders bobbed, like he was trying to shrug. "I really like you."

I wasn't sure how to respond.

Kel nudged his knee with hers. "Tell Gould what you said about his ass the other day."

Now it was Greg's turn to look alarmed. "Huh?"

"What you said to me. Tell him."

He rolled his eyes. "Oh God."

"Come on." She turned to me. "He said you have a hot ass."

I stared. "Me?"

Greg opened his mouth and hesitated a few seconds before speaking. "You gotta understand, I never looked at guys' asses that way. Like, when I was growing up, no straight guy would've been like, 'Oh, that guy's got a nice ass.'"

Kel placed her arm under her breasts to support them for a moment. "Don't Indian guys, like, kiss each other to say hello or something?"

"We hold hands. That's a totally normal Indian straight-guy thing to do."

"Sure."

"That's *different* from looking at dudes' bodies. Women're always checking each other out so you can be like, 'Am I hotter than her?' But guys don't do that." He glanced at me. "So I dunno, I was looking at you the other day, and I realized you've got some good junk in the trunk. I just wanted to say that—in a very heterosexual way."

Kel grabbed his knee and shook it affectionately. "Oh, honey. There is no heterosexual way to say that."

I looked at Greg. "I appreciate that in a very queer way." I turned to Kel. "And he can totally heteroppreciate guys' asses."

She nodded. "You're right. You're right. I just like to give him a hard time." She pushed her fingers up through Greg's hair. Gripped for a moment. "What if I told you to rim Gould?"

Greg laughed awkwardly. "Now?"

"Yeah."

He gazed at her. "I'd do it for you. But I'd have to be in the mood."

Jesus Christ. I didn't want a rimjob from someone who had to steel himself for it.

Kel moved her hand down to the back of Greg's neck. "So what if you got a nice, long blowjob from Gould. Until you were begging—*begging* for a way to earn your release. And then I made you eat his ass?"

Greg and I glanced at each other. I wasn't sure if this was an order disguised as a question, or if we were allowed input.

"I mean," I said, "If he doesn't like it, I'd rather not—"

"No," Greg said. "I'll do it."

"Can I shower first?" I asked Kel.

Greg laughed. "*Please* let him shower first."

I was pretty sure Kel would say yes. So I was surprised when she said, "You can go to the bathroom and use wipes, or a washcloth." She paused as Greg groaned, then went on addressing me. "You showered before you came over. You're clean enough."

Greg saluted me. "Just make sure you wipe away all the hepatitis."

My face burned. "I'll see what I can do." I glanced at Kel. "Should I go now?"

She beckoned with one finger. Stretched her legs out in front of her. "Come here first. Lie across my lap."

I had no idea where this was going. But I positioned myself across her thighs, supporting my upper body with my forearms on the floor. She placed a hand on my ass. Ran her nails lightly down one cheek, then the other. I shivered, my dick rising. She zigzagged one nail down the back of my thigh. I dropped my chin so that my hair brushed the carpet. She continued stroking my ass. Tapped my left arm until I hesitantly lifted it from the floor and put it behind me. She tapped the other. I placed my forehead on the carpet and offered my right arm too.

She gathered my wrists in her other hand and pinned them to the center of my back.

I inhaled and waited. She spread my cheeks, still holding my wrists in her other hand. I tensed, thighs quivering, then made myself take a breath and let the tension out. She spread me wider. "Look at him, Greg."

I flushed from my ears down to my chest as Greg scooted closer. I could feel how close he was, but I couldn't really see him.

"He looks tight," Greg murmured.

I closed my eyes. I wanted to jerk away from her hand, but I forced myself to remain still.

"He is," Kel agreed quietly. She let go and slid one finger down my crack, then tapped my hole. I bit my lip.

"Is he hard?" Greg asked.

"Oh yeah. His cock's pressing against my thigh."

I would like to die now, please.

"He's got almost as much crack hair as you," Greg said to Kel.

Kel burst out laughing, and I couldn't keep a straight face either.

Fuck yes. Talk about me like I'm not here. Embarrass the shit out of me.

"He looks good, doesn't he?" Kel asked.

"He does," Greg said softly. I heard him kiss her.

"You want to make him feel good?"

"Yeah." Greg's voice was rough.

"You want to make him come?"

"Yes, Ma'am."

I turned my head but couldn't see what was going on. A moment later, Greg's hands were on my ass, spreading me again. My stomach muscles contracted against Kel's thighs as Greg's fingers dug hard into my cheeks.

"You clean him up," Kel ordered Greg.

"With what?" he asked.

"Butt wipes, Greg. They're in the bathroom."

Shame collided with arousal, and I suddenly couldn't put a coherent thought together. Kel squeezed my wrists, and I made a small, choked sound as Greg let me go. I heard him get up and walk to the bathroom.

"Spread your legs." Kel stroked my thigh with her free hand. "He needs to see what he's doing."

Somehow I made myself do it. I lay there with my right thigh pressed against her hip, my left knee touching hers, and tried to stay present. To acknowledge and accept what was happening. Blood rushed to my head, and the carpet made my forehead itch.

Greg came back into the room and knelt beside me.

Kel shifted, keeping her grip firm on my wrists. "What's the matter, Greg?"

"I can't believe you're making me wipe his ass."

"But you're going to be a good boy and do it, right?"

"Ass-wiping is not hot in any universe."

"Agree," I said to the carpet. I jumped as Kel gave me a light swat.

She ran her nails over my cheeks again. "Who said anything about this needing to be hot for *you two*?"

"Yes, Ma'am," Greg and I said in unison.

"So let's get this show on the road. Or we'll forget about rimming and blowing, and I'll line you two up for a strapping instead."

Greg spread my cheeks and cleaned between them. His wipe-covered finger circled my hole, then pressed inward for a few seconds. I winced, but held still. Greg stood again and went to the kitchen, presumably to throw the wipe away.

When he came back, Kel pulled my head up by a fistful of hair and spoke to Greg. "He's a good slave, isn't he? Make him blow you. Use his mouth. Hard as you want, but don't come."

The word "slave" . . . God, I could get used to that.

I let Greg drag me off Kel's thighs. I ended up on my stomach on the carpet, my head in Greg's lap. He pushed his dick into my mouth, and I quickly covered my teeth with my lips and started to suck.

He arched, catching a fistful of my hair. "Oh. Ohh, yeah." He shoved my head down, and I gagged.

Hell yes. Use me.

Kel crawled over and straddled my back. Guided my left arm behind me and placed my left wrist almost between my shoulder blades, holding it there. She reached back with her other hand and flicked my hip until I lifted slightly off the floor. Then she grabbed my balls and the base of my dick and squeezed.

"Fuck yeah," Greg whispered, pumping into my mouth. "Fuck *yes*."

"You want him to suck you harder?" Kel asked.

"Please," Greg said between gasps.

I was already sucking harder, but Kel slapped my ass anyway. I bobbed as fast as I could on Greg's cock. Greg's moans became more urgent, and I worked until Kel slapped me again. "Enough."

I stopped, lifting my head until Greg's dick slid out of my mouth. Greg's thighs were flexing repeatedly, and he didn't let go of my hair.

"Okay, here's how this will work," Kel instructed calmly, her breathing only slightly roughened. She got on her hands and knees beside us. "Gould, you straddle me, facing backward. Lean forward until your ass is out."

I glanced at her uneasily. "Ma'am? Are you sure you can hold me?"

"I promise, I'll be fine."

I got up and straddled her carefully, facing away from her head. Leaned forward until my chest was against her lower back, supporting myself as much as possible with my feet braced on the floor.

"Greg," she said.

I heard him shuffle across the carpet on his knees. "Yes, Ma'am?"

"I want your cock in my mouth while you're rimming Gould."

More shuffling. A moment later, Greg's hands were on my hips. I jerked. "Easy," Greg said quietly, running his thumbs over my hip bones. He cleared his throat. "I'm gonna need Gould to scoot back a little. Is that gonna strain your neck?"

She shifted under me. "Gould, can you move back a little?"

I moved back until I could feel her hair against my ass and my inner thighs.

"Okay." Her voice was slightly muffled. "And then Greg, can you move your hips forward and, like, up?"

There was some more adjusting. Greg laughed. "Someone's gonna get hurt. We're too old for this shit."

"Oh, shut up. We've got this."

"We look like the rejected chapter of the *Kama Sutra*. Darwin Awards: Three killed playing naked Twister."

"Get rimming."

I listened to the wet sucking sounds of Kel blowing Greg. His fingers dug into my hips, and he exhaled sharply. Then I felt him lean forward. But nothing happened.

"Ma'am?" he said after a moment.

The wet sounds stopped. "Yeah?"

"Permission to dental dam? Seriously? I'm so sorry. I just . . . Please?"

For fuck's sake. Erection officially dead. Nothing like a rimjob where the guy literally had to cover his tongue in order to not vomit when he licked you. Though . . . I had never in my life met a person who had actually used a dental dam. I was sort of curious about how it felt.

"Permission granted," Kel said. "We have, like, one condom left in the drawer by the couch."

Greg rubbed my hip. "I swear it's not that you're disgusting. It's just assholes. In general."

"Yeah," I said. "Okay."

I half rested on Kel's back, my legs shaking a little with the effort of holding myself up, while Greg went to cut up a condom.

"So," I said casually. "How 'bout them Eagles?"

Her body trembled with laughter underneath me.

I went on. "I mean, this weather we're having . . ."

She tried to swat my leg. "Stop."

A couple minutes later, Greg was back in position. "I'm gonna lube you a little bit," he told me. A second later, some lube drizzled down my crack.

"Are we ready to resume?" Kel asked.

"Yep. Here goes nothing." He stretched the latex over my asshole and held it in place.

He barely caught my hole with the first swipe of his tongue. He got it on the second and third, though. It was weird, to be expecting the wetness of a tongue and get latex and lube instead.

He flicked his tongue hard against the barrier. I snapped my head up, flexing my ass and thighs, my dick pressing against Kel's warm back. It had been so long since I'd been rimmed, I'd forgotten how fucking good it felt. Even with a dental dam.

Maybe I was just jealous that he'd had the balls to ask for one. The couple of times I'd rimmed guys, all I'd been able to think about was germs and literal shit.

He started lapping quickly, like a cat. He was sloppy, and it was kind of cute. I shifted against Kel, more turned on by her low hums as she sucked Greg than by Greg's rim skillz.

Greg stopped for a moment and clutched my hips. "Aw, *fuck. Fuck,* that's good. Jesus, Kel." He spread my cheeks again, and suddenly the latex disappeared. This time, I felt the warm slickness of his tongue circling my hole.

Holy fucking shit.

I jolted, crying out before I could stop myself. He chuckled. "You like that?"

I nodded, my chin digging into Kel's tailbone.

"I'm going for it. I'm all in."

Kel shifted under me. "Are you putting your actual tongue on his actual asshole?"

"Yep. Latex tastes weird." He patted my ass. "You taste like wipe and lube."

Part of me was wishing this could be like last Saturday—just Kel and me, having silent sex. But part of me was kind of enjoying this circus. Greg had always been a talker. And while I didn't find that sexy, it was kind of entertaining.

He licked me again, pushing the tip of his tongue inside, and I gasped.

"Ask me for more," he said.

I hoped Kel would come to my defense, tell him to just keep going. But her body shuddered with another laugh.

"Please, sir." That was all I could manage.

"Please, sir, what?"

"Please keep going."

"With what?"

"Put your tongue back in my ass, dude!"

Dude? Really?

He and Kel both laughed.

Greg went back to it, circling my hole. I squirmed, rubbing my balls between Kel's shoulders. The thing was, Greg didn't stop the circling. And after a while I got desensitized. *Really* would have liked him to try mixing it up a little. He was panting and moaning as he worked, and a moment later he pulled back again to say, "Oh God. I'm gonna come. Oh no, don't stop, don't st—"

Kel's voice. "Don't you dare. Focus on Gould."

Greg tapped on my back. "Am I doing it right?"

"It's like a clit," Kel said. "Just work it like that."

"Actually—" I surprised myself by speaking up "—it's kind of . . . You can use a lot of spit, first of all. Like, the more the better."

"You want me to . . . spit there?"

"Yep. And, like, blow sometimes."

"Blow?"

"Like a stream of air. And you know how if you're going down on Kel, if you find something that works, you should keep doing it?"

"Yeah?" Greg said.

"With rimming, you actually want to mix it up. Like, different patterns, and you can put your tongue inside sometimes. Just sayin.'"

"There you go," Kel said. "Listen to Gould."

I couldn't believe I'd just told someone how to do a sex thing with me. Normally if I wasn't into what was happening, I just spaced out and waited for it to be over.

Greg went back to work, mixing it up with an impressive enthusiasm.

"Gould," Kel whispered. "Use your fingers."

I slid my hands down her ass, then up and down her thighs, warming the smooth skin. Then I ran two fingers between her legs, feeling the slickness of her cunt. She moaned softly. I spread her lips and dipped my ring finger between them. Worked it inside her, then extending my pinkie until it brushed her clit. She whimpered softly. I slipped my other two fingers into her and thrust gently, then withdrew all three and circled her clit. Her hips started rocking, and after a few seconds, she'd matched her rhythm to mine, and I'd matched mine to Greg's. Her gasps got higher and faster, then slowed. So either she'd come or given up on it.

"Oh *fuck*," I said, as Greg flicked his tongue rapidly. I squeezed Kel's sides with my legs, my hips jerking.

Kel's voice was ragged, breathless. "Come, Gould. Now."

Greg blew lightly on my hole and then lapped at it, and I felt the pressure in my balls, but I couldn't quite come. And to Greg's credit, he kept going. Reached around with one hand and stroked my dick until my breath caught and I came hard on Kel's back.

I lay there panting, resisting the urge to collapse with my full weight on Kel's back. She touched my leg. "You can get up."

I climbed off her and slumped on the floor. The dental dam lay a few inches away, and I grinned at the sight of it, then looked up at Greg. "You're not bad."

He ran a hand up through the back of his hair, breathing hard. "That was not as gross as I thought."

"That's the most romantic thing anyone's ever said to me."

He grinned too, and sang a few lines of "Can You Feel the Love Tonight." He was, in a weird way, a little like Kamen. I made my brain promise never to have that thought again.

Kel lowered herself to the floor on her stomach, chin on her folded arms. "I thoroughly enjoyed myself."

"Are you gonna fall asleep?" Greg asked her.

"Maybe."

"Because I still haven't come."

"You whining?"

"Stating a fact."

"I'll take care of you in a minute." She turned her face out. "Gould, go get a bath ready. Someone got cum all over my back."

I laughed. "Yes, Ma'am." I hesitated, then leaned down and kissed her shoulder. She made a soft sound of approval.

I went upstairs.

CHAPTER
SEVEN

"I want to show you something," Kel said later. She and I had been lazing on the couch for a while, watching TV. Greg had spent about twenty minutes brushing his teeth, and was now upstairs showering.

She went and got her laptop. Pulled up a word document. It was just a series of dated entries, one or two lines each.

> *Ball-buster*
> *Don't you mean 'Mistress'?*
> *A lot of girls don't have the stamina to be full-time Masters.*
> *You just want to get revenge on men, don't you?*
> *Sure you're not a switch?*
> *Women just aren't as interested in being in charge.*
> *Men have more spatial awareness, and that's important for a BDSM scene.*
> *You just haven't met the right dom.*
> *Sexy. I'd serve you, and then I'd fuck you.*
> *With tits like that, you ought to be a slave.*
> *If you haven't trained with Laher, you haven't trained.*

It went on.

"What's this?" I asked.

"It's a list. From back when I was training to be a master. Of every shitty thing I heard from male masters. Maybe it's stupid to keep it, but I wanted to remember."

I looked at her. "When did you start training?"

"I was twenty-five. I'd just gotten out of a . . . weird relationship, let's say. I knew M/s was something I wanted to try, but at the time,

I only knew of one school nearby—Master Laher's Academy. I didn't have a problem with Laher. I met him at an event in DC, and he was very respectful. I mean, at the same fucking event, I sat at a dinner table with five male masters, and at one point another male master came over and greeted everyone at the table except me. Like he assumed I was someone's slave and didn't have permission to speak. So yeah, Laher was one of the better ones. His school allowed female masters, and I thought about going. But there was something about the way his followers treated him like a messiah, the way his word was basically law in the community . . . I just couldn't do it."

"Makes sense."

"I searched online for other female masters, and came across Master Tan's site. It was, like, a GeoCities page, I kid you not. But I liked her ideas."

"What were her ideas?"

"She does a lot of horse-whispery stuff. She's very touch-oriented, rather than verbal. She believes in encouraging good service through positive reinforcement rather than punishment."

"And you trained with her?"

Kel nodded. "Tan and I got along really well. She said I was a natural. She made me feel like . . ." Kel stopped and glanced at the doc again, then down. "She made me feel like I could actually be a really good master, in some ways. But in other ways, I think she found me aggravating."

"Why?"

She shrugged. "I was stubborn. Kind of arrogant. She said I had to get over that entitlement if I wanted to be able to guide others."

A long silence.

Kel went on. "She never framed it as, 'This is a man's world and so you have to be extra strong' and all that. She only took on female-identified students, yet she almost never made any comments about gender. I sort of resented her for that, later."

"Because . . . ?"

"I know that maybe a woman who wants to call herself a master shouldn't let herself get butt-hurt by what men say. But I wish Tan had prepared me for how bad it was gonna be. And I mean, I've met older women masters for whom it had been much, much worse. And I know all the gross stuff guys say to women in general. But I just didn't realize how far out of their way certain men would go to make me feel like I couldn't be a leader."

I glanced through the list again. "But you didn't believe them, right? It's bullshit. Obviously."

Her smile was almost a grimace. "Of course it's bullshit. But even bullshit, when you hear it enough, has a way of making you . . . doubt." She looked at the doc again. X-ed out. "Anyway. It's late. But I wanted to show that to you."

"For what it's worth," I said as she shut the laptop, "I think you'd be a great master."

She hesitated. "I'm really not sure I'm cut out for that."

Please don't say that.

She went on. "Not because I'm female. But because I—believe it or not—I'm very private."

"Me too."

She laughed and stroked the back of my neck. "You don't say." She pinched me lightly. "I think it's time for bed."

I lay awake a long time. I was on the left side of the bed. Kel was in the middle. She'd held me for a while before rolling over and twining herself with Greg.

I stared at the ceiling, biting a hangnail.

Had Kel showed me that doc to put an end to my fantasies of being her slave? If she was trying to tell me she *really* didn't want to be a master, I'd respect that, obviously. But she hadn't said she absolutely didn't want to. Just that she wasn't sure she was cut out for it.

And could I ever really be a slave? Could I be *her* slave? Could I be her slave if Greg was part of the equation?

I rolled toward her. Watched the rise and fall of her silhouette. I thought about what Greg had said tonight. *I really like you.* Enough to see Kel and me kiss the way we had kissed in the bathroom, and be okay with it?

"You just can't be alone, can you?"

Hal's voice.

An awful night, a couple of weeks before we'd broken up. Neither of us could so much as look at the other without saying something cruel.

And my reply: *"What are you talking about? I spend fucking hours alone. Especially now that you're alwa—"*

"No. No, that's not what I'm talking about. I mean your whole fucking image of yourself is based on how other people see you."

His words played over and over. *"You just can't be alone, can you?"*

I closed my eyes. *I wouldn't have to be, if you hadn't left.*

That was stupid. I was the one who'd ended the relationship. Said we should just be friends.

Just *friends? Like my friends don't matter more than anything in the world to me? Like it didn't hurt a thousand times worse to lose him as a friend than it did to lose him as a boyfriend?*

He *left.*

I remembered, for no apparent reason, standing in the wings on opening night of *Pirates of Penzance.* And all I could hear was my heartbeat—couldn't even fucking hear the cue lines. I was convinced I'd die before I ever made it on stage. It wasn't even anything specific, like fear that I'd forget a line or hit a wrong note and look stupid. It was just that I didn't want all those people *looking* at me. Even if I hadn't had any lines. Even if I'd gotten to stand on the back of the stage, bathed in shadows and wearing a hood, I just didn't want those eyes on me.

Hal had never minded people looking. He'd *wanted* people to look. Dave said he was pretty sure Hal and Bill's scene that night had been a performance for Dave's benefit—even though Dave hadn't actually witnessed it. Hal and Dave had been arguing, and Dave had warned him not to mess around with Bill. And Hal had apparently taken that as a challenge.

I hate you, I thought to him. *I don't need you.*

"I don't think this is working for either of us," I'd told him the night we broke up.

"Could we try, Gould? I mean, I can be better. Seriously, I can be better."

I shut my eyes tighter as tears streaked down my temples. His voice—it never sounded the same in my head as it had in real life. After he died, I'd made sure to save at least one voice mail from each of my friends, so that if anything ever happened, I'd remember exactly what they'd sounded like.

"Could we try, Gould?"

"I'm sorry," I'd told him, as gently as I could. *"It's over."*

"Seriously, I can be better."

I drew a deep breath. *You didn't ever have to be better. You were perfect. You were mine.*

The next day, Kel and Greg were going to Greg's aunt's house after Greg got done with work. I was expected to have dinner ready for them when they got home at eight. No big deal. Except that all the recipes I could think of seemed unimpressive or too involved.

So I called Kamen.

He answered on the first ring. "Hey!" He sounded kind of breathless.

"Are you okay?" I gripped the phone tighter, suddenly suspicious. "Are you having sex?"

"No. Just doing something top secret."

"You know you don't have to tell people when you're doing something secret."

"I know. But I like to. What's up?"

I leaned against the kitchen counter. I was still in my work clothes, and it occurred to me that I'd never asked whether I had to get naked when I entered the house if Kel and Greg weren't there. "I need to cook dinner for Kel and Greg. I need something delicious and impressive, but that I can't possibly screw up."

"Oh my God."

"Oh my God?"

"Oh my God. I kid you not. I am gonna tell you about some garlic chicken that'll change your life."

"For three easy payments of $39.99, or . . .?"

"Gould. Listen. Can you get four boneless, skinless chicken breasts?"

I swore I heard *meowing* in the background. "I don't see why not."

"Do you have garlic powder and onion powder?"

I checked the spice cabinet. "Yep."

"Then you're basically done."

"I don't need real garlic?"

"No way, man. That'll ruin it. You powder that shit and cook it in some melted butter. You're gonna be so glad you did."

"Okay."

"I'm serious. GK and Kel are gonna unleash a rampage of gratitude on your ass. Or, like, suck your dick for hours, since you're not that into butt stuff."

"Wonderful."

"Like, GK's gonna be sucking your dick, and Kel's gonna unhinge her jaws like a goddamn snake and suck on GK's head while he's sucking your dick, and it's gonna be fucking blowjob *Inception*."

"How long do I cook it?"

"Ten to fifteen on each side. One teaspoon of each kind of powder, plus a teaspoon of seasoned salt. Serve it with broccoli or green beans or some other healthy shit."

"Thanks. You're a lifesaver."

"Anytime, man. Love you to the end of time."

"You too. Bye."

We hung up.

So I had to go to the store and get chicken breasts. And vegetables. And maybe some wine. Dessert too, probably? I headed for the bathroom, then stopped. Texted Kel to ask permission—both for the bathroom and to go to the store. She texted back yes to both a few minutes later.

Kamen texted me an emoji of a drumstick and *GARLIC FUCKIN CHICKEN!!!!!!!!*

I snorted. The rest of us had always had a little trouble taking Kamen seriously—he seemed in some ways like he'd never outgrown high school. But he was an incredibly kind person, and it was surprising how much serious stuff you could trust him with.

A couple of years ago, shortly after Bill's trial, I'd called Kamen to pick me up at the hospital after a suicide attempt. Which hadn't really been an attempt. I'd taken a bottle of Ambien, which I knew was pretty fucking unlikely to kill me, then had called an ambulance a few minutes later. Like, even the hospital staff had given me a collective eye roll. You heard people talk about how attempting suicide was "a gesture" or "a cry for help." I hated that, because I hadn't been crying for anything. And "a gesture" made it sound like I was mocking the real trauma people who tried to commit suicide went through.

I'd just been so confused. A lousy excuse, I know. But it was like the pain reached this point where . . . I don't know. I couldn't sleep. I couldn't talk to anyone. I just stayed in my apartment, and everything looked ugly—the walls, the dishes, the sheets, the view out the living room window. Eventually I couldn't *breathe*, that's how bad it was. I liked the idea of a long, dreamless sleep, and so at first it was just a handful of Ambien. And then, without really thinking, it was the whole bottle.

I'd broken down on the phone with the 9-1-1 operator—not even because I was scared, but because I was so fucking *embarrassed.*

Two days in the hospital. Normally it would have been a week, with mandatory counseling sessions. But the hospital was crowded and short-staffed, and they needed to make way for people with serious problems—not adult men who half-assed their suicide attempts. I'd spent those two days paralyzed with shame. Lying in bed, thinking about the guilt-trip I'd get from my mother—if she found out. About how Dave would probably never speak to me again—if he found out. I'd made myself literally sick worrying, and ended up having to stay a third day because I was running a fever.

So I'd called Kamen. He'd come to get me on the third day, and he hadn't asked questions. He'd taken me to get a milkshake, and then he made me stay at his place for a week and promised he wouldn't tell the others as long as I promised never to try anything like that again. I'd been mostly quiet during that week, but each night I'd lain awake in Kamen's room, staring at the guitar propped in one corner and smelling flannel sheets that held a whiff of, like, college boy—sweat and pot and cheap cologne. Imagining what would have happened if the pills had worked.

I'd always sort of believed in heaven. But at that time, the whole idea of an afterlife seemed silly.

One night I'd left the bedroom and stood in the doorway of the living room. Kamen was asleep on the couch. I'd hovered there like a kid who'd had a nightmare. Couldn't make myself wake him.

Dave would have done it. He'd come right up to you and demand attention when he was feeling down—or even when he was feeling great. Never seemed even remotely afraid he'd be rejected. Never seemed to think it was stupid or childish to want comfort.

But I'd just listened to Kamen snore for a few minutes, then had turned and gone back to the bedroom.

I checked Kel and Greg's fridge and cabinets, looking for things they might need. They were low on milk. And only had half a stick of butter left. I stared at their fridge, remembering the first few times I'd come to their house. How long it had taken me to feel comfortable here. And now it felt almost as familiar as the duplex. The counters were mostly clean, except for the small section that Kel had used to fix her breakfast. There were crumbs there. A ring from her coffee. A banana phloem. Greg was actually bigger on cleaning up than she was.

I picked up the dishcloth, wet it, and wiped down that section of the counter. Maybe I did have a long way to go in terms of learning to communicate. But I was getting better. I was here, wasn't I? I was here because I'd asked for this.

I was here because it was where I needed to be.

"That was *amazing*." Kel set down her fork and leaned back with a sigh.

Greg took a gulp of wine. "Dare I say life-changing?"

I smiled and thumped lightly on the side of my prison to indicate my approval.

I was inside a gray plastic storage bin we had dubbed "the box"— both because it was in fact a box, and because of the pleasing fem-dom symbolism of a man trapped inside a giant box. But there was a hole in the box (snicker) through which I could see Kel and a little bit of Greg.

I loved the box. They'd found the bin at a home-decorating store a few months earlier, and Kel had cut holes in the two narrow ends and sanded down the edges of the holes. I could hunch inside the box, and they could snap the lid on and then use the holes to fuck my mouth or my ass. But we'd quickly discovered that just being inside the box took me to a new level of subspace, and so now they didn't usually bother me too much when I was in there. I'd gladly lie there for an hour or more in the dark, listening to them talk and move around.

In this case, being in the box kind of sucked, because I could smell the garlic chicken, and I was starving.

It used to be when I was in the box, I thought about Hal. I imagined he was in there with me, the two of us taking up all the space, until our combined heat made me sweat, made it hard to breathe. In real life, we used to do this thing where we'd lie in bed together with our arms around each other and just . . . squeeze the fuck out of each other. Curl closer and closer until we formed this ball with no space between our skins and we couldn't get enough air and it made us both dizzy. And he'd always laugh when we finally broke apart—this laugh that was like a release of tension, relief and joy and self-deprecation, because we were both stupidly dependent on any little thing that brought us closer. Us against the world. Protecting each other.

I didn't really know what I thought about in the box anymore. Sometimes I ran through old memories: my bar mitzvah, where I'd had a panic attack because of all the people. Meeting Dave at a munch at this weird buffet that served pizza with chicken wings on it. My backward-facing car seat from when I was a baby, that my mom swore I couldn't possibly remember, but I did. I remembered being strapped in, staring at the blue-gray upholstery in front of me, listening to my parents' voices. The Central Valley Jewish Community Center, and how obsessed I'd been with the chalkboards in the classrooms there. The most random shit. Miles said that was normal, to have subspace drag up fragments of old memories. It made me feel strange, like I was doing some kind of womb-regression thing.

Kel and Greg talked for a while once they were done eating. It took me some time to realize they were discussing Cobalt, a dungeon in the city that had closed recently. They were debating whether Riddle had the space to absorb the potential Cobalt refugees.

I smiled and sank deeper. I was hungry, but it didn't matter. I was curious about what they were saying, but not curious enough to come out from wherever I was.

Eventually they unsnapped the lid of the box and helped me out.

Kel sent me to get some rope, and then she rigged a chest and waist harness that bound my right arm to my side while the left remained free. I had to clear the table, load the dishwasher, and clean the kitchen like that. It was actually awesome, since I was still pretty spaced out, but the challenge of doing things one-handed kept me focused on them, and on my role. I could hear them talking and laughing in the living room, and it made me incredibly happy. I brought them each another glass of wine when I was done. Kel undid the harness, and then they let me curl up on the couch with them.

Apparently it was Greg's turn to debrief me that night, because Kel went up to bed early and left the two of us alone to guy-chat about how things were going.

"Is this kind of what you wanted?" he asked.

I nodded. So far, I was liking this. The submission felt deeper, my service felt more constant. The only thing I still couldn't figure out was how to talk to them about the humiliation stuff. How I wanted a balance between nights like this, where I could serve quietly and obey easily, and that . . . Miles would know the word—dehumanization?— that I was looking for. "Yeah," I said. "This is good."

We sat there awkwardly for a moment before he asked, "You want to eat?"

"God, yes," I said. "I mean, yes, sir."

"Go get yourself a plate. No utensils. You can eat in here. Bring the wine bottle."

I retrieved food, wine, and an extra glass from the kitchen, then returned. Set my plate on the coffee table while I refilled his glass. I wasn't sure if I was supposed to eat on the floor or what. He hadn't said anything about that, so I sat on the couch once more, setting the plate on my thighs, and started to pick up the chicken.

"No."

My gut clenched. I glanced at him, waiting.

"Don't use your hands."

I set the chicken back on the plate. "Sorry, sir."

So that was how we ended up working our way through the wine and discussing Greg's submissive journey while I stuck my face in a plate of life-changing garlic chicken.

Greg swirled his wine in the glass. "When I first met Kel, I was pretty, like . . . shy, you know?"

"You?" I eyed the napkins on the coffee table.

"Dude, go ahead and wipe your face. I can't even look at you when you're all covered in chicken grease."

I grabbed a napkin and cleaned up.

He continued. "Talking about sex, I mean. I couldn't do it. In my mind, I could. Could tell her all the things I wanted her to call me. The way I wanted her and me to fuck. You know? But what actually came out of my mouth was bullshit I'd heard in porn, or from my friends. And some of my friends are kinda riffraff."

"Mine too." I set the napkin down. "So how'd you even get into the scene?" I felt like he'd given me the abridged version at some point in the past. But now I was curious about the details. I couldn't picture Greg *ever* being shy.

He placed the ball of his foot on the coffee table's edge. "Used to have these fantasies—tried to get my girlfriends to slap me around. Moved to the city, found Cobalt. Found girls there who *would* slap me around. But I never really looked for anything real, you know? I always wanted to feel . . . still in control, I guess. And I don't mean in the 'the sub is always in control of the scene blah blah blah' way. I mean I was, like, disrespectful to dominant women, because I felt threatened by them. Then I met Kel. And she didn't really put up with any of that shit. If I was gonna submit, I was gonna *submit.*"

"And that was tough?"

He nodded. "I was just so used to getting my way. I thought sex ended when I came, and I'd try to get her in the mood even when she was tired. I told her I preferred to go down on girls who were waxed. Really, even when I started submitting to her, I was always trying to get what I wanted."

"When did that change?"

"When she started beating my ass." He glanced at me and grinned. "Hey, look, I read some of the discussions you guys, your Subs Club, have on the Sounding Board. I really like some of them. That one you had on humiliation fetishes—and you had, like, guy and lady subs talk about what they got out of it? I agree, man. Guys are—" He snapped his fingers. "We're immediate. We're not overthinking it. We want, you know . . . Make us feel dirty, call us pussies, get us off. And maybe women, you know, they think more about the emotional component.

They want to be used and they also want to feel safe. They wanna feel like the dom's protecting them."

I took a swig of my wine. "You don't want to feel safe when someone's humiliating you?"

"Uhhhh. Pfff. I'm not— I don't get that far in the fantasy, man. I'm like—a hot woman telling me how to please her. My dick's hard, and I'm not thinking about how this'll end or how I want to feel when all's said and done. I'm in the moment."

I couldn't even imagine what that would be like. I chewed on every thought, every feeling, until it was unrecognizable. *"Everyone thinks I'm emotional,"* Dave had said once. *"But Gould's a total sap. We all just think he's stoic because he never talks about the secret Hallmark Channel inside him."* That had been a bit too on the nose for me.

Greg jiggled his leg up and down. "The only way I learn is by repetition. I do something selfish—I fail to meet her needs, and she takes me *down*. You know? She pegs my ass whether I'm in the mood or not, for as long as it takes her to have the orgasms she wants, and I see how it feels to have someone just use me as a way to get their pleasure. Or she shaves my balls so I see what it's like to do something, uh, unnatural with your body just because someone else likes it. It's powerful. She gives me an enema to remind me I'm not in control. She says I'm too focused on my dick, and so she makes me watch while she fucks herself on a vibrator, or she queens the hell out of me. *That* . . . There's nothing in the *world* like being queened."

I really, *really* wanted to know what that felt like.

Greg split the last of the wine between us. "It was a while before I started *listening* to her. Before we got to a point where I could anticipate her needs, instead of waiting for her to direct me. But now, you know, we do directed sex, and I make her come as many times as she wants, and I don't come at all, you know?"

"Yeah. I know."

"I love it. But it's weird, a little bit. Because in my culture—I mean, on my dad's side of the family, they'd think this was weird as hell. Not the kinky stuff so much, but me being the submissive one. My uncles, they're not, you know, sexist. But if they knew I took orders from my wife this way . . ."

I laughed. "They sound kind of sexist."

"No, they just— It's cultural."

"Yeah, but that's a sexist culture, though."

"Every culture's sexist."

"Touché."

"It's just, like— America, man, it's supposed to be about equality. *Supposed* to be. And my dad's like, 'Yeah, yeah, Greg, aren't you glad I came here and met your mom, because, you know, India's a good country, it's a really good country, but in America you get some different opportunities. You know? And America's very racist, true, and you're a brown dude, but you're not *too* brown, so you'll be all right.' He might not have said it exactly like that. Anyway, I'm like, yeah, irony, my dad came to the country of equality, and now I'm a slave to my wife."

"So why do you do it, then? Submit to her?"

He scratched the back of his neck. "I love her."

I grinned. I wanted to challenge him a little. "Is it because you're indulging her? Playing this little game she likes? She thinks she's a dom, and you think it's cute, so—"

"I don't! I don't feel that way. What are you, crazy? She's dom as fuck."

I snorted. "Then put up or shut up. You're a better man than your uncles."

He nodded, staring into his glass. "Now that's true."

I shifted back on the couch. "So how does the scene treat you? As a brown dude? 'Cause I know Miles, he gets asked stuff about how it feels to be a black guy submitting to a white guy."

"I don't get too much of that. Like, for me it's more subtle stuff. Definitely I've had partners who act like I'm kind of exotic."

I laughed again. "Exotic Greg."

"That's not just kink, though. In college I hung out with all these white girls who would talk about their Persian friend or their Guatemalan roommate or whoever the fuck, and how that family did such 'authentic' cooking or would send *bal mithai* all the way from Pakistan . . . shit like that. So I was, like, their Indian friend. Or Native American friend—take your pick."

"See, everyone at my college was Jewish, so I never got to be a novelty until I met Dave and the rest of my group."

"I know I was a total dick about my heritage or whatever. I'd order buffalo wings at the campus grill and then pray over them, you know? Thank the buffalo for sacrificing its wings. I was such a dick—but I do think it's cool. I did the whole Ancestry.com thing. I've got some badass ancestors."

"My friends make Jewish jokes sometimes, and I don't know. It doesn't *really* bother me. It's just weird to have a thing that makes me different, and I don't even know much about it."

He glanced at me. "You don't know much about your faith?"

I smiled and shook my head. "Not really. I feel like my parents pick one holiday every year and celebrate it. You'd think since they sent me to Hebrew day camp and Hebrew college and took me to the JCC every Tuesday when I was a kid, that they'd actually know more about being Jewish. But I swear to God, the last time we celebrated Sukkot, my dad was on his phone reading from the Wikipedia page about the meaning of the holiday."

Greg burst out laughing. "I like your dad."

"He's all right."

Greg looked at me, smile fading. He toyed with his wineglass. "You're all right too."

"Am I?"

"Yeah. You make good chicken. You're smart. You're a good guy."

I nodded. "You're a good guy too."

He held out his hand, and I wasn't sure what to do. "Dude. Low-five."

I slapped his palm.

"There you go," he said. "We're good guys."

CHAPTER
EIGHT

On Tuesday morning, I was handed a black cloth bag containing lube and a silicone butt plug and told to take it to work with me and insert the plug after my lunch break. I was supposed to wear it for the rest of the day, come home, take it out, and then display myself on the couch and wait for Kel to get home.

I think I was more nervous about keeping a butt plug in my briefcase all morning than I was about wearing it all afternoon. I felt kind of nasty, bringing my personal life into the workplace, but at the same time I loved the reminder that I belonged to Kel and Greg no matter where I was or what I was doing. At two o'clock, I finished my lunch and locked myself in the employee bathroom.

The plug took me fifteen minutes to get in—this one was wider than I was used to, and the more I anticipated the discomfort, the more I tensed up, and the more I tensed up, the angrier I got at myself, which made me tenser still. And on went the vicious cycle of plug-related woes.

Wearing it was actually pretty awesome. Despite the width, it was incredibly comfortable once it was in, and I liked thinking about Kel each time I shifted or stood or sat. Around three forty-five I finally grew a pair and texted her: *Thinking of you whenever I move.* Possibly not the sexiest text ever sent. But it was true.

She texted back: *I'm gonna wreck that ass when I get home.*

My dick was hard for a solid half an hour.

I got home at four thirty and went up to the master bathroom. Undressed and folded my clothes on the counter. The plug had a small silver ring on the bottom. I hadn't been sure at first what it was for, but I was starting to see. The plugs I was used to were so narrow it was usually an effort to keep them *in* once they'd been inserted. This bulb-shaped one was in no hurry to come out. The base was sticky with partly dried lube, and the neck was too short for me to get a good grip. So I stuck my finger through the ring, and, like a genius, decided it would hurt less if I just yanked it out instead of spending another twenty minutes trying to slowly work it free.

Mistake.

My vision seriously went black for a few seconds from the pain. I staggered around the bathroom, cursing this plug and all plugs ever. I checked for blood, found none. I washed the plug thoroughly, then put it away just as I heard the garage door go up.

Shit.

I needed to be in position. *Now.*

I ran downstairs and got on the couch. Elbows and knees, my ass up, my face buried in the cushion. Waited there, trying to slow my breathing.

I heard the kitchen door open. I was pretty sure it was Greg, not Kel, who walked inside. Keys on the counter. The fridge opened. A cough—definitely Greg's. I stayed in position. Eventually he entered the living room, but he walked right by me and into the foyer, then upstairs.

My breathing evened out, and I started to relax. My ass still ached a little, but it wasn't bad. I let the minutes pass, half listening to Greg moving around upstairs. By the time Kel came in, I felt drowsy and happy. And hard. I wanted her to touch me, wanted her to wreck my ass. Just wanted *her*, really.

I had to wait a little while, but eventually she came into the living room and stood beside the couch. She was still in her work clothes, but I could see she had her harness on, and the glass dildo. She spent a few minutes trailing her fingers along my back. Each time she lifted them, I didn't breathe until I felt them again—so light, tracing the bones of my spine, sending me deeper and deeper down. She put her other hand between my legs. Cupped my balls and ran her thumb down my dick. I shivered but didn't break position.

She climbed onto the couch behind me. Slid the dildo down my crack a few times, leaving a trail of lube. Then she positioned the head and pushed it in.

The pain was immediate. I gasped. Didn't think, just reached back and gripped her leg, hard. She stopped. Stroked my hip for a few seconds, then pushed a little farther in. I pulled away, panting.

"Gould?"

I didn't answer.

"Babe? Look here."

I pushed my forehead hard against the cushion. "You can . . . you can keep . . ."

"No." She made me sit up on my knees and look at her. "That hurt?"

I wished I didn't have to tell her. But she didn't take her gaze off me until I explained about the plug. How I hadn't been able to get it in, and hadn't wanted to go through the same struggle getting it out.

She brushed the hair back from my eyes. "Let me guess: you just grabbed the ring and yanked?"

I nodded.

She winced sympathetically. "Ouch."

I didn't tell her about almost blacking out. "I'm bad at butt plugs."

"Was there any blood?"

"No, Ma'am."

"Get back in position."

I did, and I heard her open the lube again. She spread my ass and gently pressed her finger against my hole. I folded my hands and rested my forehead on them.

"How does this feel?" she asked. All business, like a doctor.

"Fine."

She pushed in slightly. "This?"

"It doesn't really hurt anymore," I said. "Just when I pulled the plug out it. And then when you . . ."

She withdrew her finger. "I don't see or feel any damage. No blood, but there could be small tears. If there's any pain, tell me right away. You understand?"

"Yes, Ma'am."

"Sit up again." Her tone was still brusque.

I sat. She took my chin in her clean hand and turned my head so I faced her. "Do you think that was something I needed to know before I fucked you?"

"It was my fault. And I didn't think it was still bad." I tried to turn.

"No, don't look away." She kept hold of my chin. "You don't think that was something I needed to know?"

"I didn't . . . think," I finished lamely.

"I see." She let go. Seemed to consider this for a moment. Then she tapped me more curtly. "Go get the evil stick. Bring Greg down too."

I felt oddly calm for a few seconds. The *oh fuck* was a delayed reaction. "Yes, Ma'am."

I got to my feet and went upstairs. Greg was in the bathroom. I knocked lightly. "Out in a minute," he called.

"Sir? Can you come downstairs when you're done, please?"

"Yep," he said.

My heart thudded as I walked to the bedroom closet and rummaged behind Greg's shirts for the evil stick. I took it downstairs and knelt in front of Kel again, holding it out.

She took it. "Thank you."

We waited in silence until Greg came down. I kept my gaze on the carpet as he entered.

"What's up?" he asked.

Kel placed a hand on my head. "Gould and I are having a discussion that concerns all of us. He's also earned a correction."

Greg took a seat on the couch. "All right."

Kel prodded me with her foot. "Go kneel in front of the fireplace, facing us."

I did. Spread my knees and clasped my hands behind my back.

She shifted slightly in the chair. "What are we discussing, Gould?"

It took me a moment to figure out how to phrase it. "I screwed up taking a plug out. It caused some pain, and then I didn't tell you, Ma'am." I waited.

Kel snapped her fingers. I looked up. "Why do you need to tell me?"

"Because it . . . could have made things worse? If you fucked me?"

She nodded. "I might choose to hurt you sometimes. But I need to *know* what I'm doing. That was part of the agreement, right? That you'd talk to us about physical and psychological issues? That you'd be honest about any problems you were having?"

"Yes, Ma'am. But . . ."

"Yes?"

"But I'm supposed to take whatever you give me. Even if I don't like it."

She raised her eyebrows like she really couldn't believe me. "Not if I have no way of understanding what I'm giving you. You've been in the scene a long time. You know better."

Guilt jabbed at me. I did know better. I just wanted her not to care if she hurt me. Or to pretend not to, I guess.

She stood and pointed with the evil stick. "Bend over the arm of the chair. You can hold on to Greg."

I rose uncertainly. What did she mean, "hold on to Greg"? Greg got up and went to the other side of the armchair and knelt. Held out his hands across the chair.

Hell no. I was ashamed enough of having earned this. The last thing I wanted was some kind of forced Kumbaya moment with Greg.

But I bent over, and he took my hands like it was no big deal. He didn't laugh. He didn't crack jokes. He just held on. My palms were sweaty, and my mouth was dry.

Kel stepped behind me, and I tried not to tense. *You earned this. Don't fight it.*

Greg ran his thumb over the knuckles of my left hand. I exhaled, surprised. Lifted my head slightly to look at him. His gaze was steady. Made me feel steadier.

Kel rubbed my back. "What's this for?"

"Not telling you that there was a problem, Ma'am."

"What kind of problem?"

"That I was hurt."

"That's right."

She positioned the carbon stick briefly against my ass, then drew back and let go. I flexed and released my muscles, clenching my jaw as the single, thin line of fire became an all-over blaze. I gripped Greg's hands and closed my eyes. She ran her fingers along the stripe of burning skin, then placed the stick a couple of inches lower, almost across my thighs. Greg squeezed my hands. She bent the stick back again, and released.

I shuddered, letting the pain sweep through my body, then slowly fade.

She touched my lower back again. "You can get up."

I straightened. Greg kept hold of my hands and squeezed again, briefly. I squeezed back, and then he let go.

I turned to Kel. She opened her arms, and I went to her, feeling strangely peaceful now.

"Message received?" she asked gently.

"Yes, Ma'am."

"Look at me. Say it again."

I met her gaze. Her expression was incredibly kind. I was sorry, but not particularly embarrassed or upset. "Yes, Ma'am. I'm sorry."

"Over and done." She kissed me.

That simple. Over and done. Forgiven. I thought of Dave saying there was no such thing as a clean slate. *"I'm sorry." "Over and done."* I thought of the people who'd said Bill was sorry about Hal. That he'd never forgive himself. *Over and done, Bill. Right? Magic words? Did Kel say them to you?*

You had to feel it. You had to mean it. Did Kel forgive too easily? Did she mean it?

How could you use the same word to describe excusing a minor lie of omission, and offering a second chance to someone whose actions had consequences that would ripple through years, lifetimes?

I was seven and learning the forgiveness prayer, Al Chet, for Yom Kippur: "For the sin which we have committed before You under duress or willingly. For the sin which we have committed before You by hard-heartedness . . ."

I was twenty-five and Dave was picking me up from the police station after I'd attacked Bill. *"But you would never do anything like that."*

But I did.

I was twenty-eight and forgiveness suddenly seemed like the worst kind of recklessness. Like dismissing the heart's ability to hate as unconditionally as it loved. Like daring evil into the world and promising it a place to curl up and rest when it was done.

Could forgiveness be both? A gift and reckless? Well-intentioned but dangerous? A ritual repeated so many millions of times that it had lost its significance, and yet there was meaning there. Under countless hollow echoes, there was meaning. There was power, and there was a desire as frantic as lust, as innocent as a wish made on a star. A need to believe that all the bad we did was nothing stacked up against others' willingness to see our good.

I kissed Kel back and hoped there was a way to get better. To move forward. Hoped every dark moment was just that—a moment, over and done. And that the best of all good things was just beginning, for each of us.

The rest of the week passed fairly quickly. I ran a lot of errands and did a lot of chores. Spent some quality time in the box. For the most part, serving felt good, felt natural. I could usually see what needed to be done around the house or in the yard, and I did it without being prompted. I offered Kel and Greg massages when they got home, or got baths ready for Kel. I went to the store on Thursday and bought a couple of flower arrangements for the house. Surprised them that night with a candlelit dinner. I'd meant to leave them alone to enjoy it, but Kel tossed a pillow on the floor beside the table and told me to join them.

Every night, Kel shared a little of her master/slave training with me. We went over examples of low protocol—everyday services—versus high protocol—the sort of behavior and presentation expected at M/s events. Talked about events she'd been to, about the different hierarchies in master/slave households. She said Master Tan had used a guild structure—everyone started as an apprentice in her household, serving the official members. Eventually they worked their way up to becoming a master or a slave of the Tan house. At which point they underwent a ceremony similar to knighting, and were given a leather vest with the crest of the household on it.

It was all interesting, but I wasn't sure it brought me any closer to understanding what I wanted.

"What did you want?" I asked her. "Did you want to be part of a household?"

She shook her head. "Not really. I think I always wanted to fly solo." She paused. "I never did graduate from Tan's program. Came close. But took off before it was done."

"Why?"

She shrugged. "I guess the formality started to feel a little . . . like a trap, maybe? That's the wrong way to say it. I respected Tan, an enormous amount. But I didn't want to feel tied to someone else's idea of what the lifestyle was."

I was pretty sure I understood. "It seems kind of—you'd have to be *really* sure of yourself to be a master. You'd have to think you knew the right way to do things, maybe? And I guess sometimes a role like that would attract the wrong type of people."

She gave me a quick smile. "Sort of. When I trained with Tan, I was an apprentice. I served her and the other masters, and occasionally served some of the masters in training. So every master there started as a slave, in a sense. She had zero tolerance for people who were assholes, and she worked with everyone on finding an individual style. But even with all that, I still wasn't sure I fit."

I nodded.

She went on. "The thing about kink is that even though most of us try to be very openhearted and accepting of how huge the spectrum is, people still like labels. All the letters and all the acronyms and all the rules. Riddle was my dream for years and years. I thought running a club was a perfect fit for someone like me who likes being in charge, who likes people and trying new things and, you know, depravity in all its forms. But 'club owner' is a label too. When something goes—" her voice got rougher "—goes wrong, if you don't—if you can't . . ." She stopped, blinking. "People think you're *especially* stupid. For putting yourself in charge. And then not knowing the answers."

I held my breath. It was so rare that either of us brought up Bill or Hal. I waited, but she didn't say anything else. After a moment she got up, squeezed my shoulder, and then left the room.

On Friday, Dave texted me that there was a notification on the door for me to pick up a package at the post office. I texted Kel for permission to stop on the way home from work. She said yes.

I set the package in the passenger seat and idled there in the post office parking lot. Reached out and put a hand on the box.

I drove to the duplex. I didn't want to open the package in the car, or in front of Kel and Greg. Dave was at school, and the apartment was empty. I could hear our neighbor walking around upstairs.

I went to my room and sat on my neatly made bed, the package beside me. For a second, I felt so *relieved* to be back here. I lay down on the bed I didn't share, in this room that was just mine, in this house where I wasn't accountable to anyone. Rolled onto my side, closed my eyes, and breathed.

After a few minutes, I sat up. Stared for a moment at Hal's messy *Do Not Open* scrawled on the side of the box. Then I ripped it open. There were a couple of lesbian vampire novels I'd gotten him as a joke after we'd seen them in a used bookstore—I tried to imagine Cass and Ben finding those. A textbook of Hal's from when he'd briefly tried an accounting program at Hymland. Mostly the box contained the old N64 games Hal and I had bought together: *Super Mario 64, Pokémon Snap, Wave Race, NBA Hangtime, Cruis'n USA*. We'd never progressed to the PlayStations or Xbox or GameCube. We'd stuck to the N64, a relic from our childhoods.

I picked up *Wave Race* and smiled. Hal had done the best impression of the *Wave Race* announcer—that smarmy asshole who ostensibly encouraged you, but sounded more than a little mocking as you wove among buoys or barrel-rolled over ramps: "Okay . . . okay . . . gooooood . . . Nice! How'd ya do that? Maximuuum power! You almost had it . . ." And then he'd discovered that all the things the announcer said sounded like things that could be said during sex. He used to drive me crazy while I was fucking him: "Okay . . . okay . . . nice! How'd ya do that? Goooooood! Watch out! That's great—a neeeeeeeeeew record!" And I always ended up laughing, which just encouraged him.

I'd never been sure if Hal was actually kinky or not. Or if it was just something he did for the novelty, the experience. When I'd discovered the local munch and told him I wanted to go, he'd offered to come along. But he'd never said, *Oh yeah, I'm really into that shit*. When we'd finally started going to Riddle together, he'd always found doms to play with, but he never seemed to take submitting seriously. He just liked doing new things, the crazier the better. He'd come with me to a few of Riddle's educational talks and workshops, but he'd acted like some dick-wad high school student, talking during the presentations, passing notes, asking questions so dumb you weren't sure if he was really that ignorant or just being obnoxious.

We'd flirted with something like a D/s dynamic on occasion—early on, before we'd started going to munches and clubs. Each of us not quite able to come right out and say what we wanted. If I got sarcastic with him, he'd grin and say maybe I needed to be taken down a peg or two. And I'd get kind of excited, hoping he'd make good on the threat. He was always careful about how he said it, always clearly teasing, until one day I'd looked him straight in the eye and said, "Do it."

"Do . . . Uh, how?" He'd seemed so adorably confused that I'd wanted to laugh.

But I'd shrugged instead, a silent dare.

There was a moment of pure heat between us that led to nothing more than some pretty average sex. I'd been disappointed, kicking myself for days for not spelling it out for him—*tell me I have to blow you. Fuck me and make it hurt. Tell me what a pansy I am, that I can't do anything right.*

It wasn't until we'd been together for a few months that anything really happened.

I was on a tear one night about my weight. I'd learned that I could piss him off by talking about how much I hated my body. I forget why I was so wound up—probably because he'd said he was gonna stop buying anything harder than pot and then had come home with speed. But instead of taking it out on him, I'd taken it out on myself, since he tended to listen when I ragged on myself, in a way he never did if I criticized him.

"I'm a fucking fat ass," I'd told him. "And it's never gonna change. You ought to find someone else."

He'd given me that helpless, half-angry, half-uncertain look I was becoming familiar with. "Shut up. I hate when you say stuff like that."

"It's true, isn't it? You don't think I'm hot. I *know* I'm not hot."

"Gould! Fuck. Knock it off."

I wasn't sure how far I could push before he'd give up and storm off. But unless I was imagining it, we were both kind of turned on by the fight. "Or what?"

"If you keep on like that about yourself, I'm gonna . . ."

"Gonna *what*?" I said fiercely.

"Do something about it," he finished. He looked questioningly at me, almost like he was asking *Is that right?*

I wasn't sure what he was going to do. I knew what I *wanted* him to do, sort of. I wasn't afraid of him—he was, for all his wildness, a surprisingly gentle person—but it was a strange moment. He was really irritated, and I was serious about pushing him. Aroused and angry and ready for something to *change* between us. I flopped on my stomach on the bed, a subtle—or maybe not so subtle—invitation. "Oh *please*," I snapped into my pillow. "You're not gonna do anything."

It seemed like a year passed before I heard him approach the bed.

He sat on the edge of the mattress, his hip against mine. My heart raced as I felt the warmth of his body beside me, his steady breathing. I lifted my head. I could sense his gaze on me, but could only see him out the corner of my eye. He was waiting, and I was begging him silently, but I wasn't sure what for.

Then he slapped the seat of my jeans.

It wasn't a hard slap—stung a little, made me close my eyes and suck in a breath that was more shock than pain. But the *feeling* I got: like he'd knocked something into place for me, and I suddenly wasn't nervous at all.

When I could speak again, I said bitterly, "That's how you think you're gonna stop me?"

He smacked me again. It was a much sharper blow this time, and I jumped a little. I didn't say anything, and he did it again. And again.

My breathing roughened and I buried my face in the pillow. Braced the balls of my feet against the bed, and lifted my hips just a little.

Please.

He knew me. He wasn't very articulate, and I wasn't very forthcoming, but we'd learned each other. Even if this was new territory for us both, I trusted him ninety-nine percent not to go too far. And yet, it was that one percent that was making this experience exactly what I wanted.

He struck me again. He still wasn't putting much strength behind the slaps, and while the pain was already enough for me, the intensity wasn't. "If you're going to do it, *do it*," I said tightly.

He hesitated, and then his hand landed harder, and the muffled thwack of his palm on denim made my balls draw up, made me push my hips against the mattress.

"What the fuck's it matter to *you* if I know I'm a useless fat ass?" I made sure he could hear the taunt in my voice. "I'm just being honest."

There was a loud, solid swat across the center of my butt. A sting that took my breath away. I bent my knee a couple of inches—an almost-squirm. A trying-not-to-squirm.

"I can go all night," he said.

I lifted my head, my vision blurry. Stared at the wall, at the familiar chips in the paint. I wanted to tell him it hurt. Wanted to beg him to forgive me. But I figured that would freak him out. He wouldn't know if I was being serious. *I* wouldn't know.

I stayed perfectly still and didn't make a sound as he continued. He stopped after a moment, and I was afraid he was done. But he climbed all the way onto the bed and pushed my legs farther apart. Got on his knees between them, then grabbed my ankles and hauled me backward until his hips were cinched between my legs, my crotch against his. He rubbed the seat of my pants lightly, and I curled my fingers around the edge of the pillowcase.

Please.

He started playing my ass like a drum—slow, heavy whacks that got faster and harder. I winced but didn't ask him to quit.

It went on another moment, then stopped. He pulled my hips up so he could reach under me and undo my fly. I closed my eyes and let him.

He groped between my legs. I wasn't hard, but the tension had drained from my body, and I loved him so fiercely for doing this—for understanding—that I was crazy with the strength of that love, that gratitude.

I bent my knees and lifted my hips so he could yank my jeans off. Then lowered my legs on either side of him again. He started spanking me over my marine-life boxers. The pain was worse without my jeans, but it was starting to turn into something that genuinely felt good. He pushed my boxers up my thighs so he was catching bare skin with some of his lower swats. I curled my toes, a cry sticking in my throat. He didn't say anything, and neither did I.

He stopped to rub for a few seconds, and I could feel the heat trapped between my skin and the cotton. Our position left a few inches of space between my groin and the bed. I tightened my legs around his sides. He hooked his fingers in the waistband and then eased my underwear down. It caught on my dick, and he had to reach under me to fix it. With my legs spread, the boxers wouldn't go down very far, so the waistband dug in just under my ass cheeks. He placed his palm on my bare skin, scrubbing the soreness into a manageable warmth. Then he started spanking again.

The sound and the heat and the pain were all converging on me. I closed my eyes and realized he and I were breathing in unison, his breath as rough as mine, this rapid, harsh heartbeat that filled the room. I bit down on the pillow for just a few seconds, then relaxed and went limp.

He increased the speed and force, each slap impossibly loud, until tears gathered in my eyes and spilled with a single blink. I buried my face in the pillow again and sniffed. He stopped.

"Enough?" he whispered.

It never would be. Not until he owned me. Not until I was crawling for him, not until I was tied down and helpless and forced to take whatever he wanted.

But I couldn't picture him being the person I crawled for. How strange was that? I loved him, and yet he wasn't . . . right for that role. I wanted him to be careful, unsure. I wanted him to be afraid to hurt me too much.

I nodded into the pillow, trying to dry my eyes on the pillowcase before I had to look at him.

He laughed a little. "That was *hot*. Right?"

My shoulders started shaking, and I practically had to smother myself with the pillow to keep quiet.

"Gould." He jostled me. "What the hell? Say something."

I didn't understand why the fuck I was acting this way. I'd *liked* it. I had.

He rolled me over. "Did I . . .? *Gould.*"

I didn't know about subspace then. Or, I knew in theory, but I'd never realized it would feel like this. I was definitely . . . I definitely felt *good.* But there was a lot of other shit going on too, and I couldn't tell if I was sad or angry or like, over-fucking-joyed. I gazed at him blearily, unable to speak.

"Gould, *please* . . ." He sounded panicked.

I let out a breath. "'M okay."

His face lost those lines of tension. "Shit." He leaned forward. "I didn't mean to hurt you, man. Really."

"I'm sorry I said that stuff." My muscles were starting to work again, but my brain wouldn't settle. I didn't know about aftercare then either. My Google research on BDSM had given me some basics, but I'd mostly just jacked off to pictures of people getting tied up. Hadn't paid much attention to the fucking glossary. Now I looked back and realized I'd needed help coming down. That I'd been subdropping like crazy. But at the time, I just felt pathetic.

"It's okay." Hal kind of laughed. "It's no big deal. I thought you wanted—"

"I did." I wiped my eyes. *Please don't hate me.* "I'm sorry."

"Don't be. You're fine, man. It's all good."

He'd had a lot of experience trip-sitting for friends, so he basically just made like I was having a bad trip and put me to bed. Brought some ice in a wet washcloth and put it on my forehead. Then he got in bed with me, and we curled up. I shifted close to him.

"That's right," he whispered. "You're all right. I'm not going anywhere."

And because I thought I could get away with needing more than usual, since he clearly thought I wasn't myself at the moment, I whispered, "Promise?"

"Yeah. I promise."

As I'd gotten older and more experienced, I'd clung to the idea that in a scene, it was okay to need more. To say things that weren't at all manly or grownup or what I would normally say. That it was okay to need other people, to sink into the safety of promises that couldn't possibly withstand all that life had in store.

And maybe that was where I differed from my friends. For me, submission wasn't a game, wasn't temporary, wasn't some bonus facet of my identity. It was the way I kept a promise alive, it was the way I let myself need.

It was my voice.

And sometimes, when I looked back on my relationship with Hal, I wondered if that night was the only time he'd ever really *listened*.

CHAPTER
NINE

On Saturday, Kel and Greg and I made a late-night trip to Riddle. It was almost one when we got there, and the Saturday night play party was winding down. Kel and Greg put me in the kennel, where I stayed for about forty-five minutes until all the guests had left, and only a small group of Kel and Greg's friends remained at the dry bar.

One of those friends was Lady A, a beautiful black woman with graying hair and a way of looking at you like she knew every bad thing you'd ever done. There was Cuntesse, who looked like my middle school math teacher, Mrs. Donahue—with her thin, granny-curled hair and long denim dress. Sal, Cuntesse's partner. And Margie, a perky younger woman who apparently had a bedroom full of legendary dungeon furniture.

The rules tonight were that I would serve this group. Follow their instructions, and allow their corrections if they weren't satisfied. Wouldn't speak without permission. Greg had prenegotiated the corrections on my behalf, but hadn't told me what the possibilities were. I just had to trust that he wouldn't let the others do anything too awful to me. And I'd gotten a lecture from Kel before we'd left about how if I needed to safeword tonight, I should. They wouldn't think any less of me, and even though it would end our contract for this week, we only had one day left, and there would be other weeks if I wanted, and blah blah blah.

I'd pushed hard for tonight. I'd actually had to beg a little. I wanted to try more public play, see if that got me closer to the level of humiliation I was after. I tried to remind myself that I'd *asked* for this, as I stood naked in front of the group, waiting for instructions, my stomach tight with nerves. I was wearing the collar with the cat padlock, and occasionally I touched it, or swallowed hard enough to make it tighten around my neck.

The others spent some time admiring me and asking Kel questions about my training. I was allowed to keep my head down and stay quiet for that. The longer they talked, the farther away I went. I started with one image: A lake on a gray morning. Mist over the water, the uniform black V's of geese in the distance. I was stepping on slick rocks and patches of grass, heading for an inlet where boats were docked. I reached the rocky shore and looked into the murky water of the inlet. Snakes were swimming. Long and brown, shimmying their bodies like fins, their heads at the surface, sending out ripples.

Suddenly I heard Hal's voice: he was laughing, asking if snakes ate bread, like ducks. But I couldn't get the tone of his voice quite right. Couldn't figure out if this was a memory, or something I was making up. And when I looked around, I didn't see him. I was alone by the water. Even the geese in the sky were gone. It was just the snakes, troubling the surface of the water.

I jerked back to reality when Kel touched my shoulder. I looked at her, heart pounding, wondering if I'd missed something—a question, a cue. She just smiled and told me to go behind the bar and start taking drink orders. I decided to take everyone's order all at once and then go pour the drinks. Which I realized was a stupid idea once I reached the end of the line and couldn't remember of what a couple of people in the middle had ordered.

I turned and set six plastic cups on the small table by the fridge. Opened the fridge and started pulling out two-liters. I was pretty sure about everyone's order except Lady A's.

Sprite?

Unless she'd wanted Diet Coke, and Sal had wanted Sprite?

No, there had been two Sprites in a row.

Had I ever been by a lake with Hal? Had we ever seen snakes swimming? Why couldn't I remember?

The drinks. Focus.

I didn't want to ask Lady A to repeat herself and risk getting corrected for forgetting. So I poured her some Sprite.

I started distributing the drinks. Lady A didn't say anything when she got hers, so I assumed I'd gotten it right. But when I was done handing out the drinks, I heard her say, "Boy. Look here."

I turned to her.

"I ordered a Coke," she said, and threw her drink on me.

Sprite dripped from my hair and ran down my face and neck. For a second, the mortification was all consuming. To the point where I couldn't move, couldn't speak. My face was burning, and my eyes stung.

A couple of the others laughed in surprise. I stood there like I seriously didn't remember how to fucking move, and then I heard Greg's voice, amused but not mocking. "Gould. C'mere a second."

I made my way out from behind the bar. The others' voices blended together, but I focused on Greg's.

"Come on over here."

I left a trail of sticky footprints as I walked. Greg was waiting at the end of the bar. He took my elbow and steered me into the lounge area, over to the front desk, where a section of wall separated us from the bar.

He laughed uneasily. "You okay?"

I wiped Sprite off my nose. "Permission to speak, sir?" My voice was fairly steady, so that was something.

"Of course."

I couldn't quite look at him. "Please, can I not be corrected in front of them?" I was starting to lose it. My breathing was harsh, and my heart thudded. The thought of everyone laughing at me while I was corrected made me feel sick.

He moved his hand to my shoulder. "Hey. Don't panic."

I took a deep breath, not entirely sure I understood my own reaction. Being drenched in soda was hardly the worst thing that had ever happened to me. But it was like I couldn't get past the initial shock of it. Apparently I talked a big game—wanted to be humiliated, wanted strangers involved. And now that it was actually happening, I was freaking the fuck out. I finally met Greg's gaze for a second, clenching and unclenching my hand at my side. I remembered the other day, when he'd kept me calm through the correction. I stared at him, trying to make sense of what I was feeling.

He pulled me close and kissed me. I kissed him back, surprised by how natural it felt. He ran his hands down my back, lacing them just above my ass. Fuck. He really could be just as patient, just as affectionate as Kel when he wanted.

He leaned away slightly. "You already got corrected."

I nodded. "I didn't—uh. I *really* didn't like that."

"I could tell."

I laughed, starting to calm down. I stared at his shoulder and concentrated on the warmth of his hands at the small of my back. "I should have asked when I couldn't remember what she ordered."

"It's not the end of the world."

I took a step back, and he let me go. "I really suck at this. I thought . . . thought I was good at being *good*, you know. But this week is . . ."

"You're doing fine."

"I'm sorry."

"Don't apologize. Keep breathing."

"Shit, shit, *shit*. What the fuck's wrong with me?"

He gave my shoulder an exaggerated pat. "You definitely look like this is adrenaline overload."

That was about right. And *why*? Over something so stupid? I thought again about the correction the other day. About how it was over and done. I'd learned and moved on.

I was silent.

Finally he said, "So tell me more about what you didn't like."

Kel had him trained. They were both gonna ask about my fucking feelings every time we did anything ever. I couldn't think how to begin. But something strange was happening—I *wanted* to tell him. Wanted him to know.

He peered around the wall, craning his neck to see the bar, and I figured he was getting impatient. But he just gave a *we're okay* signal to Kel, who'd be watching us. Then he turned back to me. "Would it help to go to the kennel? We can talk there."

The offer was so kind, so completely ridiculous and weird and thoughtful, that I laughed and shrugged. I followed him to Chaos, to the kennel. He opened it and put a towel down, and I crawled inside, glad for the darkness. He shut and latched the door. I mostly didn't bother feeling embarrassed for wanting this. There was a flash of *I shouldn't need it*, but I didn't give a shit.

The smell of lemon-lime was stronger in the enclosed space. He didn't pull the blanket down, so I could see him as he sat on the floor outside, his shirt snagging briefly on one of the bars. I settled onto the thick fleece pad and stared at the back of his shirt. At the soft-looking skin of his neck, and the short black bristles just below his hairline. I waited for him to speak.

"So you didn't like it?" he prompted.

"No, sir." I paused. "I thought I'd be more okay with it. Serving you and Kel makes me really happy, but I guess strangers not so much."

"Why's that?"

I sighed, frustrated. "I don't know."

"You'll have to do better than that."

"I'll bring them drinks if it makes you and Kel happy, but if I mess up, I'd rather you guys were in charge of correcting me. Because getting humiliated in front of you two, it—it sucks, but it's a way of serving you. And it helps me learn. But turns out I hate when people I don't have any reason to trust—or who don't . . . who aren't thinking at all about how I feel—have the power to do that."

He nodded, but didn't try to look in at me. Just faced the empty room and talked. "I've known Lady A for a long time, and she does think about how submissives feel—even other people's subs. I'm not arguing with anything you said. Just letting you know. The group asked me beforehand about acceptable corrections, and I told them no marks, no insults, no sex. So she chose something she thought fit that bill—embarrassing but not painful."

"Okay," I tried after a while. "I overreacted."

"Nope." He said it calmly, cheerfully. "I just don't want you thinking she was being—" he snapped his fingers like he was searching for the words "—like, intentionally cruel."

I gripped the edge of the fleece pad. *But I thought that was what I wanted. Intentional cruelty. It's . . . The problem is that everyone's too nice. Even when they're being cruel, they're being nice. I still feel too much like I have a choice. Like the second I flinch, people back off.*

He turned. "Did we scare you off public play for good?"

"No." *Keep talking. Elaborate.* "I just didn't know I'd get weird about that." I hesitated. "Maybe that's something I need to work on if I really want this 24/7 thing? Just accepting what you . . . even if it's . . . difficult."

"So what do you want me to do?" he asked. "We've got more planned. But we don't have to do it."

"If I say I don't want to, am I safewording? Like, for the week?"

"Nope. Kel and I will just make an executive decision that you're done serving for the night."

Part of me was disappointed. What was the point of an ultimatum like "safeword and the contract's broken" if they weren't going to enforce it? If they were going to back down anytime I got scared?

I gripped the fleece harder. "Keep going. I want you to keep going."

And we did. He let me out of the kennel and had me blow him, which took me closer to the headspace I needed. He framed everything after that as an order. Strapped a bondage belt around my waist and cuffed my left hand to it, then brought me back to the bar to serve drinks and snacks. It worked as well as it had the other night during dinner: one-handed, I had to concentrate much more closely on what I was doing, and while I stayed focused on my job, I nearly forgot about my audience.

I let the group conversation wash over me. Concentrated only on Greg and Kel and the signals they sent me to let me know they needed something—another drink, a napkin, a foot rub, whatever. If I felt myself surfacing, I concentrated on the collar around my neck and imagined it was a real slave collar. Or I pulled lightly against the cuff attached to the bondage belt. I didn't even feel self-conscious anymore about being naked.

I love this.

It didn't surprise me, exactly. But maybe I was surprised by how *much* I loved it. Whenever I came near Kel to refill her drink or receive an instruction, she put a hand on me, and I felt so *hers*. And so proud of that.

Eventually the group headed into Chaos. I was spacey then, peaceful, and while I was a little wary of what was in store, I kept one thing in mind: *It's not your decision.* Greg and Kel cared how I felt. They wouldn't let me get hurt.

They let Bill back in.

The thought jarred me out of my trance.

They let him play in this room. They've talked to him. Counseled him. Maybe they've fucking comforted him—told him it was okay, that what happened was an accident. That it was over and done.

And then you let them touch you.

Let them give you orders.

I ran the fingers of my free hand along the collar. Kept my head bowed, my eyes on the ground.

Shut up, I told myself. *Shut up, shut up, shut up.*

Gradually the flood of adrenaline left. I started slipping under again.

Greg undid the cuff and bondage belt. I studied the red indents the belt had made on my skin. I was aware that the rest of the group had dispersed, though I didn't know who was still in the room, or who was watching me. I heard Lady A's voice, and Cuntesse's. Sal ordered me forward at one point. Placed a hand on my shoulder and told me I was doing a good job. I murmured a dazed thank-you.

I drifted, not thinking of anything in particular. Greg and Kel left me standing alone by the padded table while they watched Sal and Cuntesse do a short scene on the chain spider web. When the group came back, Kel made me sit on the table while Margie gave me a blowjob.

It was odd at first—I felt tense, uneasy. Put off by the whispers and soft laughter of other group members. But then I got lost in the sensation, letting the pleasure build and then fade, but refusing to let myself come. Eventually Margie stood, and I remained on the table, her spit cooling between my legs, the room lurching every time I tried to move my head.

"Very good." Kel placed a steadying hand on my shoulder. "Listen to Greg now."

"He is *gone*," Lady A said. "Look at him."

Greg snapped his fingers once. "Come here, Gould."

I slid off the table. Went down on my hands and knees and crawled over to him. Pressed against his leg, and noticed the box was beside him. How the fuck had they gotten the box in here without me noticing?

Greg touched my collar. "Stand up."

I did. My legs were weak, and the room suddenly felt too cold.

He turned me toward the box. "Get in."

It was a simple order, and I wanted to obey it. But something stopped me. The box was supposed to stay at home. Wasn't supposed to be used for a performance. And yet I was fucking elated that they'd thought of this, because it was a real challenge. In my state, half-drunk off a chemical reaction, it felt like a Herculean task.

I didn't move.

"Get in," Greg repeated calmly, his hands still on my shoulders.

I kept gazing into that darkness. Involuntarily, I stepped back against Greg.

He gave me a nudge forward. "In."

I took a hesitant step toward the box, then balked again.

Greg gripped my collar in front and pulled gently. I locked my knees.

My mind was foggy, and even though the box would have been a perfect way to escape the people watching me, right now it was genuinely scaring me. Which was fucking awesome. It was so difficult, in scenes, to get a real edge of fear. *Don't be careful with me. Don't back off.*

Greg stepped beside me again and slapped the back of my left thigh. I shivered, but didn't move.

Greg's voice was in my ear, low and warning. "I gave you an order."

My chest tightened. My knees stayed locked.

"I expect you to obey."

I spun suddenly to face him and dropped to my knees. Bent to place my forehead against the tops of his shoes and crossed my wrists behind my back.

Throw me off, I wanted to urge him. *Shove me the fuck away from you. Then make me get in that box.*

I heard him unbuckle his belt. "Last chance," he said.

All the air rushed out of me in a combination of fear and relief.

"Greg," Kel said quietly.

"He *likes* to be fo—"

She cut him off with something I didn't hear. It was hard to focus on anything but the pounding in my head, the panic that I kept balanced like a bubble trembling on one of those giant bubble wands. I wanted to see if I could get it bigger without it popping.

Greg knelt in front of me. Took my face in both hands. "You with me?"

I hesitated, then nodded.

He leaned close to my ear. "Can you do this for me? Get in the box?"

"Make me," I whispered, the words rushed and nearly inaudible, so that I could almost pretend I hadn't needed to say them. That he hadn't *asked.*

He hesitated, then hauled me up by both arms and spun me toward the box.

"Get in." He slapped my ass again, hard.

My skin throbbed where he'd hit me. I stared at the box, and it blurred as my eyes filled.

Did you ever go to a lake with Hal? Did he really ask about snakes and bread?

If I went in the box, I'd be with Hal, and I was afraid to bring Hal into this room, this room that was full of Bill's presence. Normally the thought of being in the box with Hal was comforting, but right now, it felt like a trap. I couldn't tell Kel and Greg, though. This was my secret, and it only added to the thrill and the fear, to have this private corner in my mind full of memories and guilt and a love I couldn't let go of, and then to detonate that mess at will.

Greg gabbed the back of my hair and shoved me down until I was bent over the box. I could feel people watching. I tried to wrench away, but Greg smacked me again and twisted my hair, and the pain jolted something in me, made me put one leg into the box. Then the other. Greg forced me into the small space. I saw a flash of the room through the hole near my head. I gripped his hand as though I was afraid he'd start shoveling dirt onto me. He held on for a moment, then shook me off and snapped the lid on the box.

I curled up and lay there for a moment in near-darkness. I could hear the muffled sounds of the others moving through the room, snippets of low conversation. A hand—a stranger's—came through the hole behind me and stroked my ass. My breath caught, then spilled out in a rush. I didn't want to be in Riddle anymore. I wanted to be home, in bed with Kel and Greg. Or I wanted to be *home* home, sitting with Dave at the kitchen table, smoking weed and talking.

Something cold and metal brushed the side of my ass. I winced and held my breath as a pair of tweezers nipped my skin. The next pinch came right where my ass joined my thigh. I clenched my teeth, willing myself not to react. A few more pinches, and I gasped quietly with each one, my eyes watering.

"Elbows and knees," said a woman's voice.

I uncurled and repositioned myself so my ass was level with the hole. Someone lubed me up, and then a toy—small and about finger-width—was inserted. I wasn't sure what it was, but it wasn't very long, and it didn't hurt, though my ass kept clenching around it. I remembered how many times I'd had to assure Kel over the past two days that there was no lingering pain from the debacle with the plug. *Let me hurt. Let me break.*

I got fucked for probably ten minutes, and I was never sure who was doing it. The knuckles that brushed my ass with each thrust weren't Kel's or Greg's. So it was some stranger, silently pushing the toy in, then sliding it out, over and over. I got lost in the loneliness, the shame, the fierce desire to be serving someone I knew.

Finally, a familiar hand slipped through the hole near my head. Kel stroked my cheek. Whoever was fucking me sped up, and Kel continued to touch me. I closed my eyes and felt an imagined warmth, someone's skin against mine. But when I opened my eyes, it wasn't Hal in the box with me.

Bill's wide, dark-circled eyes stared back at me.

I let out a raspy sigh as I gazed at him. Then my mind went blank.

Eventually, the lid came off the box. Someone touched my shoulder. My face felt stiff, my eyes sore.

"Come on out, babe." Kel's voice was soft.

I stood slowly, blinking against the dim lights of the room. Greg took my elbows and steadied me as I stepped out of the box. The others were gone, but I didn't remember them leaving.

"Gould?" Greg said quietly. "You all right?"

"Give him a few minutes," Kel said.

"I'm okay," I said. "I'm fine."

My body felt light, my breathing even. My left thigh ached a little. Everything was amazingly, wonderfully quiet.

Kel draped something over my shoulders—her sweater, a long, thick gray cardigan. It smelled like her. Traces of her coconut shampoo, of sweat and fabric softener. I pulled it tighter around me. Let the smell anchor me.

They took me to the coat closet, dressed me, and led me out to the car.

I started to feel more awake on the drive home. By the time we reached the house, we were all laughing and joking, and I'd mostly forgotten about the . . . What had it been? A hallucination? I didn't want to call it that. A hallucination implied a lack of control. I had an intense imagination, that was all, and I could have banished that image of Bill if I'd wanted to.

Then what about the time you lost?

Subspace. I'd gone a little too deep.

But it bothered me that I didn't know how long I'd been in the box. That I couldn't remember what had happened after I'd imagined I saw Bill.

Kel shut off the car in the driveway and twisted to see me. "How did Greg do tonight?"

Greg groaned. "A performance evaluation? At four in the morning?"

She flicked his arm playfully, still looking at me. "Yep."

I grinned. "He handled everything really well. Like, *really* well."

Kel turned to Greg. "Good for you."

"Is it really so shocking?"

I turned to Greg too. "Sorry about, uh, the stuff with the box. I don't know what happened, exactly."

Greg smiled, stretching in his seat. "No worries." But he and Kel exchanged a glance I couldn't quite read.

Kel shifted, taking off her seat belt so she could face me. "You should have seen him a few years ago. Anytime we had a girl sub, he was all—" she mimed petting "—'Shh, I've got you. I've got you. You're okay. You're doing great.' And I was still too nice to him at the time, because I felt guilty making this poor straight guy play with boys, so we mostly had girls. But on the rare occasion I got my way and we played with a guy, Greg was all—" she put a tentative hand on Greg's shoulder and patted awkwardly "'Hey, brah. It's cool, man. You aight?' If he even touched the guy at all."

"I was not that bad," Greg protested.

"Oh my God, you were so afraid of man cooties."

"Well I'm not afraid anymore."

Kel laughed. "Is it just Gould, d'you think? Or are you, like, a bona fide bisexual now?"

He leaned back, hands laced behind his head. "I'm just more comfortable in my masculinity." He tilted his face toward Kel. "And yeah, Gould's special. You know he is."

I shifted, pleased and embarrassed. Why? Why the fuck did it make me feel all warm and fuzzy inside to be considered some straight guy's exception to "dudes are gross"?

"I do know it." Kel reached behind her and put a hand on my knee. I smiled but stayed quiet.

Greg glanced at me again. "Look at that face. I'd make out with him all night."

I snorted and looked down. "Shut up."

Greg raised a brow at Kel. "Did you hear what he just said to me?"

"I did. And you deserved it."

"I was paying him a compliment. You always take his side."

Kel cupped his face. "Because *you* are an asshole. And Gould has splendid behavior."

Greg rolled his eyes, snickering. "Fine." He twisted so he could see me again and leaned through the space between the seats. "Would you mind being an asshole once in a while? To make me look better?"

I scooted forward on an impulse and pecked him on the lips. Drew back, smiling. "I'll try."

He stared at me for a moment. His expression made my gut twist—not in a bad way. Not at all.

"Come here," he whispered.

I leaned in a little more, as far as the seat belt would let me. He placed a hand on the side of my neck and guided me forward until our foreheads touched. We stayed like that for a few seconds. Then he kissed me—a soft, slow kiss that made my whole body surge. I groped for the seat belt buckle and pressed the button. Pulled away from Greg as I fought to get the belt off, then collapsed onto my knees in the footwell, my hands braced on the console as I rose to keep kissing him. He threaded his fingers through my hair, tongue sliding into my mouth. At first he moved it too quickly, plunging it in and out, but then he slowed, and I managed to get my lips around it so I could suck it.

He groaned quietly—barely a sound at all.

"Oh my *God*," Kel said. "Fanning myself over here."

Greg and I broke the kiss and looked at her. She was waving her hand in front of her face.

"Are all your dreams coming true?" Greg asked her.

She nodded happily. "One day I'm going to choreograph the ultimate porno starring you two."

"As long as we can sell it on the internet."

"Nahh. It'd just be for me." She opened her door and got out. "Come inside, before I get too hot and bothered."

I exchanged a last look with Greg. Raised my eyebrows. "I'd give you an honorary queer badge for that."

He reached back and patted my head, a little too hard. "Shut up."

Sunday was the debriefing. We sat at the kitchen table and ate snacks and had coffee. I got to wear clothes and everything. It was almost like an employee morale meeting at the bank.

"Honesty," Kel reminded me before we started, "is super important."

"Yes, Ma'am." I'd been feeling strange since last night—worried about that stretch of time I'd lost in the box, wondering about what had happened between Greg and me last night. Unsure what we'd all do now that our week was over—whether they'd want to go back to meeting only on occasion, like before, or whether they'd liked the week enough to want to repeat it.

Kel started with, "How did you feel this week went, overall?"

"Can I just fill out the comment card?"

Greg snorted.

She grinned. "Stand up. Bend over the table."

"Yes, Ma'am." I obeyed, trying to avoid Greg's eye.

"So let's see if I can get answers without the sass." She rubbed the seat of my jeans briskly. "How did you feel this week, overall?"

I stared at the curtains over the sliding glass door. "Good."

She reached around and undid my fly. Tugged my jeans down, exposing my rainbow boxers. "Is that an answer?"

I grimaced at the table. Tensed as her fingertips drifted over my bare thigh. "I loved this week. There were some challenging parts, but it was what I wanted."

Kel touched my thigh again. "Would you want to do a week like this again?"

"Yes, Ma'am." That, I was sure about.

"And what would you like to be different next time?"

I stared at the patterns in the table's wood. She pinched me, hard, and I winced.

"Stay focused," she ordered. "The contract's not up yet."

"Sorry, Ma'am. I think . . . I'd want to do more humiliation stuff, but maybe not in front of other people? Like, getting soda dumped on me is actually fine. It's the— I want *you* to take me down to where I can't be taken down any more. I just don't want anyone watching."

"And what could I do to take you down?"

I swallowed, not sure she'd like this. But she'd said honesty was important. "Maybe . . . say shit to me about how I'm not, like, good enough? Or if I get freaked out by something, you make fun of me for it?"

She took her hand off me. "You can pull your pants up and sit again."

I did. I looked at her, my skin prickling. "I need you to tell me I'm not good enough and *mean it*." I rushed to get the words out. "Think of the stuff you really don't like about me, and say it. Make me feel like nothing. Fucking . . . tell me I'm fat, tell me I'm weak, tell me I cry too easily. Tell me I'm worthless, that I'm not what you want." I'd said too much. I knew that right away. I could sense Greg's discomfort, though he didn't say anything.

Kel, though, didn't look horrified or anything. She shook her head slowly. "Babe. I would never say you were worthless and mean it."

"I'm not talking about you genuinely thinking I'm worthless. I just want you to make me feel that way. And how else is that gonna happen unless you say that shit to me and at least, like, believe it in the moment?"

She hesitated. "Playing with your mind like that is risky."

"Right, because I fall apart if people look at me wrong."

"That's not what I said. But yes, I do worry about your self-image."

I pushed back. "See? How the fuck am I supposed to get what I need when, if I put myself down, even a little, you're right there like, 'Oh, no, you're such a good boy. Don't you dare talk about yourself that way'? I'm not always gonna feel good about myself. I want to feel sick, I want to feel afraid, I want to feel like—like *property*. I *don't* want control. I can't only be your slave on the days I'm happy and confident. That wouldn't . . . work."

She was grinning.

"What? Is this funny?"

She shook her head again. "I just like it when you talk."

Naturally, I stopped talking then.

She reached out and took one of my wrists. Placed my arm closer to her and put her hand over mine. "I hear what you're saying. But you're talking about play that crosses from humiliation into degradation."

"So?"

"So, by definition, degradation does harm to the mind. Sometimes permanently. This is no different from you asking me to brand you, or carve my initials into you. If I say these things to you, and I make you believe I mean them, we can't take that back."

"I know. But if I'm thinking I might, eventually, want to be basically a slave . . ." *Then maybe I want to be branded. Want her carved into my body and my mind.*

"Being a slave is not synonymous with humiliation or degradation. Plenty of M/s relationships don't involve humil—"

"I get it. You asked what I want, and I'm telling you." I was surprised by how easily all this was coming out. It didn't feel like a struggle to say these words. I wasn't afraid of rejection. I could tell her these things. She'd listen.

Greg glanced back and forth between us. "I think it can work. Experimenting with humiliation, I mean. We just have to be careful."

Kel stared at me for a long moment. Finally she said, "You have to come to me with a full list next week. Hard limits and soft. What I can and can't say to you. What I'm allowed to do physically. *Anything* you think might trigger you. Just because you list something as a trigger doesn't mean it's off-limits. I just need to know about it. Okay?"

I grasped for the words I wanted. "But that takes away the . . . It won't work if I know what's coming."

She shook her head. "That's the deal, Gould. Otherwise, the whole thing's a hard limit for me."

I thought for a moment. "What do *you* want?" I asked quietly, embarrassed that I hadn't asked before.

She leaned back, tapping the leg of her chair. "I do like the idea of psychological play. Of continuing to push you. I want us to keep shaping our protocol and maybe thinking about moving to a Master/slave arrangement." She shifted, glanced at Greg, then back at me. "However. Some of my favorite moments with you don't involve humiliation or control. I like seeing what you give me on your own."

"I like that too."

"You've got to understand: I've met so many people who assume fem-dom is about humiliating men. That's a dynamic that has worked for Greg and me sometimes. But sometimes I want to be dominant in a way that . . . where I don't need to call anyone names, or ask them to get me drinks or hold the door for me or whatever the fuck. I want to *care* for someone. I want men to think I'm strong enough to care for them."

That hit me hard. I *did* want to be cared for. I would never lose my need to quietly obey, to be appreciated. But I was so ashamed of being passive that it was like humiliation was the only way to make me feel like I'd *earned* that care.

And I *did* like humiliation in its own right. I'd had these fantasies long before Hal died. I just worried sometimes that my grief had . . . twisted them, or something.

I took a breath, tried to get my bearings. "I don't need to be humiliated all the time. You know? I like the little things—eating on the floor or whatever. Just, I want to try something big. I want to see what happens if you push me until I, like, break."

Her hand tightened over mine. "Break?"

"Cry, or whatever. Get so confused that I don't even know who I am. Don't even know if I'm human. Am just completely and totally, like, at your mercy." I paused. "I like, um . . . I imagine sometimes that I'm just, like, crying or panicking or whatever, and I beg you to help me, and you don't. You just watch me suffer."

She didn't flinch. We all sat there silently.

"Why do I want such different things?" I muttered, when I couldn't take the waiting anymore. "Why can't I just be happy with one kink? Why is it this constant . . . one minute I want to feel like dirt, and the next I want someone to tell me that everything I do is perfect? I don't . . . get this, and I'm sorry I'm dragging you into it."

Kel smiled and tipped her head almost imperceptibly at Greg.

Greg leaned forward. "Remember what I told you? About when Kel and I started? And I could tell somewhere in there was a real desire to submit to a woman, but I just kept not doing that?"

I nodded. "Yeah."

He shrugged. "I don't know any kinky people who just want one thing."

I didn't say anything.

Kel folded her hands on the table. "So let's take this week off. And we'll spend it emailing, as usual. You'll get me your humiliation list, and we'll talk about it. Then next week, you'll come stay with us again. You'll serve us like you did this past week, but we'll add some new layers. And if things are going well, we can up the intensity? Okay?"

"Yes, Ma'am," I murmured.

Gould tries to be a slave, take fifteen.

"Hey," Greg said quietly. "We're gonna figure it out, okay?"

I looked at him and remembered flashes of last night. Talking to him in the kennel, being forced into the box. Kissing him in the car.

I looked at her, and she was everything. The person I wanted to belong to, take orders from, live to serve.

We *were* going to figure it out. I trusted them.

CHAPTER
TEN

D ave seemed wary of me when I got back Sunday night, like he expected me to have changed. He let me brief him on my week, though, and he didn't make any disparaging comments about Kel and Greg, so that was something. Maya dropped by Monday to hand her spare car key over to Dave and me. She was leaving town for a couple of weeks. We were supposed to go by her place every few days to see if the street cleaning signs were up and move her car accordingly.

Tuesday, I got home from work to find Miles and Dave at the kitchen table, discussing whether one of the vendors for the kink fair should have been denied because her shop had once supported a local cop who'd been kicked off the force after his stash of S&M snuff porn was discovered. Miles looked haggard. He was wearing one of his many cardigans, but it was buttoned wrong, and the shirt underneath didn't look ironed. They told me Kamen was on his way over with Ryan, and that they needed to tell us something.

"Oh God," I said. "You don't think they're getting married, do you?"

"That was my first thought," Dave replied.

Miles sat back. "Either that or Kamen's pregnant."

Kamen and Ryan's relationship had progressed very quickly. Really, so had Miles and Drix's. And Dave and D's. But Kamen and Ryan in particular had met, said, "I love you," and moved in together within four months. So an engagement wouldn't exactly have surprised me.

We talked until we heard Kamen's car pull into the driveway. A moment later there was a knock.

Dave stood. "Right. I keep forgetting we're trying that thing where we lock the front door."

After years of hounding from Miles and, more recently, D, Dave and I had started keeping our door locked. Miles and I followed Dave to the living room.

Dave opened the door, then retreated suddenly behind me with an, "Oh dear God."

Kamen entered, leading a small, stick-thin gray animal on a leash. "Come on," he urged. "Come on in. Say hello, buddy."

"Ohhhh," I said.

Ryan stepped around them and entered, keeping an eye on the animal. "Don't let him pee on their floor." He glanced at the rest of us. "He's a nervous pee-er."

Dave peered over my shoulder. "What *is* that?"

Kamen raised a fist in triumph. "It's our dog, Hemsworth."

"You got a dog?"

Kamen grinned at me. "That was the top-secret thing I was doing the other day. We were at the shelter scoping out di-zogs. Then we went back yesterday and adopted this guy."

"Wow," I said.

Kamen tried to lead the dog a little closer. "He's part Italian greyhound and part Chinese crested, so, like, he's totally fucked-up looking. Seriously, check out this face." The dog hunched, tail tucked. "These people were vacationing here from Alabama, and Hemsworth got a piece of glass stuck in his paw, and they didn't want to pay the vet bills, so they just left him at the vet's office. And the vet took him to the pound."

Hemsworth stood behind Kamen's legs, shivering, his leash tangled. He looked like a tiny greyhound except with some scraggly fuzz on his back and face. He suddenly caught sight of Miles and slunk out from behind Kamen's legs, growling. Lunged toward Miles with a series of piercing barks.

"Jesus." Miles stepped back.

"Sorry." Kamen wound the leash around his hand, reeling Hemsworth in.

Ryan leaned against the couch. "We think he's racist."

I squinted. "What?"

Kamen shushed the dog. "Well, we think maybe his old owners taught him to bark at black people. I mean, Alabama, you know?

Because he does this to our downstairs neighbors too, but not to white people." He glanced down at Hemsworth. "Easy, boy. Easy."

Hemsworth calmed slightly, but continued pacing, glaring at Miles.

"Actually," Kamen continued, "we were gonna see, Miles, if you would mind coming over sometimes so we can get him used to being around people of color? And if you have any black friends, they can come over too."

Miles sighed. "Don't *you* have any other black friends?"

"Not really. I mean, some guys at work, but I don't know if we're at that level where I can ask them to come over and make my dog not racist."

"What about Maya?" Dave suggested. "Or—" he looked at me "—GK?"

Kamen crouched and petted Hemsworth. "We're not sure if it's just, like, African Americans, or if it's all non-whites. But yeah, dude, Gould, bring GK over and we'll see."

I tried to imagine bringing Greg to Kamen's apartment. Too weird.

I crouched too and let Hemsworth come up and sniff my hand. "Hey, he likes lapsed Jews. Did you name him?"

Kamen nodded. "Hell yeah. His other name was Joshua, and I didn't want to think about my friend Dumb Josh every time I saw my dog."

That made a very Kamen sort of sense. "You wanted to think of the Hemsworth brothers instead?"

"Fuck yes. The number of times I imagine me in, like, a potentially lethal foursome with those guys is out of control."

Ryan slapped the back of his head. "Fivesome."

"Right."

Dave frowned. "So you want to get a boner every time you say your dog's name?"

Kamen whirled. "No! I just like the name."

Miles shook his head. "I had no idea you were so taken with those oafs."

Kamen straightened, passing the leash to Ryan. "Miles, give me some paper, and I will draw you a picture of exactly what I want those three oafs to do to me."

"I'd rather not know."

I slipped away to the kitchen and got some paper and a pen.

Ryan let Hemsworth off the leash. The dog stood by the couch and shivered as Kamen drew. After a moment, Kamen showed Miles his drawing. "Here's me. And that's Chris."

Miles took the paper. "Is he putting it in your ear?"

"No, turn it this way." Kamen adjusted the paper. "Okay? And that's his mouth. And look where the arrow's pointing. So when he's done with that, he starts, like, slapping my face with his dick. And then that's Liam back there in a chair, filming it."

"What's Luke doing?"

"Dude, if you can't figure out what that is, I can't help you."

Ryan glanced at the paper. "I didn't realize you'd planned this all out. Am I inadequate?"

"No! You're there too. See, you're in the bathroom, watching through the crack in the door. And then Liam sees you, and he's like, 'What the hell are you doin', you little perv? Don't make me come in there and fuck you.' And then he goes in there to fuck you, but he doesn't realize how fierce you are, so you throw him against the bathroom wall and fuck *him*—but he loves it; it's not, like, weird and illegal—and all I can do is listen, 'cause I'm still trapped in the mighty arms of Thor."

Miles nodded grudgingly. "It is a somewhat potent fantasy."

"Right? Who doesn't want to get slapped in the face with a Hemsworth cock?"

We moved to the kitchen. Kamen placed Hemsworth on Ryan's lap, then went to the bathroom.

"So," Miles said, taking his usual seat. "Once Dave moves out, where are we gonna have Subs Club meetings?"

I looked at Dave. "You told them?"

"I say we have meetings at Miles's house," Dave said glibly. "Wouldn't you love that, Miles? All of us tromping into your pristine house, bearing sandwiches, teaching your kid bad words . . ."

"Uh-huh," Miles said.

We shot the shit for a little while and tried to befriend the anxious Hemsworth.

"Hey, what's this?" Kamen called. He was standing in the doorway of my room.

"What's what?" I asked.

"You've got a box of N64 games. Also vampire books."

I hesitated. "Those were Hal's. And mine. Cass found them with Hal's old stuff and sent them." I felt Miles and Dave watching me. I didn't look at them.

Kamen came back to the table. "Do you even have an N64?"

I shook my head. "Don't know where it ended up."

"Me and Ry got one somewhere. I'll bring it over, and we'll all *Hangtime* one of these days." Kamen was good about that. He never tiptoed around anything Hal-related. Of course he would see a box of Hal's old video games and think we should play them. Really, it had been a long time since I'd seen any of them grow somber at the mention of Hal's name. A long time since any of them had mentioned Bill and what I'd thought was our mutual fury toward him.

Eventually Miles stood. "Well. As much as I enjoyed meeting your racist dog, I do have to get back to my son."

I caught him at the door and asked if he and I could get together sometime to discuss something private. He said sure, and we made a date for tomorrow while Zac was at school and Drix was teaching vampyre yoga.

Once they'd all gone, Dave and I stood in the kitchen.

"You got a box of Hal's stuff?" he asked.

"Yeah. Just junk. Cass thought I should have it."

He didn't say anything else.

I took a half day Wednesday and went to Miles's in the afternoon, stopping at the Carrden's Drugstore on the way. I sat in the parking lot for a few minutes. Watched an employee I didn't recognize come out the back and smoke on the sidewalk. Hal used to work here. I'd come by some evenings and pick him up. But he was impatient—if I was running late, he'd just start walking the four miles home. I'd usually catch him along one of the back roads. Roll down my window, ask him what a hot motherfucker like him was doing out here all alone. He'd try to pretend he was mad at me for being late, but always failed.

"You're late" had been rich coming from him, since he couldn't get anywhere when he was supposed to. It was like time didn't exist for him. You couldn't really "make plans" with him, because he just showed up when he wanted and left when he wanted. There were nights we'd all be hanging out late at someone's apartment, and one of us would look up and be like, "Where's Hal?" He would just vanish, without a word.

I squinted a little at the employee. He was about Hal's height and build, and if I blurred his face and just looked at the uniform . . .

I stopped. I'd gone through a couple of phases like this, where I'd needed to come sit in the drugstore parking lot every few days. It had creeped the others out.

I decided I wouldn't do it anymore.

Or I just wouldn't let the others find out.

"I do worry about your self-image," Kel had said. *"I need to know* anything *you think might trigger you."*

Was there such a thing as grieving too much? For too long? At what point did it become . . . inappropriate, I guess? Right after Hal had died, everyone kept telling me my feelings were natural. What about now? What about nearly three years later, when I still thought about him every fucking day? Still missed him just as much?

I put the car in drive.

Miles's house was spotless. How anyone could keep a house looking unlived-in with a five-year-old around was beyond me. On the fridge, there was a crayon drawing of what I thought was supposed to be a woman. It was labeled "The White Lady." Plus a weeklong menu listing lunches and dinners. There was also an ad, cut from a city magazine, for A2A Wear.

"Cool ad," I said.

"Yes." Miles looked pleased. "I've started expanding my advertising campaign. I'm doing two radio spots this summer."

"Awesome."

We went to the living room and sat on his couch. "So," he said. "What do you need to discuss?"

I shifted. "So, I'm . . . I know I haven't talked about this much with you. But Greg and Kel and I have been kind of trying out a 24/7 arrangement. I stayed with them last week. And I'm doing it again next week."

"Dave told me. How's it going?"

"Pretty good. But I was wondering if you could give me some advice about a couple of things."

Miles and I rarely talked one-on-one like this. I loved him just as much as the others, but I wasn't as comfortable with him as I was with Dave or Kamen. I got the feeling he found my reticence frustrating. And I definitely found his uptightness unnerving. But he knew his shit when it came to kink, and I knew it would flatter him to be asked for advice. Sure enough, his expression softened. "What's up?

"Uh, right. Okay. So, um, Kel wants me to— *I* want her to do some humiliation stuff with me. Like, pretty severe humiliation. But she wants a complete list of what I'm okay with and what I'm not, so she doesn't trigger me."

"Is that a question?"

"Not really."

He took his glasses off and cleaned them with his undershirt. "All right."

"Can you help me figure out . . . what my options are, I guess? I sort of know what I want, I just have trouble putting it into words. And you're good with words."

He went to the kitchen and returned with a legal pad and pen. Started writing. "The main thing she's probably interested in is hard limits. So let's make separate columns for verbal and physical humiliation, and subdivide physical into general, predicament, and sexual."

"Uh, okay."

He drew harsh lines down the page. "Start with verbal. Start with name-calling. What do you absolutely refuse to be called? Gay slurs? Jewish slurs?"

"Um . . ."

"It's a fairly simple question."

"I don't like the slurs so much. I mean, some insults would be okay." I shrugged, embarrassed. "I'd like it if she said stuff about my weight."

Miles lifted his head and gave me a long stare. Then went back to writing.

We spent most of the afternoon making the list and talking. It was probably the most he and I had ever said to each other at one time. I thought with a flash of guilt about the way I used to sort of ignore him back when the five of us had just met. Dave, I'd hit it off with right away. But Hal and I had been so infatuated with each other that it had taken me some time to really notice and warm up to Miles and Kamen.

At one point, I got an urge to go to the drugstore again. To just sit there for a while in the parking lot and see if I could figure out whether that image I'd had the other night of Hal and me at the lake had been a memory.

No. You went there once today. Twice is too much.

But the thought persisted. Every few minutes, while Miles talked to me about the science of humiliation and the dangers of PTSD in psychological scenes, I'd feel this little pull, like I wanted to go out, get in my car, and go back to the drugstore.

"Goodness," Miles said suddenly. "I have to pick Zac up at the bus stop."

"Oh. Sure." I took the sheaf of yellow paper he handed me and stood.

"Best of luck with GK and Kel."

"Thank you. Thanks for the help."

He escorted me to the door. Stopped me with a hand on my shoulder as I was about to leave. "Will you be all right?" he asked. "Once Dave moves out?"

I was surprised. Miles was not a fan of anything he perceived as weakness, in himself or others, and I got the feeling Dave's and my codependence made him crazy.

"Of course," I said. "I'm happy for him."

Miles gave a brusque nod. "Well." He glanced out the window in the front door. "If you would like to accompany me to the bus stop, you're welcome to."

I grinned. I loved Miles's son, and I hadn't seen him in a while. And this would be a good distraction from the drugstore. "Sure," I said. "That'd be awesome."

He'd made me sneak into Cedar Point with him once. Hal. He'd had a friend who was working the summer at the Hotel Breakers, which was right beside the amusement park. The friend had mentioned that sometimes the employees walked from the hotel down to the park's back gate afterhours, and if the gate was open, they'd go in and explore the park by night.

"You just have to steer clear of security," the friend had said.

"I want to do it," Hal told me one evening.

"Uhhh . . ." I said.

"Tonight," he clarified.

I hadn't been to Cedar Point since I was a kid. "It's two and a half hours away. And what if the gate isn't open?"

"It will be."

Thing was, I had known he was right. I did believe in fate. Believed things were meant to be, that opportunities revealed themselves when you most needed them. So we made the fucking three-hour trip. Hal drove without a seat belt, as usual. I left mine unbuckled too. Which was about as wild as things got in Gouldland. He had his friend take us through the hotel and out the back, down to the park gate. Which was open.

The friend had left us there with a warning about where the security stations were, and Hal and I had walked into the dark, silent park. We'd come to Frontier Town first. I'd peered through all the darkened windows of the saloons and shops. We passed the tall, silent roller coasters with their track lights gleaming. Sleeping food carts and diners. I'd been in awe. The roller coaster capital of the world, shut down and deserted, just for us. We crossed the railroad tracks and saw the small, old-fashioned train that transported people across the park by day. Just sitting there. So Hal of course had run up and boarded it. We'd sat together in one of the middle cars, Hal making steam engine noises and me laughing.

We'd walked until we reached the Cedar Point Coliseum. I had only vague memories of the building from my childhood, but it was beautiful—painted towers and domes, wooden balconies and arches. "The Grand Ballroom's on the second floor," Hal had said. And I was surprised he knew. I'd never heard him talk about going to

Cedar Point before, and I'd assumed his parents had always been too poor and too . . . whatever to do family vacations.

We ran into a brief situation when we realized the police station was right next to the Coliseum. The station door was open, and we could see the fluorescent lights, the officers moving around inside. We darted past the door and up the Coliseum's wooden staircase, to a balcony with four sets of doors. We tried the first door, but it was locked. Same with the second and third sets. But I went to the fourth door and pushed it, and it opened.

"Awesome," Hal whispered. We stepped inside, shutting the door behind us. Hal spread his arms. "Ladies and gentlemen. The historic Cedar Point Ballroom."

The ballroom was huge. A wide wooden floor with black folding chairs in haphazard rows. Gray square pillars, and arches that looked like they were made of Tetris blocks. An old-fashioned stage at one end. You could look at that stage and imagine you were seeing the ghosts of all the people who'd performed on it through the decades. We explored for a while. I found a hut that looked like a box office. Hal boosted me up so I could crawl through the window and stand inside. He pretended to order tickets from me.

Eventually we stumbled into a tiny side room that housed a lot more chairs and music stands, plus an out-of-tune piano. Hal banged on the piano for a bit, while I walked back into the ballroom and gazed out the windows. Below, I could see the merry-go-round's bright lights, all the horses holding still.

"Excuse me, sir?"

I jumped and whirled. Hal stood behind me. He extended his hand.

"May I have this dance?"

I rolled my eyes, grinning, and took his hand. He shuffled us across the dark ballroom, half-humming, half-singing.

"You're tone deaf," I told him.

"Oh, I see. You're in one little musical in college—"

"Operetta."

"One little operetta, and you're too good for my singing. Why don't you sing, then?"

My grin widened. "No."

"Come on?"

I pulled him closer, and rested my chin on his shoulder as we waltzed clumsily. "No," I whispered. "I don't like to."

"But I'm the only one listening."

"I want you to sing."

So he kept singing, his voice filling the wide space. I followed him around the dance floor, in love with this world that was just for us, for us and the ghosts, and this night that was meant to be.

Kel and I spent the rest of the week emailing back and forth about my humiliation and/or degradation list. She vetoed making fun of my weight, saying she'd gone through too much fat-girl bullshit in high school to do that to anyone else, even as a game. But, slowly, we got things hammered out. We decided we'd start our week together on Saturday night, after she and Greg got back from a wedding.

Friday evening I drove to Maya's neighborhood. Saw orange street-cleaning signs, and moved her car a couple of blocks over. I was about to get out, when something occurred to me. I flipped open the glove compartment. Maya's handgun was there, in a black cloth holster. I stared at it for a moment. I remembered the first time my brother had let me hold a pistol. How weirdly small and ordinary it looked, but how I'd felt sick as soon as it was in my hand. It was like standing on a skyscraper's viewing deck and looking down—you could *feel* how easy it would be to die.

I was angry at Maya for a moment, for being young and stupid enough to leave this thing here. What if someone broke into her car? The fucking gun should be in a safe somewhere, not just sitting here on top of a Toyota owner's manual and a half-eaten pack of Lifesavers.

I closed the glove box and got out of the car.

CHAPTER

ELEVEN

"We're not going to talk," Kel informed me when I arrived at their place Saturday evening. "You're not going to ask questions, protest, or tell me what you like and don't like. When I'm done with you, we'll go to bed. I don't want to hear a word from you tonight unless it's an emergency."

Well, that was a welcome change, given that she'd spent over a year pushing me to share every thought that crossed my head.

I passed that evening in silence, preparing dinner, serving it, then cleaning up. The two of them talked to each other, but not much. Kel made me eat without using my hands, and lasagna naturally ended up all over my face. They didn't let me wash it off, and Kel kept me busy for the rest of the evening, giving either terse or nonverbal orders. I vacuumed, I brought drinks, I served as a table for those drinks. I had to piss like crazy, but she didn't offer me a trip to the bathroom, and I didn't indicate that I needed one. She wasn't cold, exactly, or cruel. She was just detached, and while there were stretches of time where I was fine with that—I went into my head, didn't give much thought to her or Greg—the overall effect was disconcerting.

Just after eleven o'clock, I was still serving as a coffee table for them while they watched TV, two wineglasses on my back. I had to piss so bad that it was taking every ounce of concentration to hold still. My hips jerked involuntarily as my bladder spasmed, and one of the glasses fell to the carpet. White wine, not red. Small blessings.

Kel took the other glass off my back, set it on the actual coffee table, and then stood. Tugged my collar and my hair to get me to my feet. "Go upstairs," she said shortly. "Get the slapper. Bring it here."

I nodded. Retrieved the slapper and brought it to her. She shoved me over the back of the couch, my head next to Greg's. Greg just stared straight ahead at the TV. The correction was harsh, fast, and loud—ten blows, and I was out of breath when she was done, shocked at how much it hurt. She pulled me up again and pushed me toward the den. Bent me over the back of the love seat there, slapped my legs apart, and left me. I made myself breathe slowly.

It's okay. It's okay.

During a commercial break, Greg came in and fucked me. I was tense and my bladder ached to the point where my stomach was cramping. He pulled off the condom and left it on my back when he was done, dripping onto my skin. He exited the room without a word. I stayed there until their show was over. Then I heard another one starting. Sauce was starting to flake from around my mouth, and cum was drying on my back.

For her. You're doing it because it pleases her.

Because you're nothing.

Because you deserve this.

A few times I had to brace my feet on the floor and shift my weight off my bladder and use every muscle to keep from pissing myself. The condom fell off my back and onto the carpet. I thought about getting up to retrieve it. But I knew, even without explicit instructions, that I was meant to hold position.

Kel came in eventually, carrying the leather leash. I didn't look up, but I could see her legs. Saw her stop a couple of feet from me.

"What's this?" She snapped her fingers. I raised my head to look at her, and she pointed to the condom.

I wasn't sure if I was allowed to speak to answer a direct question, so I stayed silent.

"Get up," she said coldly. "Pick that up."

I climbed off the couch, bladder twinging, and crawled to the condom. Started to pick it up.

"With your mouth."

I placed my hands behind my back and bent to take the condom in my teeth. The movement spread my ass, made me aware of the soreness from Greg's fucking. I rose onto my knees again.

Her expression was unreadable. "All the way in your mouth."

I swallowed. Sucked the condom from between my teeth into my mouth. I tasted cum and latex. She raised the leash and whipped my shoulders with it. Over and over. I tried not to cringe with each blow, but soon my whole upper back was hot, and my mouth was full of spit from refusing to swallow.

A particularly sharp blow made me open my mouth, and drool rolled down my chin and onto the carpet.

She stopped. "What is that?" she asked again. She pointed with her toe to the wet spot. "Do you see what you did?"

I saw, and I felt sick and ashamed.

"Greg," she called. "Get in here."

I tensed. Pressed my knees together as my bladder cramped again.

Greg walked in a few seconds later. "Yes, Ma'am?"

"Look at this. This is disgusting."

I loved that I couldn't tell if she meant the mess or me. My stomach was roiling from a combination of nerves and needing to piss, and the taste of the condom in my mouth made bile rise in my throat. Greg leaned down. Grabbed my hair and yanked my head up. "Jesus Christ," he said, shaking me. "What's wrong with you?"

He shoved me away.

Kel grabbed my hair next, and shoved my head down. She ground my face into the wet carpet. I started shaking. I could feel Greg beside me, and he suddenly put his fist above my groin and pushed hard. I cried out, the condom falling from my mouth, and just barely stopped myself from pissing.

Kel kept rubbing my face in the mess. The carpet burned my nose, and my lips kept touching the condom. Finally she let go and whipped my shoulders eight more times with the leash. "Go get some tape," she said to Greg.

I waited there, hunched and aching, until Greg got back.

Kel snapped her fingers twice. "Greg, pick that condom up. Put it on his back."

Greg placed the spit-drenched condom between my shoulder blades. Then he taped it to my skin using wide, crinkly tape—packing tape, probably. Not duct tape, thank God. The condom was so wet that the tape around it didn't stick very well, but Greg had used a long enough piece that the ends clung to my welted skin.

"That is disgusting," Greg said when he was done. "Take him outside where he belongs. Animal."

I cringed, and my balls tightened. Kel clipped the leash to my collar and tugged. "Get up." I followed her through the house, the tape crackling. She dragged me out into the dark backyard, over to a square of concrete beside the deck. It was fucking freezing. The concrete was rough and scraped my knees as I crawled onto it. She stopped me in the center of the square and kicked my lower belly very lightly with the toe of her shoe. I pissed, soaking the concrete, splattering myself. Crawled back inside after her. She led me upstairs and into their bathroom. Grabbed a saline enema from under the sink and handed it to me. "Clean yourself out, then get in the bedroom. Bring me my harness and the glass cock so I can fuck you."

I took the bottle from her. She left, and I did the enema, cleaning up back there as best I could afterward. I was tempted to wash my face, but I had a feeling that wouldn't go over well. I walked into the bedroom and got Kel's harness and the glass dildo. I brought them to where she was sitting on the bed. She took the harness from me and put it on.

She positioned me ass-up on the floor and took me hard, while Greg watched from the bed, not speaking. It went on and on. A couple of times I thought the tape had come loose from my back, but it held. I was still sore from Greg, and from the enema, and by the time she was done, I felt too exhausted and strung out to care what happened next. She slapped me toward the corner of the room and left me curled up there. She got into bed with Greg, and I heard them whispering, then having sex, the sound of her orgasm making me hard. I felt so alone, so tired, and yet I couldn't sleep. This was what I'd always wanted, what I'd never been able to ask for: this feeling of total helplessness. The more I concentrated on it, the harder I got, until I was moving my hips soundlessly, imagining that I was fucking something besides air.

I listened until Greg started snoring. I couldn't tell if Kel was still awake. I had a feeling she was.

When I woke, it was daylight, and I was still lying in the corner of the bedroom. My neck was stiff, and so was my dick. Someone was touching me. I blinked and rolled over. Kel smiled at me. "Hey, babe. Let's get cleaned up, okay?"

I nodded blearily and got up. She hugged me from behind, kissing the crook of my neck. "You can talk now."

I squeezed her arm gently. "Thank you," I whispered. "That was good. That was so good."

She kissed my neck again and let me go. "You're welcome."

She took me into the bathroom, held my dick while I pissed, and then got the shower running. She peeled the condom off my back. My shoulders were still slightly sore from the whipping, and I could see in the mirror I had superficial bruising on my ass from the slapper, but overall, I felt fine. We got in the shower together, and I had to stand still while she washed me. I hissed a little as she washed between my legs.

She paused. "Sore?"

"Yes, Ma'am."

After the shower she made me bend over the bathroom counter while she got a small tub out of the drawer.

"What's that?" I asked.

She showed me.

"Backdoor Balm? Seriously?"

She laughed. "It's like Neosporin for your asshole. You'll appreciate it when you go to take a shit later."

I snorted. "I'm okay, you know. You didn't break me."

"Indulge me, then." She applied it.

This was crazy. I didn't have any privacy, any control over anything. She didn't act like watching me piss in the yard or looking at me when I had food on my face or putting Neosporin on my asshole had made me repulsive to her. She had this way of making everything about the human body seem natural, sexy, even. I felt better when I was around her, like I was someone worth noticing, worth wanting. Which was strange, since physically, I had been at my least sexy *ever* last night.

She patted my ass. "Stand up."

I did. She took me back to the bedroom. Put a robe on me and brought me downstairs. Greg had made breakfast, and we ate and discussed plans for the day. Seriously, didn't even talk about how they'd taped a used condom to my body last night, or rubbed my face in my own drool. Just talked about mundane shit. Kel apparently needed some time in the afternoon to talk to her dad, so she'd be sending Greg and me on some errands.

After breakfast, she brought me back into the bedroom and spent an hour in bed, just holding me. We didn't say anything, but she was so warm, so affectionate, that any lingering unease I might have felt from last night was gone. I tried to worship her body, but she stopped me and made me lie still. I watched her, my eyes half closed, as she kissed down my chest and over my stomach, her soft hair dragging along my skin. She raised her gaze to meet mine and smiled.

That smile left me stunned by the depth of feeling that existed in me, the fears and desires I couldn't articulate, couldn't hold on to. With Hal, love had been wild, intense, lacking in nuance. What I felt now was quieter, maybe warier. But it was the same feeling, just with more shades, more awareness.

I don't want to be in love again. I seriously fucking don't.

But apparently I didn't get a say.

"What?" she whispered.

I shook my head. Opened my mouth and then hesitated.

"Don't you dare," she interrupted, "say 'I don't know.'"

I grinned. "I'm . . . not sure?"

She swatted my thigh. Kissed my stomach again and then folded her arms across it, staring at me. Her breasts rested against my thighs, and my dick naturally tried to make the situation even more awkward by rising until it was nearly touching her collarbone. I reached forward and stroked her hair. She turned and kissed my fingers, then scooted up the bed and lay facing me. I handed her my pillow to put under her breasts, and she laughed.

"Gould," she whispered, smile fading. "You've got to tell people the things that matter."

Why? Why, when most people knew the things that really mattered? I'd gone through a maudlin phase after Hal's death where I'd pushed myself to remember the last words I'd ever said to him. All I could come up with was that I'd probably said "bye" or "later." Eventually I realized I didn't give a fuck what I'd said to him. He'd known the important shit.

I put my arms around her. Felt her shaking a little, which surprised me.

"Sorry," she muttered. "Sorry. I've been a little— The wedding, I think. It was a friend from college, and her mom was there, and just . . . seeing her with her mom made me think of *my* mom . . ."

I pulled her closer.

She ran a hand down my arm, to where my hand rested just above her hip. "I don't know why I fought with her so much. Like, what was even the fucking point?"

"She knew you loved her."

Her exhale was unsteady. "What if there were times she wasn't sure? Just these . . . little moments of doubt? You know, where sometimes you're not sure if you're just lying to yourself that people even love you at all?" She looked at me with genuine confusion in her eyes.

God, didn't I know. "Those are just moments." *They pass. Over and done.*

But you remember them. And those memories build up.

Even after I'd realized I couldn't stay with Hal anymore—couldn't live with him, couldn't be his boyfriend—I'd never stopped loving him. Or doubted that he loved me. Loving someone wasn't always the same as being kind to them.

She wiggled closer to me. "I don't even wish I'd said 'I love you' more. I wish I'd said other things—like that she was funny, and a good mother. I never laughed at her jokes, and they *were* funny. I just didn't want to ruin my sullen-teenager image."

"She was a mom. Moms see right through that shit."

She traced a light pattern on my chest. "It wasn't even like she was taken from me suddenly. I had so much time while she was dying to figure out how to be better. And even after she died— Then I was really pissed."

I tipped my head toward her, curious. "Why?"

"I was sixteen. I was pissed at everyone."

"Come on. That's not all of it."

"What do you mean?"

I gazed at her steadily, willing her to understand. "Tell me how it feels to be pissed at someone who's dead."

She thought for a moment. "It feels . . . It was like being a child and, like, you're throwing a tantrum and you forget why you started screaming—you just know something wasn't fair."

My voice stuck for a second. *Just say it.* "That's not how I felt."

"No?"

I shook my head. "Hal and I used to fight. And sometimes he'd leave in the middle of a fight, because he knew I couldn't stand that. I needed to, like, make up right away, but I was so . . . He knew I wouldn't ask for what I wanted, so he'd walk out. And I'd be so *pissed*. I wanted to run after him and throw something at his fucking head. That's how I felt when he died too. Like he'd walked out the door in the middle of something that mattered to me. Fucker."

Bill, on the other hand . . .

That had been a scattered anger at first. A tantrum. Blind fury. I'd gone to his house, and I'd hit him. And it hadn't been enough. I'd hit him again and again, but it still wasn't enough.

He'd *let* me, though. That was the thing. Like he was kind of relieved *someone* was doing this.

Maybe it hadn't been enough for him, either.

She paused. "Are we being quirky and sad and philosophical? Are we a John Green novel?"

"I think we might be a John Green novel. Except we're too old."

"And we should be having this conversation somewhere much more hipster-y than the bedroom."

"Like in our car outside an old fifties diner?"

"Maybe. In the basement of a metal sculpture museum?"

We both started laughing.

Greg came in. "I'm gonna go mow the lawn, unless— What's so funny?"

"We're being a John Green novel," Kel informed him.

He set his wallet on the dresser. "Uhhh . . . which one? The one where the beautiful, troubled girl teaches a nerdy guy about life, or the one where a beautiful, troubled girl teaches a nerdy guy about life?"

"All of them." Kel stretched, ruffling my hair. "I'm Gould's manic pixie dream girl. He and I are gonna go on some road trip to find ourselves and discover that the true adventure was in our hearts all along."

Greg had a strange expression on his face. Sort of . . . grim, or wary. I wasn't sure. It faded fast. "Sounds like a best seller."

Kel and I looked at each other and burst out laughing again, a little too hard. Kel turned to Greg again. "We're laughing because otherwise we'd cry. I miss Mom."

"Ohhh." Greg climbed onto the bed on her other side. "That kind of day, is it?"

Kel flicked a curl away from my forehead, making me flinch. "If this is a John Green novel, won't I probably die tragically at the end?"

I gripped her wrists gently. "If you die at the end, I'll kill you." That set us off laughing again, but after a moment, I propped up on my elbows, bent, and kissed her—a deep kiss. I could feel Greg watching, and when we broke apart, I turned to him, not sure how he'd react. But he leaned over Kel, and we kissed briefly too.

Then he kissed her, very gently. "I love you," he whispered.

"Love you too."

"You all right?"

She nodded.

He looked at me. "You?"

"Yes, sir."

He leaned over again, and whispered in my ear, almost too quickly and softly for me to hear: "Take care of her."

Then he was up and off the bed.

I listened to him change clothes and leave the room. When he was gone, I wrapped my arms around Kel and held her until she drifted off the sleep.

Greg woke me around three to go run errands with him. I could hear Kel on the phone downstairs. I dressed and followed Greg out the back door, waving good-bye to Kel. I felt content, staring at the house and its lit windows as we pulled out of the driveway. Thought about the duplex, which had been my home for three years. Three really important years. I wondered if I could get used to a new home. If . . .

No. Don't think it.

A little while later, Greg and I sat in a fast-food parking lot, sharing fries.

We didn't talk for a while, and when we did, we mostly bullshitted about sports and movies, and how greasy the fries were.

"Heart attack waiting to happen," he said, digging for the bottom-of-the-bag fries.

"I know." I gazed across the plaza at the hardware store. "What are we getting again? Something for the bathroom sink?"

He didn't answer. Then he looked at me and asked, "You love her?"

Not angry or anything. Just a simple question.

I shifted nervously. "I don't want to be in love with anyone. Again. Ever."

"But you do love her. Don't you?" He sounded so certain.

"I don't know."

"You're full of shit."

I watched the people going in and out of a fabric shop. "Does that piss you off?"

He shook his head. "Nah. It's a little weird, but I guess I always kind of knew. From the first time I saw you with her."

"You couldn't have known then. *I* didn't know."

"Well. I read the future, then."

I picked at a hangnail. "You really thought that?"

"She and I never bought into that whole one-person-for-everyone bullshit, so it's not like I don't get it." He finished the fries. "I'm glad she has you. She . . . she still has a really hard time sometimes. With her mom. And I think you *get* it, in a way I can't. I try. But it's not the same."

I was quiet a long time. "I don't want to mess anything up between you."

"No. We both want you here."

What do I give you, *though? I sort of see what I give her, but you . . .*

He propped his elbow on the steering wheel and ran a hand through his hair. "I can't make myself feel that way about you, you know? I would if I could."

It stung, but only for a second. "It's fine. I don't feel that way about you, either."

He turned. "Really?"

"What? You just assumed because I'm queer, I must be in love with you?" It was weird, because I really *wasn't* in love with him. But maybe, for whatever reason, I wanted him to love me.

He slid his elbow off the wheel. "I thought—"

"I really like you. I'm just not you're-my-soul-mate in love. I mean, you're straight, first of all."

He nodded. "I want you in this relationship so fucking much. But what I feel for her—it's different."

"Same here."

"You're, like, a friend who's way more than a friend."

"Dude, that's perfect."

He put his hand on the key, like he was gonna take it out, but didn't.

I took a napkin from the bag and wiped my fingertips. Thought about that night in the car when he and I had kissed. "I mean, there's not just one way to love. And being, like *in* love—whatever that means—isn't even close to the most important kind, I think."

"Huh?"

"I mean, what I have with my friends. That *stays*. Romantic love, that's . . . You can fall in and out of it. It's not very stable, or whatever."

"Are you telling me you've *ever* been in love with someone and then fallen out of it? Because if you did, you probably weren't in it in the first place."

Maybe so. Because I'd only ever been in love with one person before Kel. He'd broken my heart. Fucked up my life. And then died. And I still couldn't stop loving him.

"Man." Greg shook his head. "When I first married Kel, we were at each other's throat. Damn, marriage—you wanna talk about a 24/7 relationship full of humiliation and pain and watching each other piss . . . But I loved her through every second of it."

I laughed. "Same here. Hal and I used to fight like crazy."

"I can't picture you fighting with anyone."

"Well, it happened."

He picked up his Coke and took a drink. "Look at us talking about deep stuff."

I dropped the empty fry container into the grease-streaked bag. "So are you actually attracted to me at all? I mean, do you *like* fucking me?"

"You shouldn't ask me this now."

"Why?"

"She's got me butt-plugged. It's, like, messing with my prostate and making me feel *really* gay right now."

"So you're totally gay in this moment?"

"Like eighty percent. It's either the butt plug or you."

"You think I bewitched you into gayness?"

"Hell yeah."

I grinned. "You might have to face your bisexuality, you know."

"That's what everyone who knows I'm playing with you says! They're like, 'You're bisexual, Greg. Bisexuality is a spectrum, Greg.' I'm like, 'Yeah, I know!' I know what you read on your freaking sexuality blogs or whatever. And if I was bisexual, I'd say I was bisexual. But I'm not bisexual. I'm a straight guy who's very open. And you're different, man. You know you are."

"So you think you're gay for me?" I teased.

"Nooo! That's like a diss to gaydom, you know? Like, oh, you can just be a little gay if you feel like it. No, man, if everyone and their mother is allowed to call themselves queer and have it mean whatever the fuck they want, then why can't I be straight and . . ."

"Have it mean whatever the fuck you want?"

"Yeah, basically!"

I shrugged. "Doesn't make any difference to me. Aside from, you know, bi-erasure and how that's bad. I'm just throwing it out there, though: you can be bisexual and only experience attraction to *one* same-sex person in your entire life. You don't even have to fuck them or anything to earn your bi card. There only has to be the attraction."

"God, can we please just go buy some hardware?"

"Absolutely." I unhooked my seat belt.

"I'm not gay."

"I know."

"I'm not bi either."

Honestly, I didn't give a shit how he wanted to identify. I just liked seeing him get flustered. "Look, I'm a solid Kinsey five, but Kel's hotter to me than any person I've ever met. So . . ."

So that was out on the table.

He opened the door. "I gotta look at some drills before my brain explodes."

"I want to make a joke about Freud and drills, but—"

"Enough! As your secondary master, I order you to be silent, slave."

I laughed and got out. "I talk about this shit with my friends all the time. For *fun*."

He walked around the car to join me. "I pity you a little. I do."

I punched his arm. We started across the parking lot together. Suddenly I felt his hand in mine, and I almost stopped dead. I forced myself to keep walking, a smile creeping onto my face.

He glanced sideways at me. "Don't laugh at me. I'm Indian."

"Hey," I said as the automatic doors opened. "I'm not laughing."

CHAPTER
TWELVE

I'd thought those almost-declarations of love might change things between all of us. That I would feel different, behave differently, now that I'd sort of admitted to myself that I loved these two. But the rest of the week passed quietly, as did several weeks after that. We kept up our pattern—one week together, one week apart. Kel had a busy couple of weeks in mid-March: covering shifts at the store for a coworker who was sick, and spending evenings at Riddle with Greg preparing for April's Spring Fling. I went with them and helped clean and make decorations with a few other volunteers. When it was just Kel and Greg and me, I stayed in the kennel, or else let Kel tie me to the padded table in Chaos.

It was strange to be in the club on weeknights, when it wasn't open. With all the lights on and the rooms empty, it looked like a different place. It reminded me of nights last year, when I'd stay late after the weekend play parties and help Kel and Greg clean up. There was something beautiful about being in a place that a crowd had just left. A dungeon after a party. An amusement park after closing.

We continued to experiment with ideas from my humiliation list. It turned out that name-calling didn't do much for me. I did get a rush from being called dirty or disgusting or told I was working too slowly or getting things wrong. But it never lasted. Physical humiliation worked better—being told to stand in a corner, ass out, with my hands on my knees. Tied so that I was on display or off-balance. Having Kel jerk my dick down or to the side while I was pissing, and then making me scrub the bathroom floor on my hands and knees.

They even started a game where they'd be in different rooms of the house and they'd each have ink pads in all different colors, and each color signified a certain act, or a type of toy or restraint. I didn't know the code system, but they did. Kel would put a thumbprint on my back or shoulder or ass—somewhere I couldn't see, then send me crawling to find Greg. He'd do whatever the ink color indicated—whip me, plug me, cuff me—and then put his own mark on me and send me to find Kel. Greg in particular seemed to enjoy that game.

I still wasn't sure whether I was getting what I wanted or not. Humiliation in such small doses didn't really break me down. I either needed longer scenes, or for them to get nastier. Because this stuff didn't feel any more humiliating than the ground we'd already covered—having to put in a butt plug at work, or being forced into the box at Riddle. So finally, Kel promised me a long humiliation scene on the last Saturday of March, where she would break me down as far as she felt I could safely go. Where my hard limits would be respected, but I would have no say in what actually happened.

We decided that Greg wouldn't be involved at all. That Kel and I would do the scene in the downstairs office, which was uncarpeted and had plenty of open floor space. The fact that Kel considered lack of carpet to be significant made me uneasy, but we'd agreed no blood, so I was guessing wax play or watersports. When that Saturday arrived, Kel sent Greg and me to the movies for the afternoon so that she could set up the office. She made us both go commando and told me I had to get Greg off at some point during the movie. His job was to keep me hard through the whole thing. Afterward, I barely remembered anything about the film—I was just focused on using our jumbo popcorn to shield the front of my pants as we left the theater. Greg casually reached out and took the bucket away from me as we crossed the lobby.

The theater was close to Cardden's Drugstore, so on the way home I had Greg stop. Made up some story about needing a new toothbrush. I realized as soon as I was inside that this was a mistake. That I wasn't supposed to do this anymore. I bought a toothbrush and left quickly.

By the time evening rolled around, I was nervous, but in a good way. Kel let me eat and then do an enema a couple of hours beforehand. We spent some time on the couch in front of the TV, just chilling out. I couldn't settle down, though, and I got the sense she was every bit as restless. At 8:45, she sent Greg to the office to get it ready. Told him to go upstairs when he was done.

She and I walked to the office at nine o'clock, and shook hands like we were about to enter an arena. I was naked. She wore jeans and a T-shirt. We grinned at each other, and she slipped a finger under the collar around my neck. "When we walk into that room, I own you."

The pit of my stomach jerked. "Yes, Ma'am."

She leveled her hand in front of me. "This is 'Are you okay?' If I use it, what I need from you is a nod or a head shake." She'd insisted on that provision. Not a safeword, exactly, but a way for her to check in, make sure I was still at least somewhat coherent. A safeword would, as always, end not just the scene, but the week's contract.

"Yes, Ma'am."

"Then let's do this."

She opened the door and ushered me in.

The room smelled lemony, like furniture polish. She turned on the computer desk's lamp. The floor was spotless, gleaming. There was a chair in the center of the room, a TV tray beside it. On the computer desk sat two plastic pitchers full of ice water and lemon wedges, and two glasses. The box stood in one corner, and there was a black canvas bag under the chair.

She pointed to the floor. I knelt. She walked to the chair and sat. Curled her finger at me. I crawled toward her.

She snapped her fingers.

I stopped, looked at her. She shook her head. Got up and strode over to me. I cringed slightly as she moved behind me. She lifted my legs, pulled them straight, then set them down, so that I was supported on just my hands. Then she sat in the chair again and motioned me forward.

I started toward her on my hands, dragging my legs behind me. By the time I reached her, my dick was hardening, and I was slightly out of breath.

She spread her legs wider. Pointed between them.

I knelt up. Leaned forward and breathed cautiously on the denim. She tipped her head back. *Please, yes. Let me do this for you.* I wanted to taste her. Wanted to make her come, show her how much I needed her.

I reached for her fly, but she planted one bare foot in the center of my chest and shoved me with it. I sprawled backward, putting my hands behind me to catch myself. I stared at her for a moment, stunned, my chest throbbing where she'd kicked me.

She made the beckoning motion again.

I knelt again and moved slowly, like she was a wild animal who might let me close if I was nonthreatening. She kicked me back again, harder this time. I tried not to let any frustration show. I didn't know if I was doing something wrong, or if this was for her own amusement. Her silence threw me off too.

You're not even worth speaking to, I told myself. *You're nothing to her.*

When I got to my knees a third time, she kicked me immediately, but I braced myself and didn't go over. I stared at her, looking for a clue. Her expression was blank, and that scared me. I was used to her smiling when she cued me. And even when she didn't smile, her eyes usually held amusement or affection. But right now I couldn't read anything in her face. She held my gaze for a moment, then jerked her head toward the jug of ice water on the table.

I crawled to the table and then rose. Picked up a glass and started to pour water into it. She snapped her fingers. I stopped. She pointed to the jug and the glass, then herself. I brought the jug and glass over and set them on the TV tray beside her chair. Poured water into the glass, hoping that was right. I set the pitcher down and handed the glass to her. She sipped, watching me over the rim of the cup.

I went to my knees, since that seemed more appropriate than standing. She immediately set the cup down, picked up the pitcher, and dumped it on me. I gasped as the worst of it hit me in the face, ice chips, lemon slices, and water streaming down my back and chest and onto the floor. I sucked my stomach in and tried to breathe through the chill and the shock. The night at Riddle with Lady A came back to me, and the memory of that shame got under my skin, physically *hurt*.

She grabbed my elbow and jerked upward. I struggled to my feet, and she lifted the glass of ice water. Gripped my dick and plunged it into the cup.

I jerked, stifling a shout. The water was so cold, and the head of my dick pressed directly against an ice cube. My balls drew up into my body. I panted sharply. *You're nothing. You're a toy for her amusement.*

After a few seconds, she let me go. Pushed me to my knees, then handed me the cup and mimed drinking it. Heat spiked through my insides, and my difficulty drawing a full breath made me light-headed. I winced and tipped the cup to my mouth.

I drank the dick water as fast as possible, trying not to think about it.

You're a thing. It doesn't matter what you want.

I choked a little, and she pressed the glass against my face until the rim dug painfully into the bridge of my nose. Then she snatched it away and set it aside. Directed me silently until I was on my elbows and knees on the wet floor. She pulled something out of the bag and showed it to me. It was an anal spreader. I'd known she had one, but she'd never used it on me. From what I understood, it was kind of like a speculum. It had a forceps-ish part, and a handle that cranked and forced your ass open.

She lubed it up and came around behind me.

You fucking stupid piece of shit. She's going to use you until you cry. And then she's going to punish you for crying, you weak, pathetic little thing.

She pressed the tongs into my ass. I winced as she cranked me open until my hole was spread so wide I was shaking with the strangeness of it, the feeling of cool air where it absolutely shouldn't be. Her finger probed the area lightly, but never went all the way in. She kept me like that for what seemed like an eternity, teasing me slowly. A pause, and then something damp, cold, and pulpy nudged between my cheeks. A few drops of liquid landed inside me, and it stung like hell. A citrusy smell. She was squeezing the piece of lemon into me. A few more drops, and my stomach started to turn like I was going to be sick. I pressed my forehead hard against the floor, trying to keep still as the burn spread through my body. My hole spasmed around the forceps, but the device held me wide open to her.

I imagined begging. *Please, Ma'am. Please,* please *tell me how to get it right. Please help me.* I wondered what she'd do if I spoke.

I heard her walk to the desk, where the second pitcher stood. Heard water being poured into the glass. A second later ice water splashed against my ass and into my hole. There was nothing I could do but gasp and dig my nails into my palms. I choked as I tried to draw a breath, clenching so hard around the forceps that my whole body shook. She left me trembling there for several long minutes. The fear started then—small at first, but growing. I didn't like being held open like this, could feel how exposed I was, how easy it would be to make me hurt.

You don't deserve comfort. You should be ashamed of yourself for wanting any.

She went back to the chair and the black bag. She returned to me, crouching behind me to remove the spreader. The sensation as the forceps came out was strange—I was left empty and throbbing, the ache a reminder of her power, of my lack of control.

She set it aside and tapped my left arm until I lifted it, then placed something in my hand: the flat, heavy walnut stick. With a pat on my ass, she came to stand in front of me. Made a swinging motion.

It took me a second to realize she wanted me to hit myself with the stick.

I stared at her. *This is for you. I told you I'd do anything for you, and I meant it.*

I extended my arm behind me. Landed the stick as hard as I could against skin numb and clammy from the ice water. It hurt. God, it hurt. She waited, and I did it again, refusing to wince at the pain. Again, as hard as I could. It took me a few seconds before I could even lift my arm after that one.

After twenty, I was struggling not to cry. But I didn't pull the blows. I kept going until my ass felt bruised, until I was gulping for breath, but she didn't relent, and neither did I. We kept eye contact— she watched my pain grow into something almost unmanageable. And her expression never fucking changed.

Yes. Yes yes yes yes. This was how I wanted to feel. Pathetic and used. Not worth touching for any reason other than to cause pain. And it scared the shit out of me, it fucking terrified me, to want this so much, to know how badly I'd be willing to hurt myself for her, if she asked.

Eventually she gestured at me to put the stick aside and motioned me over to where she sat. She picked up a coil of coarse rope and a pair of shears from the bag. Put me on the floor on my side, my right leg bent slightly behind me.

She didn't talk to me or touch me while she was tying. There was a muscle-deep ache in my ass, and the backs of my thighs felt swollen. She rigged a harness that would keep my leg bent, and placed a knot just under my right knee. Then another one on top of the pressure point at the base of my big toe. Each time I moved, the knots dug into the two points, creating a shooting pain from toe to knee.

Please don't. Please. I'm sorry, Ma'am. Please.

She moved her chair back a couple of feet. Patted her thigh.

I crawled forward. The knots pushed into my leg and foot. After a few seconds, my leg gave out, and I fell sideways on my right hip. She waited until I'd gotten onto all fours again, then snapped her fingers and sent me back to my starting point. Made me try again. Any time I had to stop to get a handle on the pain, she made me go back and start again. Tears welled in my eyes.

What right do you have to cry? Fucking useless piece of meat.

I was crying silently when I finally reached her. I was disappointed in myself for taking so long, for fucking up so many times. She dried me off briskly with a towel, then tossed the towel aside. Leveled her hand in front of me, and I nodded quickly. *Keep going.*

I was in a strange headspace now—not that floaty, drifting space I entered when I was in the box or the kennel, but somewhere a lot harsher and more confusing. I was getting hit, not with fragments of memory, but with snarled emotions, colors, small sounds that suddenly seemed amplified.

She stood and undid her pants and pulled them down, along with her underwear. Hauled me onto my knees by the hair and forced my head between her legs. I started licking, trying to ignore the pain in my knee, the wet skin around my hips being chafed by the rope. She didn't give me a chance to think or to use any kind of technique— she just kept shoving my face against her until it was covered in fluid—hers, plus my own tears and saliva. She came like that, holding my head where she wanted it and rubbing against it until she was satisfied. Then she knocked me onto the floor.

I lay there for a moment, breathing shallowly, and my thoughts started coming unwound like ribbons. *She doesn't care about you, maybe she never did, maybe nobody does, maybe Hal never did. Why would anyone? She's not your master. A master would* need *you, and she doesn't. She doesn't need you.*

Kel retrieved something from behind the computer. Stood in front of me and snapped her fingers. I tried to get up, but the pain in my leg froze me. She didn't punish me—just watched me struggle to get back on my knees. I finally looked up, panting and sobbing.

She held our jar of marbles—black and white mixed together. My fear grew into something enormous and irrational. My heart pounded so hard that the rhythm of it seemed to make the room around me pitch and spin.

She leveled one hand again. I nodded.

She overturned the jar above my head. Marbles poured down my back and scattered all across the room—under the desk, into the corners, and around her chair. I shook one out of my hair.

She gestured to me to pick them up.

Dragging my bent right leg to avoid pressure on the knots, I picked up every marble and put them all back in the jar.

She immediately dumped them again.

Gritting my teeth, I repeated the process. The jar was between her feet, and with each trip I made to put more marbles in, she dug her heel into my side or pressed on my balls with her toe, and when I got the last marble in, I offered her the jar, my arms shaking.

She emptied it again.

All rational thought seemed to scatter with the marbles. I felt a soul-deep despair—an explosion of frustration, anger, and fear; I was electric with shame, and the agony in my knee and foot touched my other nerves like a flame to the wicks of candles, creating small pockets of pain everywhere. It was like a white sheet had covered my mind, and I couldn't see the room, couldn't see her, couldn't feel anything but a pulse that moved my whole body.

I sucked in a breath and blinked until I could see the room again. I started forward, but she stopped me. Knelt beside me.

She undid the rope around my leg and foot. I felt an insane gratitude toward her, despite knowing she was the one who'd caused the pain in the first place, and I wanted to be in her arms, but I knew that couldn't happen. A moment later, the blood rushed back to the spots that had been tied, and I let out a low, strangled moan.

Be quiet. Be fucking quiet.

She went to the desk and poured another glass of water, then returned, setting the glass on the chair.

Please, Ma'am. Please stop. I begged silently for her help, her mercy. But she didn't even look at me.

She used rope to tie my wrists behind my back, then pulled me to my feet, kicking a couple marbles aside. My right leg buckled, but she was ready and caught me, holding me up. Once I could stand on my own, she stood behind me, gripping my jaw, and helped me drink. I was still unsteady, but she didn't offer any comfort beyond the water. She placed the heel of her hand on my lower abdomen and waited.

No. No, please.

Tears streamed down my face. *Why do you still have a mind of your own? Stop thinking. Stop feeling. Just do.*

She pushed. I didn't need to go, didn't want to piss on the floor like a dog. But I wanted to obey.

Urine splashed my legs and pooled around the marbles.

When I was done, she looked at the mess on the floor and clucked softly. I was breathing in shuddering gasps, afraid I'd throw up in front of her. She pressed down on my shoulders, lowering me onto my knees in the puddle and gestured to the marbles. I couldn't use my hands anymore, which meant . . .

I looked up at her. She stared back at me, calm, waiting.

You can't.

Please, no.

She waited.

Slowly, I leaned forward. The smell of piss was acrid. I picked a marble up in my mouth and held it between my lips and teeth, then dropped it in the jar. I went first for the marbles at the outer edge of the puddle. Tried to send my mind somewhere else so I wouldn't have to think about what I was doing, wouldn't have to taste piss or feel the overwhelming humiliation of having her watch me do this, but it didn't work, and my breathing didn't slow, and everything was too fast and too loud.

When I got to the marbles directly in the puddle, I started shaking and couldn't stop. She placed a hand on the back of my neck for a moment, stilling me. Stroked my throat with her other hand. Through my haze, I recognized what she was trying to say. If I didn't calm down, I'd probably choke on a fucking marble.

I took a few deep breaths.

Stop crying.

Accept it.

When I was quieter, she patted my neck and let me go.

By the time I was done putting the marbles back, I was completely disoriented. Exhausted and in agony, my stomach twisting every time I moved, humiliation eclipsing every other feeling. She dumped the jar again, but instead of picking them up, I lunged at her. There wasn't much I could do without my hands, but I knocked her with my shoulder, fighting blindly. Marbles skittered across the floor, and she caught me, holding me until I lost the energy to struggle. I was crying hard and soundlessly. She grabbed me by the hair and pushed me down onto my stomach, until I was lying in the puddle of piss. I tried to keep my head above the floor, tried kicking at her, but she pushed, and I finally went limp, resting my cheek on the wet floorboards with a slow, shaky exhale.

You're nothing. You're nothing.

I closed my eyes, but she jostled me until I opened them again. Her hand was horizontal in front of my face. I blinked at it, confused.

Nod. Nod, or she might stop. And you're close. You're so close.

I wasn't even sure what I was close *to*.

I forced myself to nod.

She left me there and dragged the box out from the corner. Tapped the edge of it.

I can't.

She tapped the edge again.

Slowly, I dragged myself to my knees. My face and hair were wet with piss, and my eyes and nose were streaming.

I climbed into the box. There was no point in fighting.

Why would you fight? Why didn't you fucking serve her, like you promised?

I hoped she'd leave me in the box for a while, so I could be alone. She pressed on my shoulders until my head was down, my ass up. I heard sounds I half recognized, then she spread my cheeks and slid a thin nozzle into my ass. I sobbed harder. She emptied the bottle of saline solution into me. I could feel her knuckles against my bruised skin as she twisted and squeezed the bottle to get the last of the liquid out. Then she pushed my ass down and slammed the lid on the box.

I lay there in the dark, breathing hard. I was pretty sure I knew what was going to happen now, but I didn't want to believe it.

The minutes ticked by, and pressure built in my gut. A matching pressure built in my chest, and then vanished suddenly. I felt a moment of complete peace, complete silence. I breathed out. I was so close. So fucking close to being nothing more than a collection of thoughts, a body to be acted upon. I inhaled slowly, sniffing. Almost started laughing. I tried to wipe my nose on my hand, but gave up. A painful cramp made me curl tighter, but I breathed through it.

For her. You're suffering for her.

Because it pleases her.

I held on as long as I could. I didn't beg. I didn't struggle. The cramps came and went. And eventually I lost control.

The lid came off the box, and Kel's hand tangled in my hair. She pulled me onto my knees and then forced my chin down, made me watch as the bottom of the box filled with liquid. She still didn't speak. It was mostly just water, since she'd let me clean myself out earlier, but I still retched as it pooled around my legs and feet.

Something snapped in my brain, and then there was a sensation like I was sinking, like I was literally drowning in the shame. The room kept shifting, and for a few seconds I had no fucking idea where I was. Briefly, I was in Bill Henson's hallway, and he was leaning against the wall, pinching his bleeding nose. Each sob that burst from me brought a sharp pain to my chest.

I was in Hal's apartment—paint peeling from the walls, dishes piled in the sink. He was armed with a mop and I had an antique dinner bell, and we were facing off against a cockroach that was sitting smugly on our kitchen wall.

Someone was repeating my name, sounding scared.

No. I tried to hold on to the vision, so I could have just a few minutes with Hal, but it faded. Hands clutched me, and I shook them off, but they didn't stop. They were trying to rip me away from Hal.

I remembered making myself throw up, over and over. A mass of white pills. The inside of the ambulance, full of colorful bags and kits.

And I remembered wanting him, so badly, in that hospital room—just wanting him *there.*

I snapped back to the room. I sucked in a breath, then screamed, slamming against the walls of the box.

"Gould. *Gould!*"

My throat suddenly opened up, and the words rushed out: "I can't see him ever again. Please. Please let me see him. Please just let me see him one more time. *Please—*" I broke off, crying too hard to finish.

Kel placed an arm around my shoulders, whispering, "Okay. Babe. Shhh. Okay. It's over."

I took a deep breath, then collapsed, sobbing against her shirt.

That was the problem. How did I make her see that was the fucking problem?

It's over. I can't have him back. Not ever. I'll never hear his voice again, and I'll never be who I was when he was alive.

When he was here, I was someone people could love. He made me *better.*

If I let him go, I don't know who I'll be.

I squeezed my eyes shut.

I didn't protect him. I let him go. I'm holding on to him now, like that can make up for letting him go when it actually mattered.

"Could we try, Gould? I mean, I can be better. Seriously, I can be better."

I gripped Kel harder. I understood now that humiliation was almost a comfort to me. It felt new every time, and yet it was familiar as a sort of backdrop to my life. Like chronic pain people learned to absorb as part of their existence. Like living near railroad tracks for so long that you stopped hearing the trains, or carrying a virus without ever showing symptoms. I felt like I'd been born with shame humming through me. Certain words or situations brought it to the surface, and then I felt shocked by the power, the threat of something that had been there all along.

And Hal had felt that way too. You'd never have known it, because he acted like he wasn't afraid or ashamed of anything. Like he believed he'd breeze through life without troubles, that every gate would always be open to him. But he'd known what it was like to never quite get it right. Whether you flouted the rules or obeyed them to the letter, whether you feared danger or embraced it, life would find ways to knock you off-balance.

Instead of staying by his side, instead of us each shoring up the other, I'd walked away. And now . . . now I was getting exactly what I deserved.

Stop crying.

Accept it.

I took another deep breath.

It's over.

CHAPTER
THIRTEEN

I was pressed against something warm. I lifted my head, my chest tightening as I moved. My throat was raw, but I didn't remember shouting. I was in Greg and Kel's office, kneeling in front of Kel's chair. Kel was stroking my damp hair, talking quietly. The sweater was in her lap—the thick, gray cardigan she'd put on me the night we'd played with the group at Riddle. The one that smelled like her. A blanket was draped over my shoulders. The smell in the room was fucking awful.

Kel shifted slightly. "Good. Good, that's right. Come back now. It's okay. I know, Gould. I know."

I blinked, gazing around. Greg was sitting at the desk, and he looked as nervous as I'd ever seen him.

I tried to speak, but nothing came out.

"Babe?" Kel ran the back of her hand down my cheek. "Can you look at me?"

I shivered as she touched my shoulder. It had been so real, that memory of Hal and me. But the truth of where I was and what had just happened was too horrible to process. I was wet and smelled like piss and shit, and I didn't know how she could stand to touch me.

She turned to Greg. "I don't know if he—"

"No," I said hoarsely. I wasn't sure what I was saying no to.

She turned back to me. "Gould?"

I wiped my eyes. Forced my voice steady. "I want to shower. Please, Ma'am."

She still looked worried. "Can you tell me what just happened?"

"You know what just happened!" I snapped.

"It's all right," she whispered. "I promise, it's all right."

"I couldn't hold it." I felt younger. Saw my childhood room. Felt damp sheets tangled around me, felt my heart pounding post-nightmare.

"I know, babe." Kel rubbed the back of my neck. "You weren't supposed to. No reason to be embarrassed."

The whole point of the scene had been to embarrass me. But it had done something else. I felt split wide open. It was still frightening, but not terrifying. Disorienting, but some part of me felt very stable. My breathing was getting slower, my mind clearer.

I swallowed several times. "I want a shower."

"Greg," she said calmly. "Take him to shower, then get him in bed, please. I'll bring up some water."

I almost clung to her as she got up. But Greg was there right away, and he eased me to my feet, took me upstairs.

I stood under the shower and kept shivering, even though the water was hot. Emptied almost a whole bottle of bodywash onto myself, got soap in my eyes. Greg stayed in the bathroom the whole time. He helped me out and dried me off, then led me into the bedroom. Kel was nowhere in sight. He didn't press me to talk, which I appreciated. He handed me some sweatpants, boxers, and a T-shirt from the closet. I dressed and got in bed when he told me to. He brought me a cup of water from the bathroom. I tried to set it aside.

"No," he said firmly. "You're dehydrated. Drink."

I did.

He stayed with me, sitting on the edge of the bed. He didn't say anything, and didn't touch me for a while. Then he slowly put a hand on my side. I flicked my gaze to his, but didn't say anything. The bedside clock read 11:22, and the next time I looked at it, it was 2:06. The lights were off, and he was snoring beside me, but Kel wasn't there. I lay awake a long time, waiting for her to come up. But she never did.

I woke up around eleven the next morning, and she was still gone. Greg lay in bed next to me, reading. He told me she was running errands. I waited until he went to the bathroom, then headed downstairs.

The office was completely clean. She must have stayed up all night working on it. It smelled like bleach and some kind of linen-y air freshener, and there was no trace of anything we'd done.

"Gould?" Greg's voice startled me. I hadn't even heard him come downstairs.

I turned to him. "What?" I'd probably meant *Yes, sir?* But I really wasn't in the mood for that shit.

He paused when he saw me in the doorway to the office. "Come on into the kitchen. We'll fix lunch."

We took a side trip to the bathroom, where he lifted my shirt and pulled down my pants.

"Buy me dinner first," I muttered.

"You look all right. Anything hurting?"

"I'm fine."

My ass ached inside and out, and one of my arms had some light bruising where I'd been grabbed. But nothing too bad. My mind felt quiet. He dropped my shirt, pulled up my pants, and rubbed my shoulder. "You all right? Kel said the scene was rough."

"It was what I wanted."

He didn't ask any more questions.

When Kel got home, Greg and I were watching basketball in the living room. She stooped and kissed him. Hesitated, then kissed me. Cursory, impersonal.

I felt a flash of anger. *You don't get to do that. You don't get to do all that stuff to me and then refuse to look me in the eye.*

I kept watching TV. She went to the kitchen. After a while, Greg got up and followed. I stayed where I was and turned the TV up.

Eventually, I heard raised voices. So I muted the TV for a moment and listened.

"—just disappear!" Greg's voice.

Then Kel's: "I need some space. You said you could step in if I—"

"It doesn't work that way. I will help you with whatever *you* need. But right now, you need to be there for him."

Kel's voice dropped, and I couldn't hear it anymore. I turned the volume back on and watched the game.

Greg returned about ten minutes later. Kept up a muttered commentary on the basketball game. I got up without asking permission and went to the guest room. Settled there with a book. I never got called to make dinner, so I just stayed there until Greg told me to come down and eat.

After dinner, Greg got out Scrabble and set it up on the floor. Kel and I sat on opposite sides of the board. She barely looked at me. We played in silence for fifteen minutes, and then Greg tossed the bag of tiles aside. "All right. This is ridiculous. You—" He pointed at Kel. "Aftercare. You can't just withdraw after a scene like that."

"Thank you, Greg," she said icily. "I've never topped before."

I opened my mouth. "I'm really f—"

He turned and pointed at me. "And you. If I hear 'I'm fine,' out of you, there will be the direst of consequences. You two need to talk to each other. Talk to *me*. I still don't know what happened."

Kel and I didn't speak.

Greg looked at me again. "From now on, I'll treat your refusal to talk as a breach of contract. You too, Kel—you've got responsibilities here. Welcome to the temporary regime change. Somebody *start*."

I shrugged. "The scene was kind of intense. I overreacted. I'm okay now."

He turned to Kel. "Is that how you'd describe it?"

She shook her head silently.

Greg put his arm around her. Kissed her cheek. "Honey?"

She glanced up and met my gaze, her eyes dark. "I needed to know all potential triggers." Her voice was low, uneven.

"Yeah?" I shot back, suddenly furious. "Well I need you to not act like I suddenly disgust you."

She flinched. "That's not—"

"Trigger warning: I sometimes think about my dead friend, and I don't know where or when that's gonna happen. I would think *you* of all people would understand that!" I was shocked at myself. I'd never yelled at her. Ever.

"Okay." Greg picked up the board and put it aside. "We're talking. That's good."

Kel never broke eye contact with me. "If you were thinking about Hal yesterday before the scene, you should have—"

"Told you? Like I have to tell you about every goddamn feeling I have?"

Greg held up his hands. "Okay. Kel, I don't know that this is an issue of Gould withholding. Gould, this only works if we all communicate."

I stood. Anger shot through me, spreading like a spill, an accident, something that wasn't really mine or my fault.

It is *mine.*

I am *angry.*

"Okay," I said. "Great. Then explain to me why you never talk to me about Bill."

They both looked surprised.

"Bill?" Greg asked.

"Yeah. You know, Bill Henson? He's a real fucking legend, apparently. Has a sex act named after him and everything."

They exchanged glances. Greg turned back to me. "What do you mean?"

"I was in Riddle. A few weeks ago, when you put me in the kennel. I heard these people talking about Bill Henson-ing. Where you—" I stopped, closing my eyes briefly. "You put a rope around your partner's neck and choke them. Pretend you're—you're, like, trying to kill them or whatever. It's a game to people now. You let him back in. You *forgave* him. And now people are making him into some kind of..."

I watched them exchange glances again.

"You know," I said to them. "You know what I'm talking about, don't you?"

Kel blew out a breath. "We've heard the term, yes."

"For what it's worth," Greg said, "I think it's a phrase used by a very few insensitive people for shock value, not an activity people are actually engaging in."

"I don't fucking care whether people are *doing* it or not!" I shouted. "Why did you let him back in?"

He got to his feet. "Let Bill in Riddle, you mean?"

"Why?" I demanded again, taking a step back in case he tried to come near me. "It *was* reckless. It *was* criminal, even if he got acquitted. If you fucking, I don't know, poured gasoline on someone and then tossed a lit cigarette on the floor next to them, you can't be like, 'Oh, their death was an accident; all I meant to do was get rid of my cigarette.'"

"We talked about that a lot." Greg kept his distance. Kept his voice calm. "Witnesses say Hal asked Bill—"

"No. Don't give me that 'Hal asked for it' bullshit."

"No. No, no, no. It doesn't excuse Bill, or make it Hal's fault. But we did consider, in our assessment of the situation, the fact that tops do sometimes feel pressure from bottoms to engage in risky behavior. Just as bottoms sometimes feel that pressure from tops."

My stomach knotted. I knew pressure could work both ways. I also knew that Hal, when he had his mind set on doing something stupid, was very hard to talk down. But I'd seen so much victim-blaming bullshit piled on Hal over the past three years, and I couldn't believe Kel and Greg had bought into it too.

Kel spoke. "Gould, you wouldn't believe some of the things men asked me to do to them when I was younger, and trying to get some experience as a dom. I'm talking wanting to be burned, maimed, knocked unconscious. One guy begged me to break his leg with a mallet. *Begged* me."

"Did you do it?" I asked flatly.

She shook her head. "But I did do some things I wasn't ready for. Things I didn't understand, and that could have ended badly."

"What does that have to do with anything?" My voice was cold. "What does Hal asking Bill to do breath play have to do with *anything*? You can do breath play without leaving someone alone with a rope around their neck. The act wasn't the problem."

"I know. The problem was Bill's inexperience. His assumption that he'd taken the necessary precautions by leaving the rope loose, leaving Hal's arm free—"

"He told everyone he *was* experienced! He was always fucking bragging about his experience."

"Did you ever actually hear him say those things?"

I racked my brain. "No, but other people . . ." I hadn't liked Bill. I never had. There was something about him, an arrogance that made me feel like I didn't have to know him to know we wouldn't get along. But no, I'd never heard him say anything about his own domming prowess. Other people had told me Bill thought he was hot shit.

Kel turned a Scrabble tile around and around between her thumb and forefinger. "I talked to him when he first became a member of Riddle. And quite a bit after Hal. He does have a sort of overbearing personality, I know. But he never claimed to me that he was anything but a fairly new dom looking to explore." She met my gaze again. "The rumors that he'd lied about his experience, or that he'd overstepped subs' boundaries started, as far as we could tell, *after* Hal's death. I had to consider both possibilities: That the rumors were true, and people only came forward once they felt confident they'd be believed. Or that people hated Bill so much for what happened to Hal, they'd add fuel to the fire anyway they could."

I opened my mouth. That wasn't what Dave said. Dave swore those rumors had been flying since the day Bill set foot in Riddle. But I couldn't remember. "And what if it was the first one?"

"I don't know the answers, Gould. I don't know that it *is* either-or. I'm just telling you what we had to consider."

Greg looked uncomfortable. "A lot of people came to us with stories. You wouldn't have believed some of the things we heard."

"So you *listen* to those stories," I snapped. "You don't fucking victim-blame."

Kel winced, but I didn't feel sorry for her. She took a couple of deep breaths and placed her elbows on her knees. "We all know what Bill did was negligent. That it broke a basic safety rule. It's just that . . ." She put an arm up and then let it fall, shaking her head helplessly. "You know? We think what's the big deal if we answer just one text while we're driving. Or we have sex without a condom, or we leave a baby on the changing table for a few minutes, or we cross when there's a Don't Walk sign, or we smoke a pack and a half a day." She blinked rapidly for a few seconds. "*Life* is full of basic safety rules we break."

My voice shook. "So does that mean everybody deserves a fucking get-out-of-jail-free card? 'Hey, we're all stupid, so group hug?'" I felt like I was losing ground. But I could also sense a weight lifting off my shoulders. Even if my thoughts were too jumbled to pick apart, even though I had no idea whether I agreed or sympathized with what they were saying, it was still a relief to be talking about this.

"If you had a child," I went on, "and that hypothetical texting driver hit and killed your kid, would you think, 'Oh, sometimes I text while driving too. I should try to be understanding?'"

"I know. I know. Believe me, I've been through all this."

Greg folded his arms across his chest. "We fucked up too, that night."

I tensed. "What do you mean?"

Kel swiped under her eyes. "We should have had a DM at every door. I should have been walking around, checking on things. Where was I when it happened? Yakking with Greg at the bar. Afterwards . . . during the whole investigation, I was sure we were gonna be shut down, or worse. And I knew we deserved whatever we got." She swallowed. "If there's no second chance for Bill, then there's no second chance for me. For us."

I gazed at her warily. "So you let him back in because you feel guilty? Or like you're capable of doing what he did?"

She wiped under her eyes again with her thumbs. "I don't know. Maybe, in a way."

"Bill is the one who killed Hal," I said tersely. "No one else."

And I was the one who hadn't given Hal a second chance in our relationship—who'd promised him I would always be there and then failed to protect him. And Dave was the one who left Hal with Bill that night. Kel and Greg and the DM were the ones who weren't watching. And Hal was the one who'd asked for a risky scene when he wasn't sober enough or experienced enough to be trying it.

But Bill *was the one who put the rope around his neck. Only Bill.*

Greg said, "We mentored Bill because it seemed like there had been enough hate and blame. Because punishment doesn't always *teach* people."

Kel glanced at him. "Or it doesn't teach them the right lesson."

Greg nodded. "And we let him back in so we could keep an eye on him, frankly. I know we failed to be vigilant in the past, but we . . . we wanted him where someone could help. If there was a problem."

"I don't know that I'd do the same thing again," Kel said. "It sounds so naïve now, but at the time, it *did* feel like a step toward healing the community. Letting him come back."

I tried to start with one image. Over and over. But everything I created slid from my mind like a flimsy backdrop, leaving blank space underneath.

"You're nothing like him," I said fiercely to Kel. "You'd never do anything as stupid as what he did. I know you." I had to believe that.

She blinked, and a couple of tears spilled down her cheeks. "What about last night? What about this morning?"

It took me a moment to realize what she was talking about.

"Seeing you like that," she said. "I was so scared. And instead of trying to fix what I'd done, I . . ."

I stood there numbly. "You didn't do anything. Last night. That wasn't your fault."

Greg went to her and helped her up. He put his arm around her, and she leaned against him. Let out a huff that was part-sob, part-laughter.

Then slowly, she shrugged him off and faced me. "Come here."

I can't.

"Please?" She held out her arms.

I gazed at her, not quite meeting her eye.

You're hurting her. This obsession with Bill, with Hal. It doesn't just affect you.

It's your own fault you're fucked up, but she's *the one who feels guilty.*

She waited.

Either you let it go—Hal, Bill, what happened; you accept that it's over—or you'll have to let her *go. Let* them *go. Because you can't keep lying to them. You can't keep refusing to tell them the things that matter. You can't keep convincing yourself that the only person who ever* really *saw you was Hal. They do too. They see you. They're trying. But you have to let them in.*

I stepped toward her.

Nothing will bring Hal back. Not hating Bill. Not burying yourself in memories. Not asking Kel to strip you down to something less than human.

Her arms closed around me. She rubbed the back of my T-shirt. "I'm sorry I wasn't there for you. After the scene. I'm sorry I can't bring him back, and I'm sorry I let him—"

"No," I said, so sharply I could feel her tense. "That's not your fault."

You have to face what's here and now. Have to face who you are without him.

I pulled back slightly. "I'm sorry I didn't talk to you."

She wouldn't let me go. She yanked me harder against her and held me.

"You're mine?" she whispered.

I nodded slowly. Let my chin rest on her shoulder and put my arms around her. Felt how she was shaking. "Yes, Ma'am."

I glanced over her shoulder at Greg. He was watching us with an expression I'd seen before, fleetingly—the day Kel and I had been a John Green novel. The day we'd all first talked about M/s. The occasional night when Kel fucked him and then rolled over to hold me. Wistful, resigned. Grateful but uncertain, like he wasn't sure how to measure his loss against his gain. The way I'd felt when Dave had started dating D: glad Dave had someone to take care of him, to love him, but hurt in some hard-to-define way. Because that had been *my* role. And I hadn't been sure a new member of the Subs Club family could make up for my fear that Dave now needed me just a little less.

"Take care of her," Greg had said to me that day in the bedroom.

I will. And I'll love her. But never without you.

It's both of us—all of us.

This only works with all of us.

This only works if I let go.

A peace settled over me after that weekend—like someone had flipped a switch. No more trips to the drugstore parking lot. Very few thoughts of Bill. If I thought about Hal, it was just fleeting memories that made me smile, and then disappeared. It was as though that scene, frightening as it had been, had been a purge. I stopped thinking so much. I stopped struggling so hard. I just gave in, and let myself be theirs. Let Kel care for me.

Kel brought up grief counseling. I refused.

"Sometimes I just really miss him," I told her. "I didn't realize that scene would bring that out, but I promise, I don't need counseling."

She let that go, but made it clear I had to keep talking to *her*. All M/s-related discussions were tabled until I could prove to her that I was ready to be honest and open. And until she was sure she could handle it if something did trigger me that way again.

She was careful. She was strict. She was kind. We stopped being so precise about when I came over. I'd spend a few days with them, and then a few days at home. Sometimes I'd go over to their house just for a couple of hours after work. We took a couple of steps back, kink-wise. Did more familiar activities, and steered clear of all but the mildest humiliations. What surprised me was that a lot of our conversations had nothing to do directly with Hal, or my grief, or even with the terms and conditions of our relationship. Instead, she and Greg got me talking a lot more about my job. About my friends and family. It only smacked a little of Operation: Secret Therapy.

Greg wanted to hear more about my family's halfhearted Jewish holidays. In turn, he told me about his childhood trips to India with his father, who loved his home country, and his mother, who tried to love it but couldn't stand crowds. Kel was particularly interested in my two older brothers, and how it felt to have siblings who were almost complete strangers to me.

"Are your parents obsessed with you because you're the baby?" she asked.

I laughed. "No, they're obsessed with my brothers. I was a late-in-life experiment they could have done without. So they mostly just throw money at me."

That seemed to bother Kel. She was still bringing it up a few days later. "So your mom doesn't visit you?"

"A couple of times a year. She doesn't travel well. My dad will stop by sometimes on business trips."

Not long after that, Kel and Greg took me to dinner at Kel's younger sister's house, introducing me as their friend. I liked kids a lot, and spent most of the evening playing with Kel's four-year-old nephew, distracting him from punching Kel's boobs.

It was the little stuff we'd never figured out how to do. For a year, we'd been so focused on getting the most playtime out of our occasional weekends together that our knowledge of each other's real lives was still patchy. We hadn't quite learned how to be together outside of their house, outside of Riddle. No, we couldn't tell the world what we were to one another, but on a couple of occasions when we were in the park, or in a store, Kel would kiss Greg and then immediately turn and kiss me.

That, I decided, was the best, most perfect embarrassment imaginable.

April arrived, and on the night of Riddle's Spring Fling, I was happier than I'd been in a long time.

Kamen and Ryan got there early. Dave joined a while later— he wasn't technically a member anymore, but Kel and Greg let him in, and I even saw them talking and laughing together at one point. We got into some serious Cards Against Humanity with a group of former Cobaltians, and then Kamen's mom, Mrs. Pell, came over to us and started doling out rib-crushing hugs. She'd been in the scene for years, and she loved our group. "Where's Miles?" she demanded as she squashed Dave.

Dave grunted. "I think he's at home trying to drive a wooden stake into his partner's ass. I mean, heart. Sorry."

Mrs. Pell slapped his shoulder. "David."

"What? If Miles is gonna date a vampyre, I am contractually obligated to joke about it."

"He actually is supposed to be here," Kamen said. "But I think his mom can't get to his house to babysit until, like, ten."

Mrs. Pell leaned in and hugged me, then jerked back. "Ow!" She glanced down. "Hon, is that a key in your pocket or are you just happy to see me?"

"Mom!" Kamen said. "Don't make sex jokes with Gould."

I pulled my massive key ring out of my pocket. "Sorry. This is getting kind of out of control." I held it up to Dave and indicated one of the keys. "I still have Maya's car key. We gotta give that back to her."

Dave shrugged. "She said not to worry about it. She has like three spares."

"Dude," Kamen muttered. "She's gonna be twenty-one soon. Next thing you know, she'll be playing here." He didn't look thrilled about that.

"Is someone a little overprotective?" I asked.

Mrs. Pell laughed. "Honey, I snuck into my first dungeon at sixteen."

Kamen clapped his hands over his ears. "Mom. Don't."

The night wore on, and I lost myself in the pleasure of being with such good people. Miles and Drix made it eventually, and we commandeered the couch and chairs in the lounge. I saw Ricky at one point. He caught my eye and did a visible double take. His expression shuttered quickly. I made myself smile. Gave him a slight nod. After a moment, he nodded back.

"This is a good party." Dave indicated the room. "I asked Kel and GK earlier about some decoration ideas for Kinkstravaganzapalooza. They said they'd help." He glanced at me, as if for approval.

I'd told him about the scene with Kel. I hadn't given him all the details—either of the scene or of the conversation afterward—because I knew he'd freak. But I'd let him know that the scene, difficult as it'd been, had helped me. And since then, he'd been stepping up his effort to talk about Kel and Greg like they were my partners rather than his enemies.

Around midnight, there was a break in the dubstep-a-thon, and then suddenly Enya's "Only Time" came on.

Dave punched the air. "Yes! Holy shit! I requested this, and they listened."

I rolled my eyes, laughing.

"Do bitches love Enya?" Dave asked. "Or do bitches love Enya?"

"Bitches love Enya," I agreed.

Dave started singing. Miles joined in after a couple of lines, and we were all singing by the second verse. Kamen did the "dee dah day, dee dah does," and even when we reached the point where we didn't know any of the lyrics except "only time," we made some up so we could keep singing.

When the song ended, Dave leaned against my shoulder. "Why do bitches love Enya so much? Is it her ethereal Celtic beauty?"

Miles sipped his iced tea. "Is it her voice, which is angelic and seductive all at once?"

"Her philosophical lyrics?" Kamen volunteered.

I shoved Dave's shoulder. "I know why *this* bitch loves Enya."

Miles turned to me. "Why?"

I grinned. "Because a certain daddy covered in waxing bumps once boom-boxed him John Cusack–style with an Enya song."

Dave ducked his head. "Shut up!"

"*Really?*" Miles said. "When was this?"

Dave shook his head. "He was the first dom I really played with. We fell a little bit in love but not really at all."

"He boom-boxed you?" Kamen asked.

Miles looked confused. "With an Enya song? How would that even work? Boom-boxing is a declarative act, indicative of romance and triumph. Blasting an Enya song doesn't say 'I'd like you to be my boyfriend.' It says 'I'd like you to be my guru.'"

"Hey," Drix raised his plastic cup and gave a slight nod. "Nothing wrong with that."

"It was very romantic!" Dave protested. "You weren't there." He turned to me. "And you're right, he did have a lot of waxing-related skin irritation. He was the first hairless daddy I ever encountered."

Kamen looked around at our circle. "Does everyone remember their first dom?"

Dave nodded. "Boom box guy. And Gould's was Hal. I remember I saw the two of them the day after they 'experimented' with that shit. And they kept, like, schoolgirl giggling every few seconds."

I smiled. "Um, no. Our first foray into that was weird and did not make us giggle."

"Please. I walked into your place, and you two were laughing like you'd invented the fart or something. And I asked why, and Hal told me."

"Hal wasn't actually my first," I said after a while. "There was a guy in college who tied me up with his belt."

Dave whistled. "And here I thought nothing dirty ever happened at Hebrew college."

Kamen chugged his drink and crushed his cup. "Mine was Coming-Inside-You."

I snickered. "That guy's obsessed with newbies."

Dave did an impression of the silver daddy we'd nicknamed Coming-Inside-You: "Oh, oh, oh, you're so tight. You're so *tight*! I'm coming inside you. Are you ready? I'm coming inside you . . ."

"Shh." I swatted his shoulder. "What if he's here tonight?"

Miles joined in. "Oh my G-o-o-od, I'm still going . . . I'm still going . . ."

"And dude," Kamen said over them. "He always wore condoms. So it was like, 'Yeah, you're coming inside me, technically. But the cum's not *staying* inside me.'"

I turned to Miles. "Was yours Bowser?"

He shook his head. "There were a couple of guys before that. Not very memorable."

We sat for a while in silence. Even Dave didn't speak. I watched Mrs. Pell laughing with Greg at the bar. Watched Regina trying to hook up our friend Girltoy with Rachel the rope top. Spotted Ricky at the snack table playfully fighting over the last of the cheese cubes with a woman I didn't know. Drix and Ryan were off checking out a piece of furniture they hadn't seen before. I scanned the club, letting my gaze pass over the doorway to Tranquility. It was like pressing on an old bruise—a small ache, but nothing I couldn't handle.

Someone tapped my leg. Dave was holding out his hand. I took it, then offered my other hand to Kamen. He took it with a quick smile at me, then turned and gave Miles his other hand. Miles took Dave's, completing the circle.

Dave squeezed my hand. "You guys are my best friends. And we'll always be best friends forever, right?"

"What the hell, dude?" Kamen shot a look at Dave. "Of course."

Dave grinned. "I'm quoting *The Fox and the Hound*."

I groaned. "That's the most depressing movie ever."

"What about *Homeward Bound*?"

"Shut up," I ordered. Dave laughed.

"Okay, everyone!" Kel called from the bar. "We're gonna start cleaning up here in a few minutes."

Everyone booed. My friends and I started carrying our plates and drink cups to the trash cans. I jumped at a hand on my shoulder.

Greg was standing behind me. "Hey."

"Hey."

"Are you going back to your place? Or do you feel like coming over tonight?"

"I can come over tonight."

He smiled. "Okay, good. Because we have something special planned."

I wasn't sure how to respond, and before I could, he wandered off to help Kel.

I stood there, grinning stupidly.

Dave elbowed me. "Something special planned? Something . . . slavey?"

"Stuff it."

"You know I'm gonna make you tell me all about it."

"You know you'll never get a word out of me."

He stuck his fingers in my armpit. I yelped and jerked away.

He faked like he was going to try it again. "I have ways of making you talk."

"We'll see." I kept an eye on him as I tossed my plate in the trash. "We'll see."

When Greg, Kel, and I got to their house, they sent me upstairs and told me to wait. The bedroom was dark except for the small lamp on their dresser. I undressed and knelt in a corner of the room. After about fifteen minutes, Greg came in.

I waited, my heart pounding as his approaching footsteps sounded behind me.

I arched into the hand he placed on my shoulder, not caring if I was supposed to stay still. I'd had such a good night, and I wanted him to know how happy I was to be here, how excited I was for whatever they had planned.

He laughed softly and dragged his fingers along the back of my neck. I turned impulsively and kissed his hand. He moved it up to stroke my cheek, cupping my jaw and running his thumb over my lips. "Stand up."

He had me lie on my back on the bed. He played with my dick for a while, gently, but with a focus that took me by surprise. This wasn't something he ever really did on his own—he mostly only used me in ways that benefitted his boner. But something was different about him tonight. I couldn't tell if he was still riding the high from the party, like I was, or if there was something else going on.

I grew more suspicious as the handjob went on. "Did Kel order you to do this? Otherwise you'd just fuck me, right?"

He gripped my chin with his other hand. Met my gaze and flashed me a grin. "Is that what you think?"

I smiled back. "I don't know, sir."

"As a matter of fact, it was my idea. And I can make this feel very good—" he tightened his grip "—or very painful. Which do you prefer?"

I couldn't answer. His face was suddenly very close to mine.

He pulled me up by the hair and kissed me. God, he and Kel kissed so differently, but I loved both styles—Kel's deep and certain, and Greg's harder and almost overeager, his stubble scraping my lips and chin.

He pushed me down onto the bed. Pinned my wrists above my head. "You're mine tonight. My boy. My slave. Understand?"

My balls throbbed. "Yes, sir." *Fucking his. Yes.* I'd do whatever he told me.

"Roll over," he ordered.

I did. Hesitated, then spread my legs without being asked.

His warm hands slid down my back. I concentrated on the rough patches at the base of his fingers—not quite calluses, but not as smooth as the rest of his palm. He gave the area between my shoulder blades a series of light, damp kisses, pausing with his lips against my skin to hum. I shivered, burying my face in the pillow. I could feel the wet spot my dick was making on the comforter.

He didn't take things any further, just held on to my shoulders and breathed roughly against me, the air cool against the moisture patches where he'd kissed me. Eventually he licked a path between my shoulders, up to the base of my neck. I rounded my shoulders and rubbed my dick on the bed. He hovered there for a moment before his teeth closed on my earlobe.

"Mmmhh." I lifted my head slightly. Caught the shadows of the room, the golden glow of the lamp, before my eyes fell shut and I started sinking. He worked the tip of his tongue against the edge of my earlobe while increasing the pressure with his teeth. Nipped hard suddenly, and I bucked, startled out of subspace.

"Focus." I could hear the amusement in his voice.

I lay there on my stomach, my fingers curled in the sheet, waiting.

He flipped me onto my back again. We kissed hungrily, my hands up under his shirt, my fingers combing through the hair on his chest. I circled his hardening nipples with my thumbs, and his nails dug into the soft space under my ribs.

"Fuck me," I whispered. I knew I didn't give the orders here, but it was worth a try.

He grinned. Placed a knee between my legs and rubbed it against my balls until I was panting. Then he stopped. "Not yet. I've got something else in mind."

"Like what?"

He leaned down and kissed my cheek. "Kel and I want to ice brand you. I've offered to do it on behalf of us both."

I knew a little about ice branding from Miles. A temporary mark made with salt and ice—Miles claimed it didn't hurt much, but Miles liked to be cut with knives, so it was all relative.

I didn't answer.

He sat back slightly. "What do you think? Kel and I have done it to each other before. It lasted a few days on her, and a few weeks on me. I'll do it somewhere discreet, so you don't have to worry about anyone seeing."

I nodded slowly.

"Gould? Can you use words?"

I laughed. "Yes. You can . . . anywhere, even if it's not discreet. Except, like, not my face."

He gazed at me a moment, those large eyes serious. Beautiful. He reached out and placed his fingertips just under my collarbone on the right side. "What about here?"

I sighed happily. "Yes, sir."

He brushed his hand up the side of my neck, to the back of my head. I closed my eyes. He leaned in and kissed me one more time. I kept my eyes closed, felt the warm wetness of his mouth, the softness of his lips, his fingertips pressing into my scalp. "Wait here."

He left the room. Came back a few minutes later and sat on the edge of the bed again. Wiped down a spot on my chest with a wet cloth. Then he opened the pour side of the saltshaker. "How about a *K* and a *G*?"

"Yes, sir." I shifted, excited.

He poured the salt carefully, making a *G* about two inches high, and then a lopsided *K* beside it. He shaped the letters with his fingers, then squinted down at them. "Okay. I don't have the best handwriting, especially in salt. But it'll do." He picked up the ice tray. Cracked a couple of cubes loose. "This is gonna hurt a little. But not, like, hot-iron branding, I promise. Okay?"

I smiled. "Okay."

He plucked a cube from the tray and brought it toward me.

I squirmed nervously. I'd wanted to take this quietly, without moving, but I felt restless, in the wrong headspace.

"Hey?" I whispered. The ice dripped on me, and I flinched.

"Hmm?"

I reached out and placed my hand on his knee. Gripped.

He rubbed my shoulder. "Just relax," he said softly. "Stay still for me."

Those words: *for me*. I loved them just as much when he said them as when Kel said them.

He placed the cube carefully on top of the *G*. Held it there. I didn't feel much at first except the cold. Then a mild sting, which increased until my skin started to prickle and throb. Water ran down the side of my chest as the ice melted. I swallowed and gripped his knee harder. After several moments, he removed the ice. The mark was grayish and puffy—not what I'd been expecting. "It'll turn red a little later," he assured me. He gave me a few minutes to recover, stroking my thigh until my dick was hard again. Then he put a second cube on the K.

When he was done, he wiped the salt off the burn. I looked down at the swollen skin. I couldn't make out the letters at all. "Uhhh . . . the Monet of ice-branding, right here."

He laughed and punched my shoulder. "You just wait and see."

"Beautiful," Kel said from the doorway.

I started. "Jesus! I didn't hear you come up."

She stepped inside. "I may be your all-knowing dom, but I'm not your lord and savior."

"Hey, He's not *my* lord and savior," I grumbled.

She sat on the other side of the bed, watching us. Reached out and touched the *K* on my chest. "That'll look nice later."

"Good. Because right now it looks like a moldy piece of eggplant." She laughed.

Greg spit in his hand and made a fist around my dick. Stroked it slowly. That shut me up. The pleasure merged with the faint ache from the brand, and soon I was breathing fast, fighting to keep my hips still.

He knelt on the floor beside the bed and kept working me, a steady rhythm that didn't change, even when I needed him to go faster.

Kel let out a long sigh.

I lifted my head so I could see her. She was running her hand between her legs, stroking herself over her pants. Then she tugged down her zipper. Popped the button and shoved her pants to mid-thigh, revealing her green cotton underwear. She rubbed two fingers over her crotch, letting out a breath. I watched the swell of her breasts on her next inhale. I imagined I was the one making her come. That she was queening me, and I could barely breathe, could only lick and suck her like the toy I was. Her property, her servant, her slave.

She slipped her fingers into the side of her underwear and circled her clit.

"You're so hot," she whispered, voice breaking on a gasp. "So fucking hot, Gould. I love watching you come. If you come, it'll make me come. Can you do that for me?"

I wanted to. More than anything.

I felt dizzy. Her fingers moved more rapidly, and her gasps were punctuated by soft whimpers. She cried out, and my balls drew up.

"Come for me," she ordered.

Greg pumped me harder, but I couldn't come. Disobeying her felt awful and frustrating, and the more agitated I got, the less possible it was to push myself over the edge.

She stood and walked around to my side of the bed, kicking off her pants as she did. Pushed Greg aside and pulled me up, then eased me onto the floor. I sat between her spread legs, trying to catch my breath. She stroked my chest and kissed the side of my neck. I knew what I wanted, but as usual, I couldn't get the words out. Finally I slid down, walking my feet forward until I was on my back, my head between her legs.

"Please, Ma'am," I begged. "Please."

She bent her legs, lifting up so she could slide her panties off. Then she got on her knees and shuffled forward. Lowered herself onto my face. She sat lightly at first, letting me explore, letting me worship her. She was so fucking wet, and as desperate as I was to please her, I didn't rush. Used my tongue gently, until she started rocking back and forth, grabbing my hips and squeezing. I lapped faster, slipping my tongue inside her briefly, then pulling out to lick the base of her clit.

"Yes!" She slapped my thigh. "Yes! Right there."

I licked in a zigzag.

"Oh shit, Gould, fuck. Yes. Come on."

She seemed especially sensitive on the left side, so I pushed my tongue against that spot, over and over, until she was breathless. Then I moved back again to tongue-fuck her. She sat hard on my face, forcing my tongue deep. For a few seconds, I couldn't breathe, couldn't think, could only work my tongue inside her. Each time I tried to inhale, I got her smell: her skin, her sharp sweetness. Then she rose, giving me a chance to grab a breath. We did that until she eased off and rocked back so that my tongue was on her clit again. I was amazed by how well she could control me just by shifting her weight.

I swallowed, feeling her shudder as she rutted against my chin. Greg's hand was back on my dick, and he was jerking me faster now. I tried to keep my focus on her.

She pumped her hips, her cries growing louder, then squeezed my thigh, letting out a long, ragged moan. "Fuck yeah," she whispered. "Fuck. *Yeah.*"

A second later, Greg swiped his thumb over the head of my cock, and I came hard. I kept licking, cleaning her up, but she stopped me with a light slap to my hip. She wrapped a hand around my wrist and used her thumb to stroke the crook of my thumb and forefinger. Then she swung off me and stretched out so we were lying side by side. I blinked, shielding my eyes from the glow of the lamp.

She laughed. "Are you seeing, like, colorful blobs in the shape of my pussy flashing behind your eyelids?"

I grinned, wiping my mouth on my arm. "Yeah, kinda."

Greg was sitting on my other side, by my legs. "There's cum all over our carpet."

"You could clean it up," Kel suggested.

"Nah. I wanna hear it when you tell him."

"Tell me what?" I asked.

Kel turned her head toward me. "Sooo . . . This might now be kind of . . . anticlimactic, for lack of a better word."

I snorted. "Okay."

"But basically, we want to try it," she said.

"Try what?"

She sat up, propping her back against the bed. "If you're still interested, I'd like to become your master."

I couldn't speak for a moment.

"We've been talking about it," Greg said. "And we're both on board. If things continue to go well, maybe in a couple of months, after the kink fair—"

Kel smiled. "We could draw up a longer, more official contract. We were thinking a period of six months, to start. And we'd be master and slave."

"Plus weird guy who watches," Greg added.

She leaned over me to swat him. "Plus my second-in-command."

"If you want," Greg repeated to me.

"If I *want*?" I managed finally. "Of course I want." I started to sit up.

She placed a hand on me. "Stay there."

Settling back on the floor, I looked up at her. "Would . . . I mean, would things be different than they are now?"

She drew a circle on my stomach with her nails. "We'd do some renegotiating, based on what we've learned about each other. This contract would be more specific. You'd be welcome to spend as much or as little time here as suits you. I know you like living with Dave, so it's fine if you stay there. We'll work out online protocol for when we're apart. But we'd like to make it official. And we'd like to pick out a collar together."

I pressed my cheek against her leg. Caught her wrist, and brought her hand to my chest. Placed it over my brand.

"I love you," I said.

"I know," she whispered. "I love you too."

Greg got on his knees and raised his arms over us. "I hereby bless this union . . ."

Kel groaned. "Well, that was almost a beautiful moment." She grabbed Greg's sleeve with her other hand and pulled him against her. "Come here. It's your union too."

"You're right," he said to her. "I love you. Very, very much." He glanced at me. "And you . . ."

I clapped a hand on his thigh. "There are lots of ways to love someone."

"Exactly."

He took my hand and hers, and for a while, it was just the three of us in the quiet room.

CHAPTER
FOURTEEN

We didn't get to bed until around four. And even though I slept in, I was still tired for most of the day. I took a nap after lunch and didn't wake up until evening. I lay in their bed—*our* bed—blinking at the ceiling.

A formal contract. A collar.

Maybe not much would change. But just the idea of being able to address Kel as "Master" made me so fucking happy.

I loved them. I did. In different ways, but with absolutely everything in me.

And if I started having trouble again—with obsessing about Bill or going to the drugstore, or anything like that—maybe we could negotiate that. They could forbid me from going to the drugstore, and correct me really harshly if I did . . .

Careful. You don't use her to punish yourself for what you're feeling. You talk to her instead.

I still had some work to do. But I was truly, finally at a point where I felt I could do it. I grabbed my phone and started looking up collars online. Got so overwhelmed by the choices that I had to set the phone aside. *We'll look together. They know a lot of shop owners too. And there'll be vendors at the kink fair . . .*

I rolled out of bed and headed downstairs to the kitchen. I heard them talking in the dining room—a small room in the turret, which they almost never used. At first I didn't try to listen, but then I got curious.

"—in the future, for Riddle." Kel's voice.

"—thinking about . . . what we . . ."

" . . . she said. It's . . . or Rachel."

I moved closer to the doorway. Because nobody in the history of the world has ever had anything bad happen as a result of eavesdropping.

"Why would she tell me this now?" Kel asked.

A chair creaked, and Greg said, "Probably because she's seeking attention, just like everyone who came forward after the trial to be like 'I saw this the night of Hal's death.' 'I heard Bill say this.'"

"But Rachel's not like that."

"Maybe she is. Do we really know her that well?"

I froze. *Rachel?*

"Well, she's not typically the sort to come up in the middle of a party and be like, 'Hey, so here's some dirt on Bill Henson.'"

"So she just approached you out of nowhere?"

"No. We were talking about the demo she agreed to do for Kinkstravaganza-whatever-they're-calling-it. And she got kind of a funny look on her face and said there was something she's been wanting to tell me for a while."

"What exactly did she say he said?" Greg asked.

Kel was quiet for a few seconds. "She said she heard Hal and Bill negotiating the scene. And that Hal asked Bill specifically to tie him up and then leave him."

What the fuck?

"And leave him?" Greg repeated.

Kel continued. "She said Hal told Bill, 'I want you to tie me up and walk away. Leave me, just like everyone else fucking does.'"

I didn't feel much of anything at first. Because Hal wouldn't say that. Why the fuck would he say that?

"I still think it's bullshit," Greg said. "Why wouldn't she come forward with this before the trial?"

"I don't know," Kel replied. "Would it have made a difference? It's like Gould said—just because Hal said, 'Do this' doesn't mean Bill had to do it."

"Leave me, just like everyone else fucking does."

"Did she say whether Bill agreed? Was Hal angry? Was Bill? I don't get it."

"She said she didn't hear what Bill said."

Greg sounded frustrated. "Why say it now? Why tell *you*? I really don't see why it's this dark secret?"

"Because it's intent, maybe? Not to kill. But maybe it makes it more than just carelessness?"

"So what? Is she gonna tell someone? The cops, or—"

"It's not like Bill can be retried."

Neither of them spoke for a while.

Then she said, "Should we tell Gould?"

My heart pounded harder.

"What good would it do to tell him?" Greg asked.

"I don't know. Part of what drives him crazy is wondering, I think."

"But is it just gonna upset him? This isn't an answer. This is just more speculation."

"If we're having this conversation, I feel like he should be here."

Greg's voice rose slightly. "He doesn't have to be part of every conversation we have."

Silence. "What's going on? You said you wanted to make it official. You said you wanted this as much as I did."

A short, harsh sigh from Greg. "I'm fine. It just takes some getting used to, is all. No matter how much we like him, he's not a part of this marriage. He hasn't been through all that we've been through together. He doesn't even know a *fraction* of what we dealt with after Hal died."

"And we don't know what he went through, either. God, getting him to talk about his relationship with Hal is like—"

"It's not your job," Greg said abruptly. "It's not your job to 'get him' to talk about it. Either he has to learn to speak up, or learn to cope with keeping it in."

"I know."

"What kind of relationship is it gonna be if you have to play therapist to him?"

"Greg."

"I know how much you care about him. But sometimes you treat him more like a pet than a man."

"That's enough," Kel said sharply. "Just because he's not like you, just because he's a little fragile—"

"Okay. Okay, okay." Another sigh from Greg. "I'm sorry. I'm tired. I do want this. I do. But it's difficult."

Nothing for a few seconds. Then a soft sound. A kiss.

"I know," Kel whispered. "I know it's different."

In movies, the eavesdropper usually flees, crying, before they've heard all there is to hear. But I stayed, and actually felt much worse when they moved on to talking about something else. A few minutes later, they were laughing.

I walked back toward the kitchen, letting the hum of the fridge muffle their voices again. *"Leave me, just like everyone else fucking does."*

If Hal had said it, he could have been talking about Dave. Dave and Hal had fought that night, and Dave had left and gone outside to smoke.

But what if he was talking about me?

I'd left Hal. I'd given up on him because his problems were too big, his refusal to grow up too off-putting. I'd stayed his friend, but I'd taken away the kind of love that had made him feel like the only person in somebody else's world.

And if Hal had been talking about me, that meant I was the one who'd driven him to play with Bill.

I closed my eyes. Greg was right. So many people had come out with stories about Bill and Hal during and after the trial. It had been impossible to know what was true.

Bill has the answers.

He's the only one who has the answers.

I walked back upstairs and quickly dressed. Greg was right about this too: I wasn't part of their marriage. I didn't belong here. Not permanently. Not in any truly meaningful way. I pushed people away. I spat their kindness back in their faces, and they didn't even realize I was doing it. Because as long as I stayed quiet, they never knew how awful I was. They assumed I was shy. Or wise. Or fragile.

". . . more like a pet than a man."

What else could I have expected from Greg? I'd come in here and rearranged his marriage. Taken up Kel's time and attention for a year, and then demanded more because I wasn't stable enough to be alone.

"You just can't be alone, can you?"

And could I really expect Kel's patience to hold out?

It was time for me to grow a pair. Take a risk. Make a choice.

"You just can't be alone, can you?"

I won't ever have to be, I imagined snapping back at Hal. *I'll always be stuck with you.*

By the time I reached the duplex, I had a choppy outline of a plan. I changed clothes. Turned off my phone. Made myself sit still for a moment in the kitchen.

The walls looked empty, and there were boxes in the alcove by the bathroom—Dave had already begun packing some of his things.

I started with one image: the duplex, the day I'd moved in three years ago. Sun shining through the huge kitchen windows, falling on the massive, varnished table Dave's father had built. I'd been slowly moving in ever since Dave's old roommate had left. But that day, I'd brought my last boxes of stuff and made it official.

Dave and the others had helped me carry my things in, and then we'd ordered sandwiches from Mel's, and Dave had broken into the giant case of gluten-free beer he'd gotten just for the occasion. I'd been awful since Hal died. I'd known that. Withdrawn and unavailable. But that day, I'd felt like things really were going to be all right.

The Subs Club had started as a way to get justice for Hal. And even if the other members had lost sight of that mission, I wasn't going to. I didn't want to spend every day wondering what had happened that night at Riddle. What Hal had said to Bill. What Bill had said to him. What he'd looked like, tied to that bench. Wondering if what had happened was my fault.

I knew the gist of what people had said at the trial. Cinnamon the ponygirl had been the only witness, and she'd told Dave last year that she could hear Hal laughing while he was on the bench. Could hear Bill and Hal whispering, said they sounded like they were having fun. She'd said nothing seemed creepy about the scene at all. And then Bill had left—supposedly to get some water for Hal. He'd been gone a long time. Long enough for Cinnamon to start to feel uncomfortable. She'd looked over at the bench and seen how still Hal was. She'd gone to check.

People had seen Bill crying afterward. Having a complete breakdown beside the bench after Hal's body had been carried out of the club.

But he could have been acting.

If Bill had left Hal alone at Hal's request, Bill was even more of an asshole than I'd thought. Because that was obviously not the kind of request a healthy, stable person made, and to take advantage of Hal's insecurity . . .

You asked Kel to try to break you. You tried to talk her out of prenegotiating that scene. You asked her to use every one of your insecurities against you.

Well, we all fucking knew I was hardly a model of stability.

What if it had gone further than that? What if Hal had asked Bill to leave the room so he could kill himself?

No. The rope caught on the bench.

But what if?

I stood and gathered my keys. Was about to leave, when I heard the front doorknob jiggling furiously. Finally Dave burst in. "I *hate* that we're locking that door," he declared, storming past me into the kitchen.

Against my better judgment, I went to the kitchen doorway.

"Gould," he called, slamming through the cupboards. "I need you. Come here."

Just like that. As though there was no chance I'd tell him I was busy, that I had to go.

I walked into the kitchen, my hands in my pockets. He pulled a package of trail mix out of a cupboard. Slammed the cupboard shut, tossed the trail mix on the table, then walked up and threw his arms around me. "You are the only person in the world," he said into my neck, "who makes any sense."

Said no one ever.

Except Dave.

I put my arms around him instinctively, even though my brain still felt numb. "What's wrong?"

"D and I had a fight."

"About what?"

Dave stepped back, scrubbing his eye with the heel of his hand. "About money. And how I need a lot of it for school, and he wants to help me, but I don't want him to be my chubby, pornstached sugar daddy."

He started crying suddenly. I mean *suddenly*. He'd always been a crier.

"Hey," I said. "What's up?"

Dave tipped his head back, then snapped it down again. "He's not even pornstached anymore. He shaved his mustache!"

"What?"

"Now his upper lip area looks like a stupid, naked parrot beak, and I don't know what to do."

I had to go. I had a plan, something I needed to do, and here Dave was complaining about a *mustache* . . .

And yet instead of walking out the door, I rubbed his shoulder. "Hey. Hey, it'll grow back."

"It's not about the mustache! It's about change and how we're all changing. And I hate it, and I love it, and I'm not gonna freak out about it because I already did that to Kamen last year. But I don't want to leave you alone. I don't want to sell the duplex."

"You do know we don't own it, right?"

"Whatever. I don't want someone else to live here. D's house is filled with silence and sawdust. Where will I go if it doesn't work out between me and him?"

"You love his house. And you love him."

"I know. I just . . ." He curled and uncurled his fingers. "I'll miss you. You'll either move into some sad little one-bedroom, or you'll go be GK and Kel's slave, and I hate slavery."

I didn't answer. Didn't want to tell him it was over. Didn't want to tell him why. The less he knew, the better.

We were both silent a long while. Then Dave went off again. "*Why* did he shave his mustache? And if he had to, why couldn't he let me do it so I could practice barbering?"

You have to go now. He'll be fine. He has Miles and Kamen if he needs to vent.

But I couldn't leave him there, still sniffling like a child.

"Come here." I held out my hand.

He looked at me suspiciously. "Why? I want to be mad. Are you trying to make me less mad?"

"Just come with me." I led him to my room. Dragged him toward the bed. When he balked, I let go of his hand and flopped on the mattress. "Bed party."

Bed parties were Dave's invention from way back. They used to happen with all five of us—Dave would insist we cram onto the nearest available bed and snuggle in a pile. But a bed party could happen with only two people.

His face softened. He climbed onto the bed and stretched out beside me, facing me. I pulled the covers up over us.

I looked at him, thinking about the years we'd spent as friends. His parents had moved to Canada as soon as he went to college, and mine didn't visit a lot, so we'd started calling each other our family. Miles and Kamen were part of that family too, but there was something about Dave . . .

I don't have to go yet. I can stay and make sure he's all right.

He gazed back at me. I could feel something between us—a hint of whatever used to drive us to kick our pants off and start jerking each other off, back in the day. Which, okay, horniness, probably—but there'd been more to it. Like what Hal and I used to do, erasing the space between our skins. Dave and I had felt this desperate need to be as close as possible, to tell each other, without words, how much we loved each other. In some of my less kind moments, I'd kissed Hal deliberately in front of Dave. Like a dare: *If you love me so much, then why are you letting Hal have me?* Or a taunt: *I don't need you. If you left me, I'd be fine. I'd still have Hal.* And when Hal's and my relationship had started going to shit, I'd found myself wondering sometimes what life would have been like if I had dated Dave instead.

Dave laughed awkwardly. "I feel like we're about to make out."

I didn't say anything. For just a second, I wanted so badly to kiss him. To remember those soft noises he made, the way he sometimes laughed into my mouth. I wouldn't, for the world, have done anything to jeopardize what he had with D, but it suddenly seemed unbearably stupid that the line between safety and trouble was a matter of whether or not our lips touched.

As if he were reading my mind, he said, very softly: "All it takes is one, like, second. How crazy is that? One second where it just feels right and—" He snapped his fingers.

"Stop," I said.

He gazed at me a moment longer. "I won't do it. I'm just saying I want to and you want to. And what's the fucking— You know? What's the difference between me holding your hand and me kissing you? What's the difference between a European man-on-man mouth kiss and the kind of kiss that makes us bad people?"

I closed my eyes for a few seconds. Then opened them and leaned forward, touching my lips to his. He pressed back gently. My body stirred at the contact, but it wasn't the fierce rush of heat I got when Kel or Greg kissed me. I just felt like I couldn't get close enough to Dave. Like it was a shame he and I were two separate bodies.

He let out a breath.

"I love you," he said. "I always have. From the minute I met you, I knew you were, like, *necessary* for me."

I placed my head under his chin, holding him. I knew what he meant. Like Greg and Kel, I'd never believed in this true love, one-soul-mate-for-everyone bullshit. I'd been drawn to Hal's sense of adventure. The ruthless way he fought against rules and expectations, the way he offered comfort only when you'd earned it. But I'd been drawn to Dave's kindness. He could be judgmental, overly dramatic, and downright mean, at times. But he had this invincible belief in human goodness and trustworthiness. A belief that had been shaken hard by Hal's death.

"I'll never leave you," he whispered.

"You either," I said, tightening my arms around him. I wanted to mean it. I *did* mean it. No matter how tonight turned out, he had my soul. I thought about how sad it had made me years ago to see all those people in Riddle who didn't have a perfect dungeon friend. And later, how sad it had made me to see all the people in the world who didn't have a perfect *friend*, period. Someone you could fight with and forgive. Dave was maybe the only person in my life I didn't hold to the standard of *You shouldn't have gotten away with it*. I'd let Dave get away with fucking anything.

He swallowed. "Do you ever feel like we were meant to find each other? You know? Like we gave out something like . . . like friendship pheromones?"

"I do think some things are meant to be."

He shifted, his chin digging into the top of my head. We didn't do anything beyond the kiss. Because the labels and rules and those unbearably stupid lines that looked like the bars of cages were sometimes a comfort.

I'm sorry. I really am. I hoped he could sense that. *I love you.*

The bed party lasted about an hour, during which he fell asleep and drooled in my hair. When he was snoring, I disentangled myself and left him sleeping there in my bed. I slipped out the front door, locking it behind me.

CHAPTER

FIFTEEN

I drove to Maya's neighborhood. Unlocked her car with the spare key still on my key ring, and took Roxie Hart from the glove box. I tucked the gun deep into my pocket and climbed out, looking around like I thought a cop might jump out of the bushes and arrest me just for holding a handgun. I locked her car, got back in mine, and drove.

You're crazy, I told myself. *This time, you've really lost it.*

I took a deep breath in, then out. Drummed my fingers on the wheel when I stopped at a traffic light.

You can't do this. It's wrong. It's . . . People will think . . .

I didn't care. I was fucking tired of being good.

I got on the interstate and headed out of the city. I passed a plaza with a three-story Old Navy. Passed a sign for the county fairgrounds.

One night, toward the end of our relationship, I'd asked Hal to meet me at a county fair. Maybe I was trying to get back the magic of our night at Cedar Point. But the fair was nothing like that—it was loud and dirty, full of screaming kids and tween girls in booty shorts and toothless carnies. But I stood at the gates, waiting for him, and I watched the lights of the Ferris wheel and imagined that this night could save us. But he'd arrived in a bad mood, pissed at his parents and at his life.

"You're doing okay," I'd told him.

"No, dude. Everything fucking sucks for me. You know? I'm dirt poor, I work in a drugstore, my parents have never done one nice thing for me, so now I'm some poor white-trash stereotype. And it's not gonna ever change."

We'd walked down the midway. Kept getting offers to pop balloons with darts. "Think about what you do have. You've got me, and the other guys. You've got a place to live."

"My place is shit. I hate being there."

"You've got the synagogue. You've got the BDSM community."

He'd snorted. "For fuck's sake. 'The BDSM community.'" He shook his head. "And the synagogue? Really? I'm only Jewish because my mom converted. Because she just sat there her whole fucking life letting shit happen to her and praying to Jesus for whatever she wanted—*stupid* shit. I'm talking iPhones and more drugs and a fucking waffle iron. And then she decided JC wasn't doing it for her, so she fucking— I think she'd milked the Christian community for handouts and wanted to try the Jews." He clenched his hands into fists and put them up to his temples. "I can't do this. You don't understand. None of you understand because you're all so fucking . . . doing-just-fine."

"I do understand," I'd said quietly. "But at some point you need to move forward. Don't you think?"

He'd sneered. "Oh, is *that* what I need to do? Thank you so much. If only I'd fucking known that all I had to do was move fo—"

"Hal, shut up. I wanted us to have a nice night."

"It's so easy, isn't it? To leave your problems behind? To just forget, and have a 'nice night'?"

I gripped the wheel, not wanting to remember anymore. I'd been such a prick. He hadn't always been good to me. But maybe I'd been worse to him without even knowing it.

You can't make a satisfying story of grief, because it's constant motion—no beginning or end. You're always answering imaginary calls for rides—pulling into the empty parking lot behind Carrden's and telling yourself you arrived just a few seconds too late, he's already walking home. So you take the route he'd use if he were walking. You drive too slowly, the beams of your headlights spilling along the gravel shoulder, and you're waiting, waiting for a glimpse of his beat-up sneakers, his shirt stuck to his back with sweat. You picture him turning around—squinting through the light, giving you an exasperated smile. Climbing into your car and saying, *You're late.*

Grief is that. You're always missing him by a few seconds, and you live out in your mind an endless string of moments where you find him. You wait by the gate of the empty fairgrounds at night and you build yourself a carnival of lights and ghost laughter and sweaty, toothless ride operators, and foam tie-dye lizards on wire leashes. You create a ticket-taker and increase your own impatience. And then he's walking toward you, and he doesn't have enough money for a ticket, and can you spot him?

So you spot him.

You're always spotting him. You look for him in other people's faces. In the way they walk. In every joke you know he would have laughed at, every movie you know he would have liked. In some ways, he's less of a ghost than you are—because look how much of yourself you've given up to keep him alive.

Bill lived in one of those drab suburban neighborhoods, where the houses look like toys and kids rollerblade in the streets. I remembered his house from the last time I'd been here. When I'd shown up to beat the shit out of him.

By the time I parked, I was nervous—not about what I was planning to do—Do *you have a plan?*—but about the possibility that if I got arrested, Maya would get in trouble for being the owner of the gun. So I sat there in my car and googled the gun laws in our state to make sure she couldn't be held liable for what I did. I'd lucked out on that count, since there *were* plenty of states where the gun owner was responsible for anything that happened with the gun. Next, I YouTubed a demo on this particular gun, making sure I knew how to use it.

It reminded me of my suicide attempt, where I'd started by googling whether or not a whole bottle of Ambien would kill me. And once I'd taken the pills and called the ambulance, I'd tried to look up what my odds of survival were if they pumped my stomach. Then I'd stood over the sink and made myself throw up, hoping I could help the hospital staff out.

I really was pathetic.

I got out of the car and walked up the driveway, awkwardly holding on to the gun in my pocket.

I'm not really going to do anything.

I'm fucking crazy. This isn't me.

I told that voice to shut the fuck up.

I knocked on Bill's door. Peered through the glass. The house was dark. I didn't hear anything. I thought for a second that he wasn't home, and I was incredibly relieved.

Pathetic.

I heard footsteps. I stood back a little so he wouldn't see me through the glass.

He opened the door.

He looked different than I remembered. Taller, thinner. He'd grown a goatee. Little veins stood out in his temples, and his hairline was receding. But he had those wide, dark eyes I remembered. Purplish circles underneath. He was still in his work clothes.

He seemed surprised, then wary, then angry. "You're not allowed to be here." His voice was low, clogged-up, like he had a permanent cold.

"I need to talk to you," I said.

And what would I do if he said, *No, I'm calling the cops*? Show him my piece?

What the fuck was I thinking?

And, Jesus, if the police came to escort me off the property, they'd search me and find I was packing heat, and then they'd think I'd come here to fucking murder Bill.

He stared at me hard for a moment. "Why would I talk to you?"

I tried a little honesty. "Because I can't do this anymore. I need some answers, and they can only come from you."

Don't make me pull out the gun. Don't make me pull out the gun.

He sighed and seemed to collapse a little. And then he pulled the door open. "Come in."

We went to the living room. I hadn't really seen anything last time except the front hall. And I hadn't looked too closely at that, since I'd been busy punching him in the face.

The living room was very . . . granny-ish. White and pale-blue and lacy with, like, decorative plates and a piano and shit. On the piano was a picture in a gold frame. Bill and Ricky, posing in front of Bill's house. I looked away, my anger rising.

He sat in a cream-colored armchair, and I sat on the floral love seat, a glass coffee table between us.

"What questions can I answer for you?" he asked sarcastically.

I felt the gun, heavy in my pocket. It occurred to me that the reason he'd let me in was that he didn't see me as a threat. Even though I'd fucking punched him. He'd probably taken out the restraining order because it was a subtle form of revenge where he came off looking like a victim. Not because he really thought I was dangerous.

"Do you know?" I asked.

He stared at me. "What's that?"

"Do you know how wrong it was? What you did?" I sounded perfectly calm. Kind of badass.

He seemed to collapse a little more. There was no sarcasm in his voice when he said, "Of course."

"What you took from me . . . was so much more than just him."

He'd taken some younger, happier version of me. A piece of my friends' shared history. He'd turned all my memories of Hal into eulogies, and maybe that wasn't his fault, maybe it was mine, but it was so fucking hard not to blame him.

His brow furrowed. "I don't think this is a good idea." He started to stand.

"Stay here," I said calmly, "and answer my questions."

He settled back in the chair. The veins in his temples bulged.

"Did Hal approach you to do the scene?" I asked.

He nodded.

"Was breath play your idea?"

Bill shook his head. "His."

"What were you thinking when you left him in that room?"

"I wasn't," he said simply. "I was thinking he'd need some water when we were done. I'd left one of his hands free. He said he . . . said he wanted to keep the ropes on. I didn't think . . ."

"You could have called for a DM to get water."

"I didn't think," he repeated.

My own thoughts grew harder to track. *Focus.* "Did he . . ." I started. I couldn't form the question I wanted to ask.

"Look," Bill said quietly. "There's nothing you can ask me that dozens of people haven't asked already. I can't give you what you're looking for. There's nothing I can say that will bring him back, or make you feel better, or let you know how sorry I am. I don't remember exactly what he and I said to each other. I remember he was laughing . . ." He shook his head, smiling a little. "I'd never seen anyone do that. Just give themselves over so completely. I don't—"

"Why are you smiling? You fucking asshole, why are you smiling?"

"What do you want me to do?" He held his hands up slowly. "I stay away from your club now. I don't bother you. What else can I do?"

Die, I thought, and was shocked by how much I meant it in that instant. *You could die. And then it would be fair.*

But that wasn't right. It wouldn't help. And the longer I sat here, the more I could see what a mistake this was.

I started with a moment, an image. With a twelve-year-old boy walking home from school on a street lined with trees. Walking quickly, glancing between the trunks every now and then to see past and future versions of himself. A five-year-old sitting at the table, a plate smeared with food, and then a small white dessert plate that remained empty in front of an eight-year-old while two adults ate slices of yellow cake—because you could lose privileges when you acted out. A thirteen-year-old, terrified of his own bar mitzvah, being herded into the living room to greet the guests. An eighteen-year-old, all acne and flab and wild curls, stammering "Hey" to a hot classmate in Accounting 101. A twenty-three-year-old, in love for the first time with a guy in smiley-face boxers. A twenty-eight-year-old, kneeling in front of a woman and a man who made him feel necessary, valued.

And all those moments led here, to this moment that wasn't fair or brave or what it should be. That was reckless, a mistake.

I pulled the gun out of my pocket. It snagged on the fabric, and I fumbled to get my sweaty thumb on the safety.

I waited for Bill to notice I had the weapon, feeling a familiar anxiety that he *wouldn't*—that nothing I did, even the boldest, craziest shit, was worth noticing. Except Greg and Kel had taught me otherwise. They saw me. They listened.

I was worth noticing.

I mattered.

And right now, I was throwing that all away.

Bill stared at the gun for a long moment. Then he glanced up at me, and he sort of half smiled like he was on one of those eighties sitcoms where the actors glance up from whatever they're doing during the opening credits and smile at the camera. It was like he thought this was a prank. "What are you doing?"

"What the fuck does it look like?" I snapped. My hand wasn't shaking, but it was sweaty, and I was afraid I was going to drop the gun.

He glanced at the gun again like he was ... disappointed?

Be scared, you asshole. Be fucking scared.

"Did he tell you to leave him?" I asked.

He was still eyeing the gun. "What?"

"Did he tell you to *leave him*?" I demanded. "Did he tell you to tie him up and then walk away? Did he say that was what everyone else did: leave him?" The words rang in the silence that followed them. I raised the gun. "Answer me."

He met my gaze, and for a second he looked so unafraid, so convinced of his own answer that I actually believed his next words. "No. He never said anything like that."

I felt relieved. Even if he was fucking lying, I felt relieved.

"For what it's worth," he said eventually, sounding hoarse and old. "If I had gone to prison, I'd have killed myself. I'd have found a way." He paused. "Ricky has helped. But I still feel very ..." He shook his head.

I wanted to tell him he should have done it anyway, prison or no. But I couldn't speak. And I couldn't make myself believe what I wanted to say. I was so out of place in this scenario. I was never meant to hold a gun. Was never meant to get revenge, seek justice. I was meant to stay quiet. And that was what made me furious.

I held out my arm and fired at the picture of Bill and Ricky on the piano.

I missed, of course.

The sound was deafeningly loud, and when I looked, there was a hole in the wall behind the piano.

Slowly, my heart pounding, I set the gun down on the coffee table and raised my hands in surrender.

Bill sat there for a moment, staring at the hole in the wall and taking shuddering breaths, and I couldn't tell if he was terrified or angry.

Then he turned to me. Gulped a few times. Spoke quietly but firmly. "I won't tell anyone you came here. I won't tell the cops. Okay? But you gotta leave right now. Understand? You gotta let me live my life." He paused. "I promise, it's plenty miserable. I promise, I don't like myself very much. But there are good moments too. I can't help that."

I didn't answer, just stared straight ahead with my hands up.

You're crazy. Everyone's going to know now, how sick you are. Everyone's going to see.

He leaned out of the chair, extending his arm toward the coffee table but keeping his gaze on me. "I'm gonna take this and unload it. Okay?"

I nodded, numbly, wishing he'd pick it up and shoot me. I sort of thought he might.

But he picked it up and unloaded it, pocketing the bullets.

"That belongs to someone." My throat was dry, my voice barely audible. "She needs it back."

He sat as slowly as he'd risen. "I'm gonna call someone to come get you. Someone you know. And she'll make sure the gun gets where it needs to be. All right?"

I blinked, trying to nod. I couldn't imagine who he'd call. His voice was different. Softer, kinder. And I hoped, for just a moment, that this was the voice he'd used with Hal. *I'm gonna get you some water. And then I'll be right back. All right?*

"Just relax," he said, taking out his phone. "We're gonna get things straightened out."

Mrs. Pell took the gun from Bill and made me give her my car keys. She and Bill talked quietly in another room. Then she brought me outside and shepherded me into the passenger seat of my car. Started to drive to the duplex, but I asked her to go to Kel and Greg's instead. She reluctantly agreed.

She didn't say anything at first. I thought maybe I'd horrified her so much she couldn't even speak to me.

"I talked to Bill quite a bit during his mentorship," she told me finally. "I won't tell you you're wrong to hate him. But he's not a monster, Gould."

"I know," I said dully, staring out the window.

We arrived at Kel and Greg's. I got out, flushing as Mrs. Pell got out too and walked with me up to the door. She knocked.

Kel answered, looking worried. "Where were you?" she asked me. "Greg and I couldn't—" She caught Mrs. Pell's eye and went silent.

They made me sit on the couch. Kel stood in front of me. Leaned over, running her hands down my arms. "You okay?"

I nodded. *Never better.*

They went to the kitchen. I could hear their voices, but couldn't tell what they were saying. That was okay. I didn't want to know.

Mrs. Pell came out a few minutes later. "Hon? Do you want me to stay?"

I shook my head.

"I can drive you home if you want. Dave could look after you?"

I glanced at the wall, fucking exhausted. Shook my head again.

She told me to get in touch if I needed anything, and then she called a cab and left.

I heard Greg come downstairs. More voices in the kitchen. I knew they were making some decision that I didn't get to be a part of, and I put my head in my hands and sighed.

Footsteps. I looked up again at the sound of a glass set on the coffee table. Kel had put water in front of me. Greg wasn't there. I supposed he didn't want to handle this—too much emotion for a straight dude, and I wasn't a part of this marriage, after all. I could feel Kel watching me as I picked up the glass and drained it.

"Gould?"

Just her voice—her voice was all it took to break me. I wasn't stable and I wasn't obedient and I wasn't who they'd thought I was.

I stood and started for the foyer.

"Gould." Her voice was firmer now. She was behind me, and I turned and waited. There was nothing I could think to do—kneeling and bowing my head wouldn't work here. I couldn't ask her to tell me what to do with all I was feeling. So I waited, and my right arm trembled a little, as though with the memory of the shot I'd fired into Bill's granny-blue wall.

"Please stay." Her arms were folded—defensively, like she was afraid.

I walked to her. I could hear my own breathing, rough, but not out of control. My lips tingled like I'd been stung there, like there was poison swelling them. I wanted to kiss her and didn't know if I was allowed.

She looked wary as I approached, and that made me feel worse than anything.

I hesitated, and then with a burst of breath, I put my arms around her.

She immediately put her arms around me too, and held me too tight, until it hurt.

"I'm sorry," I whispered against her shoulder. "I'm sorry."

She backed into the kitchen, one arm still around my shoulders. She sat me at the table, and then she took the seat beside me. Clapped a hand so hard on my thigh I jumped. "Tell me what happened."

"I just hate him. And I can't stop."

"I know. But—"

"I heard . . . what you said. About Rachel. And me being . . ." The whole story sounded so stupid now.

"Oh, Gould." Her voice was so quiet, and that did me in.

"I think about Hal. All the— All the time. When I'm in the box, I'm thinking of him." I tried to hold the sobs back. "I'm w-with him."

Kel stood. "Babe." I leaned against her when she stepped beside me and put her hand on my shoulder. Closed my eyes and let the tears run down my cheeks. I imagined Hal laughing at me, but not in a cruel way. Just . . . exasperated.

Greg came in then. Stopped in the doorway.

I swallowed. "S-sometimes I just want him back s-sss-s-s-so much."

Kel stroked my hair, not saying anything.

"I l-love you," I murmured shakily. "Both of you. I wish I wasn't like this."

I'd never had breakdowns like this around anyone but Dave. Part of me wanted him here with me instead. Didn't want Kel and Greg to see this. But they had to know. I had to tell them somehow.

There was a knock on the door. Kel went to answer it, and I heard raised voices. A few seconds later, Dave burst into the kitchen. "What the hell, Gould?"

I swiped at my eyes. "What are you doing here?"

"Kamen's mom called." Dave walked toward me, face pale, panic in his eyes. Kel was standing in the doorway, like she wasn't sure whether to intervene.

"What did you do, you idiot? What did you *do*?"

I couldn't answer, because he'd lifted me out of my chair and was half hugging, half strangling me.

"Miles will be here in a minute," he muttered. "And he is going to have something to *say* to you. You are gonna get the very prissy, very righteous wrath of Miles Loucks. And I am not going to do *anything* to save you from it."

Kel stepped forward. "Dave. Let him . . ." I saw her hesitate and fall silent.

"I fucked up," I murmured into his bony shoulder.

He punched me lightly in the back. "No shit. Asshole."

Kel cleared her throat. "Bill's not pressing charges."

Dave turned and glared at her. "Yeah, I guess Bill owes you one. For being his crying shoulder all these years and all."

I shoved him away, hard. "Be nice to her!"

He stared at me, yanking his shirt straight.

"You didn't have to come here. You should ha—" I started. But at that moment someone pounded on the front door, and we all went to see who it was.

"Dude." Kamen stepped inside and homed in on me. "My mom says you went to Bill's? With a fucking *gun*?"

"Yeah, I went to Bill's with a gun. Does Miles know, or am I going to have to repeat this when he gets here?"

"I'm right here," said Miles from the porch. "And I know."

They all crowded in the foyer, looking at me.

"Great." I turned back toward the kitchen.

"I'll get some more chairs," Kel said.

But before she or I could leave the room, Kamen's voice stopped me. "*No*, Gould. You promised. You fucking promised!"

"Promised what?" Miles demanded.

I turned to stare at Kamen in horror. *Don't you dare . . .*

"What's going on?" Dave looked from me to Kamen. "Kamen, did you know he was gonna do this?"

Kamen didn't break eye contact with me. "Tell them. Tell them about after Hal died. And how you promised you wouldn't hurt yourself again."

What the fuck? I didn't *hurt myself again.*

"That's my business," I said furiously.

"For fuck's sake, what is going *on*?" Dave asked.

Kamen turned to him. "I picked Gould up from the hospital after Bill's trial. Because he—"

"Because I took a whole lot of pills," I finished.

Typically, it took considerable effort to render Dave speechless. Gold stars to me.

My voice was shaking with anger. "I took some pills. I called my own ambulance. It was cowardly, like every fucking thing I do."

They were all talking at once, and I turned, meaning to get the fuck *out* of here. But Kel was standing in my way.

"Shut *up*!" she yelled to everyone else.

They fell silent.

She looked as furious as I felt. "You never told me."

I was so not in the mood for this. "Yeah, well I never told anyone but Kamen. So join the club."

Her cheeks were red, and I realized I'd never seen her truly angry before. "That is something I *needed* to know." Her voice was so fierce it was almost unrecognizable.

"Oh for fuck's sake, we're not talking about scenes."

"We are talking about my responsibility toward you!" she shouted. My friends remained silent. She lowered her voice. "That scene we did was risky enough. And now you're telling me you had me degrade you, make you feel worthless, had me put you in an altered mental state—when you'd made a *suicide* attempt?"

I couldn't answer.

"I trusted you." She bit off each word. "We agreed to trust each *other*. What if I'd sent you somewhere you couldn't come back from? What if I'd fucking brought on a sub drop that led to you hurting yourself, killing yourself?" Her voice rose again. "You want to turn me into Bill? Is that it? Make me live with that fucking guilt and grief every day of my life?"

"Well, you forgave him no problem!" I snapped. "How long would it take you to forgive yourself? A few days? Couple months, tops?"

"That is not the issue!"

"Don't yell at him," Dave shouted at Kel. "He's obviously not *well* right now."

She whirled to him. "Stop treating him like he can't take a little fucking responsibility!"

Dave stepped up to her. "Yeah, well, you weren't even there with him after that scene, so if anything had happened, it would have been y—"

"Stop it!" I shut my eyes, then opened them again to face the room. "All of you! I make my own choices. All right? My own fucking choices, however stupid they are." It felt good to shout, so I kept at it. I started with Dave. "You were supposed to be on my side. You're supposed to hate Bill too. That's why we started the Subs Club. But you don't give a shit about that anymore."

I turned to Kel. "There are some things I don't want to talk about. Can I have *anything* that's just mine?"

I faced Kamen. "And you—*you* promised. You swore you wouldn't tell."

"Uh-uh," he said. "I'm not backing down, man. That promise was because you promised you were okay."

Miles held up a hand. "Enough. Let's just get Gould home, and—"

"I am not your five-year-old!" I roared at him. "I'm tired of being coddled. Of being treated like I'll fucking break. You hear me? All of you? I don't want to tell you all every detail of my past, because it doesn't change what I want, or who I am *now*. I know I'm fucked up. I know. But just give me a little fucking *space*."

They all stared at me.

"I am leaving," I announced, with exaggerated politeness. I may have even bowed a little. "You all are welcome to stay and discuss me. But I frankly don't find the topic that interesting."

I strode around them and out the door.

I realized as soon as I was outside that I was gonna have to walk home, or call a cab. So I started walking. But I didn't even make it half a block before a line of cars pulled up beside me.

CHAPTER

SIXTEEN

"I'm fine," I repeated for the millionth time. Dave and I were sitting on the couch the next day. "I do *not* need to go to therapy."

"Oh please. You expect us to believe you went to Bill's house with a gun, had a nice chat with him, got some closure, screamed at all of us, and now you're fine? Go to therapy."

"I don't want—"

"Go to therapy."

"It's my choice!"

"You are really stuck on this choice thing, aren't you? Yeah, dude, I know it's your choice. And you know what else I know? You don't particularly like being given choices. So I'm telling you: talk to somebody."

I shook my head. "Kel and Greg aren't gonna want me if I'm . . ."

"What? Human? Grieving? Mentally stable?"

"You know what."

"Yeah, that sounds like the kind of people they are. They love the fuck out of you and care about your well-being, so if you do something for your personal health, they'll be like, 'Oops, nope, don't like you anymore.' Enough bullshit."

"I don't like talking."

"You, sir, are surprisingly stubborn for someone so compliant."

I was silent awhile. "Maya's not answering my texts."

"Well, you did steal her gun to commit a crime."

I know. "I checked the laws to make sure she couldn't get in trouble."

He slapped the back of my head. "You fucking idiot."

"Ow."

"That did *not* hurt. If I were Greg and Kel, I'd whip your ass black and blue."

I didn't answer.

He scooted closer to me. "I'm kidding. Mostly."

On an impulse, I pulled my legs up onto the couch and put my head in his lap.

He ran his hand over my hair. He smelled like Vibrant Hills bodywash. "You let me go on and on about D's mustache. And that whole time, you were—"

"Shut up."

He gripped my shoulder. "How am I supposed to never leave you if you leave *me* to go to jail?"

"I'm done now," I mumbled. "I won't do it again."

"Against my better judgment, I believe you." After a moment, he spoke again, his voice rough. "Or if you leave me for fucking good?"

I turned my head, pressing my face against his knee.

He stroked my shoulders.

"I won't," I said, voice muffled. "I won't."

"It's gonna be okay," he said, more gently.

I didn't look up. Concentrated on his hand on the back of my shirt. Tried to anticipate the patterns he'd use, where his hand would go next.

I started with one image, one moment—this blond kid who'd showed up at a munch in spleen-crushing jeans, and who'd introduced himself to me with, *"Miles says you and I should be friends."* I don't remember where I ended.

Kel and Greg kept calling. I didn't answer. But they came over that evening. Greg apologized for what I'd overheard. Kel apologized for yelling at me. I apologized for yelling at her, and I wasn't sure how I felt about any of the apologizing—whether it actually made anything better. But it was all very polite and considerate.

"I'm gonna spend some time getting better," I told them. They were sitting at the kitchen table across from me. "I'm gonna try counseling."

Kel nodded. "I know some kink-friendly counselors, if you want recommendations."

I gazed out the window. The neighbors' kids were running over the flowerbeds with a remote-controlled truck. It was some time before I spoke. "I thought, at first, that it might . . . fix me? What we were doing."

They didn't say anything.

"I know that's stupid. It just helped, for a while. I felt so good sometimes, when I was with you guys."

"Us too," Kel said.

I sighed and ran a hand through my hair, still looking out the window. "I'm sorry I fucked up what we had. I really wanted you to be my master."

"I still want that."

"No, you don't."

"Jesus, Gould," Greg said. "You don't know how much."

"Don't bullshit me. You're right. I *would* mess up your marriage. I—"

"Listen to me." Greg's tone made me jump. "I said that because this *is* new territory for me. For all of us. And it's . . . confusing. But that doesn't mean I don't want to try."

It was like the words hit me and slid right off. Mostly. Some part of me wanted to believe him.

I heard Kel shift in her chair. "But I think you know that you need some time to help yourself."

I nodded. The kids' mom had come out and was yelling at them. "Sort myself out," I said under my breath.

Kel reached across the table. Tugged my sleeve. "And I want you to know that we'll be around. Okay? Whenever you want us."

Yeah right.

"Gould. I'm serious. We're not walking away from you."

"You might as well." The mother was ushering the kids inside. A perfect spring day ruined, just because adults wanted tidy flowerbeds. "It's not like we can do any of our usual stuff. If I'm like this."

Her chair creaked. "Let's give it a while, okay? Let's spend some time talking, and let's make sure you're feeling better before we get back into playing."

I continued to stare out the window. "Talk. We talk so much. We talk and talk and talk. What good does it do?" I turned to her. "The Subs Club. Talking. You and Greg and I. Talking. My future therapist and me. Talking. Does it do any good?" I shrugged.

"It does more good than you'd think."

I doubted it. She was still watching me—I could feel it. I finally met her gaze. Her eyes were filled with the same regret and confusion I remembered from the night we talked about Bill. It almost made me want to tell her: how much I loved her, how hard it would be for me to let her go. But I stayed quiet.

"It must have been really frightening," she said finally.

I frowned, not sure what she meant.

"That's what I should have said. Instead of shouting at you. It must have been really frightening, to reach a point where you wanted to—"

I glanced away, embarrassed. "I don't remember how it felt."

Dave came out of his room and stood in the alcove, watching us. "I turned my music up and everything. But I keep accidentally eavesdropping." He looked at me. "If you want me to go away, I will. But there are some things I want to say to GK and Kel, if you'll let me. Nothing bad, I promise."

I faced Kel. "You okay hearing from him?"

She sighed. "Go for it, David."

Dave pulled out the chair next to me. Slung his arm around me and faced Greg and Kel. "This guy is *everything* to me. Okay? Nicholas Sparks himself would vomit if he could witness our level of devotion. And this guy—" he scrubbed my shoulder with his palm "—*sucks* at talking. I mean really. He's awful."

"Thanks," I muttered.

Dave kept his hand on me. "You *do* have to be careful with him. Not because he's weak or breakable or anything. But because some people are like that. They're just, like, too gentle for the world. If we didn't have people like that, the world would be one hundred percent cynical and depressing. Instead of just seventy percent."

"*Dave.*" I shook his hand off me.

"See? Miles would probably legit punch me. He just shrugs me off."

Greg laughed awkwardly, but shut up when Kel glared at him.

"Gould is really special," Dave said. "I don't care whether everybody else sees it or not. I see it, and I think you do too. He needs a little extra looking out for. And he *does* need to treat you well in return. That means being more honest with you, sure. But *you* have to be patient, and I think overall what I'm saying is pretty much the standard, 'If you break his heart, I'll kill you.' Except times a thousand."

My face was hot. "Can I talk now?"

"Sure, bud." Dave patted me again.

I looked at Kel and Greg. "Dave is full of shit. I am awful. At talking. And in other ways. I want you to know that you don't have to stay with me."

"Bullshit," Dave told them. "Stay with him."

I elbowed him and continued addressing Kel and Greg. "I'm serious. I'm going to work on getting better. But you don't have to hang around for that. You should be able to focus on each other." I glanced at Dave. "And I have this guy. I really will be okay. You don't have to stay because you feel bad for me."

Greg leaned forward across the table. Looked directly at me, and said, "So it's that easy for you to let us go?"

"Uh, no. I'm just trying to be realistic."

His voice was low and very serious. "You are a part of us. All right? If you want out, we can't stop you. But *we're* not going anywhere."

"Damn straight," Dave said. "You would regret it for the rest of your lives if you bailed on him."

Kel smiled. Placed her foot on top of mine under the table. There was a moment where everything went completely still. "You know? Dave and I don't agree on much. But on this one, I think he's right."

CHAPTER
SEVENTEEN

The community center downtown was decked the fuck out. There were two small platforms serving as stages for the demos, lots of artful Kinkstravaganzapalooza signage, courtesy of A2A, and a handful of local vendors—leatherworkers, photographers, furniture makers, and toy retailers. It was awesome to look around and see the fruits of our labors. Well, mostly Maya's labors. She was talking to me again, so that was cool. But we'd all helped out, and I'd really thrown myself into the preparations over the couple of weeks leading up to this.

The past three months had been pretty good. I went to counseling once every two weeks, and I tried to talk openly with my friends about how I was doing on the Hal front. Oddly enough, since my confrontation with Bill, my anger at him really had faded. I don't mean I was suddenly like, *You know, he's actually a pretty okay guy.* But I lost that burning hatred, that sense he was the source of all my problems.

He'd let me go, and that was probably more than I'd deserved. I was trying to make good use of my second chance.

I'd had a lot of contact with Kel and Greg initially. They'd even worked with me on establishing my therapy goals. But after a couple of months, something had shifted. I guess it had started when I'd asked them, half-jokingly, if they thought we'd ever be able to put the master/slave relationship back on the table. Maybe I'd expected Kel to say no. Expected her to say, *You're not ready, and you probably never will be.* But she'd been interested. We'd played together a few times over the summer—never very intense scenes, but that was okay. And maybe I'd gotten used to having my hand held. Maybe I was a little nervous about trying to go back to where we were before.

So I'd sort of stopped talking to them.

I know. I know.

Old habits die hard.

They'd been calling and texting and emailing me for a few weeks now, and I'd only responded when Dave or my therapist made me. It sucked, to treat them this way. But it was too . . . I don't know. I kept imagining what they must think of me. What it would be like for them, to take on a slave they couldn't trust. How did I know when I would be ready? What if I thought I was doing better, but got it wrong? I couldn't do that to them.

I was feeling better, though. Overall. Less anger. Less obsessing over the past. I'd been talking to my parents more. They'd actually come up to visit last month and my dad and I had a really good talk about Hal, and how I was having a hard time letting go.

Dave had postponed moving in with D. I felt shitty about that. I'd literally begged him to go ahead with the move, but he'd refused, saying he was staying in the duplex until I had my feet on the ground again. If nothing else, it had been good motivation for me to go to my counseling sessions. If I couldn't get better for myself, I'd get better for him. And for Greg and Kel too, because I didn't want to let them go. Even if we couldn't sign the contract, I wanted to be able to have some kind of relationship with them.

I really needed to tell them that.

"Gould!"

I looked around. Girltoy was approaching. She had on an orange pleather corset, ruffled bloomers, striped stockings, and sparkly fairy wings. Her shoulders and arms were covered in tattoos of keys.

She hugged me. "How awesome is this?" She stepped back. "The Subs Club did such a good job."

"It was mostly Maya and Ryan. And Dave."

"Yeah, I already told Maya how friggin' schweet this is." She glanced around again. "Well, hey. It's good to see you. You haven't been to Riddle for a while, and we've missed you." I could tell by her tone that even if she didn't know exactly what had happened between Bill and me, rumors were flying. But she didn't fish for information.

And I didn't volunteer any. "I'm trying to find Dave. He's been running all over the place."

"I think I just saw him over by the Spank-for-Charity booth. Come on." She led me through the crowd. We didn't end up finding Dave. But twenty minutes later, we headed to stage B to listen to Kamen and Ryan's BDSM safety song. I spotted Dave, D, Miles, and Drix in the front row, along with Mrs. Pell. Girltoy and I joined them.

Kamen stepped up to the mic, guitar over his shoulder. "Hi, everyone. You all having fun?" A cheer went up from the crowd. "Okay, awesome. So, I'm Kamen, and this—" he motioned to Ryan "—is MonsterMeg." The crowd applauded. "Today, we have a song for you about basic BDSM safety. And while we hope you'll find it amusing, we want to let you know that BDSM safety is no laughing matter. People get hurt and even die in BDSM accidents. So remember that. But also have fun." He stepped back. Looked at Ryan, and began to strum and sing:

"BDSM is lots of fun
And there's a million ways to do it
But when you're havin' kinky sex
You've really gotta think through it.

"The first step is negotiating,
Which means telling your partner what's cool,
And telling them what's never okay,
And laying down some rules.

Ryan jumped in: "I don't like to be fisted."
Kamen replied: "Hey that's totally rad.
How do you feel about nipple clamps?"
Ryan shrugged. "Not great but not that bad."

Kamen took over again. "Then let's skip the clamps for right now,
But we'll check in again someday.
Because pressuring you about a soft limit
Is totally not okay."

Ryan took the next verse: "Hey thanks for understanding—
I'm defs not saying never.

Just the fact that you're not pushing me
Makes me feel a whole lot better."

Kamen turned to the audience and sang out:
"You should check in really frequently
About how your partner feels.
And if he—or she or ze or they—doesn't like what you like,
Then you just gotta fucking deal."

"Even if your partner is your sub
Or your toy or pup or slave,
They can still back out at any time,
Otherwise it's rape."

Dave leaned over to me and whispered, "That's our boy."

I grinned and glanced down the line. Saw Miles nestled against Drix. D was bouncing his leg along in time to the music. His mustache had grown back, something I knew Dave was happy about. I looked back at the stage, where the song was still going on.

"If you're sharing toys between partners,
Make sure that they're nonporous . . ."

I peered over my shoulder at the line of booths. Spotted the Riddle booth, manned by Greg. Kel was in front of it, talking to him. She turned and headed my way. For a second, I thought she was coming to talk to me. But she went through a door that led out into the community center's lobby.

I got up and followed her through the door. She was almost to the staircase that led down to the basement when I called out to her. "Kel."

She turned. "Hey. I was wondering if I'd see you today."

I didn't really have a plan for what to say next.

She walked up to me. For a second, I sort of hoped she'd grab me and kiss me, and that everything would suddenly be fine between us. But she stopped right in front of me, and did that magic thing of hers where she made herself seem taller than me.

"You haven't answered my calls. Or texts, or emails. For weeks."

I stuck my hands in my pockets. "I know. I'm sorry."

She studied me. "I made you a promise. I said I wasn't walking away from this. So my question is, are you?"

I shook my head. "No. I'm just ... worried I'm not gonna be what you want. What I did—not trusting you, not telling you about ... that was unforgivable."

"For God's sake, Gould. It's far from unforgivable. It just scared the shit out of me. All I can do is tell you again that I'm sorry for how I reacted. And that I hate thinking about not having you in my life."

The door creaked open behind me. I turned to see Greg.

"Hey," he said. "What's going on?"

"We're being an Adele song," Kel deadpanned.

I laughed. "I think in order to be an Adele song you have to come find me years later, after I've moved on and am happy with someone else. And passive-aggressively tell me you're glad for me."

Greg stepped forward. "You haven't moved on? You're not happy with someone else?"

"Um. No."

"Then why aren't you talking to us?"

"I don't know," I admitted. "I feel like I really screwed up."

Kel grabbed me and kissed me so fiercely that my eyes widened. She pulled back. "We'd like you to come to our house tonight. And bring enough clothes for a week." She patted my ass. "Even though you won't really be needing clothes."

I stared at her. "Are you *sure*?"

Greg shrugged. "It's up to you."

"Don't think we're not gonna be talking about therapy goals," Kel added. "If you come over."

I stuck my hands in my pockets. "Oh, that's great. Yeah. Real sexy stuff."

She batted her eyes. "I know. For me, though, babe. I'll bet you can do it." She threw me a smile and headed downstairs to the bathroom.

Greg grinned at me and shrugged.

I stepped toward him, feeling awkward at first. But he closed the gap between us, and we hugged. It felt good, familiar.

He went back to the fair. And I was left standing there in the empty hall, trying not to smile.

I looked out the glass doors at the gray city.

"You fucking idiot," I imagined Hal saying. *"Go to their fucking house."*

Hal was gone. But I got him back in dreams. I got him back in memories. I batted the years away from my eyes like smoke and saw us as we had been—young and wild and clawing at each other to escape some imagined prison. Happy and reckless and seeking adventure in each other's body. Protecting each other. I got him back a million times, and each time I was more thrilled than the last. I showed him all I'd learned. About being human and growing up and letting people down and hoping to be better. About how to surrender and how to ask questions.

And when he would lay down with me sometimes in those dreams, he was a calmer Hal. A softer, happier man than life had allowed him to be. And maybe he tried for a second or two to view my quiet, settled life with disdain. But he always ended up smiling. Looking at me with admiration and a maybe little envy. Loving me more than he'd ever thought possible.

Someday, after a long life where I continued to grow and love and fuck up and dream, I'd see him again. I'd hold him for real. And we'd keep getting closer until there were no spaces between his skin and mine, and we'd stay like that for as long as we needed to.

I took out my phone and texted Kel and Greg that I'd see them tonight.

"God, when are they gonna get here?" Dave was pacing the kitchen restlessly, boxes of his stuff covering the floor from here to the living room.

"They'll be here," I said. "Relax."

"Ermahgerd, I'm so nervous."

The others were on their way over with a U-Haul so we could help Dave move. I tried to reach out and grab him. "Ermahgerd. Serttle dern."

He laughed. "Ermahgerd, yerss, sir."

"Weirdo."

"You should say that to Greg sometime. 'Yerss, sir.' And Kel. 'Ermahgerd, yerss, Merm.'"

"That sounds like it could be 'Mom,' though."

"Nooo. It's clearly 'Ma'am.' Or with Kel...would it be 'Merster'?"

I nodded. "We are...currently in discussions about her becoming my merster." He walked by me, and I swatted his ass. "Seriously, stop pacing."

He mock-yelped. "Ermahgerd, dern't spernk me." He paused. "The ermahgerd voice works really well with kink stuff, doesn't it?"

I tried it out. "Ermahgerd, nerpple clermps."

He snorted with laughter. "Ermahgerd, a werdern perddle." He sat down across from me.

"Ermahgerd, a lerther wherp.

"Terping frerm the bertom."

"Tertal Perr Exchernge."

"Ermahgerd, *Ferfty Sherds of Grey*."

"Ermahgerd, ernemas!" We were laughing so hard we couldn't breathe.

I looked up and nearly had a heart attack when I saw D standing behind Dave. "Oh my actual God!"

Dave whirled to see what I was freaking out about, and jumped about a foot off his chair. "Jesus fucking mother of... How do you *do* that?"

"I am a conduit for stealth." D glanced at me. His mustache twitched. "I was informed you two had been locking your door."

"We're leaving it open today for our helpers." Dave faced forward again and leaned back as D put his arms around him.

"I see." D kissed the top of his head. "And what were you two cackling about?"

"It's a meme," Dave said. "That's, like, a thing on the internet where—"

"I know what a meme is."

"Okay, do you know 'Ermahgerd, Gersberms?'"

"No."

"It's this meme of a girl holding up some Goosebumps books, and, so, okay, 'ermahgerd' is an exaggerated way of pronouncing 'oh my

God,' and then you apply that pronunciation to whatever you're 'oh my God-ing.' In the case of the original meme, it was Goosebumps— or, 'Gersberms.' So now we're doing it with kink terms. Like, 'Ermahgerd, sherberi.'"

D's face didn't change throughout Dave's explanation. But when Dave was done, D turned and silently walked to the fridge. He took out our Ziploc bag of deli turkey and began eating it from the bag like chips.

"Ermahgerd," Dave whispered to me. "He is nert ermyersed."

D tossed the empty bag in our recycle bin, despite the fact that it was clearly trash. He gazed out the window. "The others are here with the truck."

Through the window, we saw Subs Club members jumping out of a U-Haul like ninjas. Kamen, Miles, Drix, Ryan, and Maya hurried up to the door.

The next hour and a half was *loud*. Music blared, and people talked, and boxes were schlepped out to the truck. I didn't even have time to get emotionally devastated until I scanned the room and saw that there were only a few boxes left.

The others were gathered around the table, "resting." I walked to the fridge on the pretext of getting some water.

"Gould!" Kamen looked shocked. "Are you crying?"

"No." I grabbed a bottle of water. "I'm not crying. I'm not a crier."

"Oh, please." Dave walked by carrying a shoebox full of receipts. "You need to see Gould try to watch the end of *Homeward Bound*."

Kamen stared at me suspiciously. "Dude. Really?"

"No."

Dave set the shoebox on the table. "I'm serious, just pull up the end of *Homeward Bound*. Go on."

I sighed. "I can watch the end of *Homeward Bound* without crying."

Dave raised his eyebrows at me. "How much do you wanna bet?"

"Fifty bucks."

The others gathered around as Dave pulled up the *Homeward Bound* ending on YouTube. "Prepare to lose, Gould."

Even D came over to investigate. The *Homeward Bound* kids were out in the yard when they heard a bark. A moment later, Chance came bounding over the hill and barreled into Jamie, licking his face. Okay, cute and everything, but I wasn't going to . . .

Sassy ran down the hill and leaped into Hope's arms. There was a stirring in my chest. *Not gonna lose fifty bucks over this.*

Peter looked hopefully into the distance, but then his face fell as he realized Shadow hadn't made it. He turned away, muttering about how it was too far, and Shadow was just too old.

Why did my lungs feel so tight?

Someone was already sniffing beside me. Pretty sure it was Kamen.

The camera focused on the top of the hill. Suddenly, Shadow appeared on the ridge, gray-faced and regal. The mother gasped softly and glanced over at Peter, who was still facing away. My heart started hurting.

Peter turned slowly.

"Oh God." On the other side of me, Maya broke down, sobbing.

The music started to play as Shadow took his first limping steps down the hill toward Peter. My eyes burned, and my throat was clamped tight, but I held strong. I could see Dave's hand on the edge of the table, gripping so hard the knuckles were white.

Shadow and Peter reunited, and Chance's voiceover started, talking about how the years fell away and Shadow was a puppy again. A single tear rolled down my cheek.

There was a triumphant whoop from Dave, undermined a bit by the fact that he had tears streaming down his face. "What'd I say? Huh?"

"Yeah, yeah." I reached into my pocket, took out my wallet, and handed Dave three twenties. "Keep the change.

Dave danced away with the money.

D was staring out the window, eyes glistening. I was pretty sure I heard him mutter, "That golden retriever is resourceful."

I checked behind me. "Where's Kamen?"

"He just needs a minute," Ryan said.

I heard a honking nose-blow from the bathroom. Kamen emerged a moment later and returned to the table, his eyes red. "God! Why did you guys do this to me on a day when I'm already sad about things?" He stood next to Ryan, still wiping his nose with a wad of toilet paper.

Ryan rubbed his back. "Shh. Shadow's home now. It's fine."

"Those animals traveled so far just to find those people."

"I know. But it's not real."

Kamen bumped Ryan with his hip. "How are you not crying? Are you a robot? Is everything I thought I knew a lie?"

"Shh, shh." Ryan pulled him closer.

Kamen wiped his nose with the back of his hand. "If I got separated from you, I would walk a thousand miles to find you."

"All right, Vanessa Carlton." Ryan looked up at him. "I hope you'd just text me before I got that far away."

"But if, like, we were both gonna get on a bus to somewhere but I accidentally got on the wrong bus and it took me to Canada."

"Then I hope you'd, I don't know, book a flight back here."

"But if it was in the desert."

Ryan frowned. "In Canada?"

"Why don't you want my sacrifices?"

"I *do* want your sacrifices." Ryan pulled Kamen down to kiss him.

"Do you think Hemsworth would find us? If we lost him?"

Ryan rolled his eyes. "The only thing that dog can find with any certainty is his own asshole."

That seemed to cheer Kamen up. "Yeah-hea-heaahhh, that's my boy!"

We finished loading the U-Haul. The others piled into the truck while Dave and I lingered in the kitchen, doing a last check.

Dave shoved his hands in his pockets. "I don't know why I'm acting like I'm checking out of a motel. I can always come back if I forgot anything."

"What if I start locking the door?" I joked.

He didn't laugh. He took one hand out of its pocket and offered me the sixty bucks. "Here."

I closed his hand around it and pushed it away. "Keep it. You might need it to buy a juicer, or Chevron curtains, or chain mail underwear to protect you from D, or something."

He snorted and looked away. "Don't ever be a stranger. Call anytime. Really. Come over. I'll leave D's front door unlocked."

"Dave. I'll be around."

He glanced at the slightly emptier kitchen. "I guess this meeting is now adjourned."

"Oh my God, you cornball. Let's get your stuff over to D's before you go all *Our Town* on me."

"Gould?"

"Yeah?"

"I'm really, really glad you're my friend."

I cuffed him lightly, then pulled him into a hug. "Me too."

He squeezed me tighter. "Ermahgerd. I lerv Gerld."

"Ermahgerd," I whispered back. "I lerv Derv."

It took us a couple of hours to unload Dave's stuff at D's. And D's spartan house looked much . . . brighter when we were done. We ordered food, and D shared his whiskey. By the time I drove back to the duplex, night was falling, and I had a lump in my throat that wouldn't quit.

I walked into the empty living room and flipped on the light, willing myself not to feel anything. Start with one moment, one image—a wasteland, a ballroom, a bedroom, an island. But I couldn't settle on one image. Everything ran together, and I found myself standing in the living room, staring at the mantel and the stack of Kinkstravaganzapalooza magnets we'd left there after the fair. The tiny stuffed leprechaun Kamen had brought us for St. Patrick's Day. I don't know how long I stood there, but eventually a car door slammed outside. A few minutes later, the front door opened behind me, and I was like, *This is it. This is when a murderer finally comes to kill me because I've been leaving the front door unlocked all these years.*

But when I turned around, Kamen was standing there with a six-pack of gluten-free beer and dusty N64 dangling cords everywhere.

"Hey," he said. "Want some company?"

CHAPTER
EIGHTEEN

Three months later.

W hen I let myself into Kel and Greg's house, it seemed empty. I pulled my key out of the lock and shut the door cautiously behind me. "Hello?" I called.

I thought I heard voices upstairs, but I wasn't sure.

There was something shiny on the foyer table, beside a vase of dried flowers. I walked over to investigate.

A thin silver collar lay on top of a few folded pages and a pen. I picked it up. Fucking gorgeous—strong and gleaming and elegant, with a small but surprisingly heavy padlock.

I stared at it for a while, overwhelmed by how lucky I was.

I brushed the pen aside and opened the folded papers. The first was a handwritten note that said. *Come upstairs when you're ready— we'll put it on.*

The second was the last page of our slave contract, with vows from each of us.

I'd seen the words before, in the last draft we'd all gone over together. But now there were three signature lines underneath the vows. One for the master, one for the second-in-command, and one for the slave. The first two lines had already been signed and dated. I glanced over the vows again and smiled. Thought about reading them a few more times. Saying them out loud to the world. Instead I picked up the pen, signed the last line, and folded the paper.

Some things were private.

I walked to the stairs. I definitely heard voices: whispering, giggling, hushing each other. I grinned and headed up.

You started with one moment. In a car seat, facing backward, listening to your parents' voices. You grew and the seat turned around and you could see trees rushing by, eyes in the mirror, a profile as she turned and smiled. But you were still strapped in, safe, limited. You grew older still, and your parents weren't there and you were riding without a seat belt and with a driver who made you feel invincible and vulnerable at the same time. You rode to Hebrew college with your suitcase sliding in the hatch. You drove home from Cedar Point listening to the snoring from the passenger seat, the radio on, and the stars in a shower across the sky.

Life moved too fast, and you started to feel little moments of emptiness pulling at you like hunger pangs. You were at a party—beer and balloons and out-of-season Christmas lights, and you looked around suddenly and asked, *Has anyone seen him?* You went outside to check and ended up in a cold world where you were always putting your foot through ice, and you couldn't get back to the party.

An endless string of transformations. You thought you were taking control by riding without a seat belt, by daring the most gruesome outcomes to chase you and snap at your tires. But it only takes one man and one mistake. One moment when no one is looking.

You *did* learn to seize control. By facing the emptiness that was never really empty, the loss that never quite swallowed what you'd gained in its wake. And you learned that control was a malleable thing—not a hazard unless you craved or lost too much of it, not a victory unless you made good use of it.

Why was the memory of a voice never as beautiful as the real thing? Because even in memory, you got stage fright, you missed the notes. But every once in a while you nailed it, and you sank into that memory, into a place where what you'd lost intersected with what you had to believe you were yet to find.

I lived for those moments.

I have never stopped loving.

Explore more of *The Subs Club* series:
riptidepublishing.com/universe/subs-club

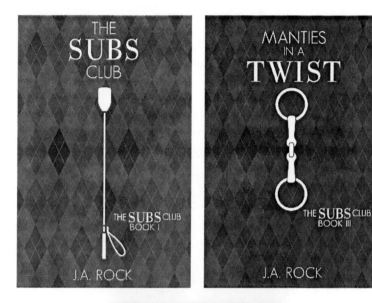

Dear Reader,

Thank you for reading J.A. Rock's *24/7*!

We know your time is precious and you have many, many entertainment options, so it means a lot that you've chosen to spend your time reading. We really hope you enjoyed it.

We'd be honored if you'd consider posting a review—good or bad—on sites like **Amazon, Barnes & Noble, Kobo, Goodreads, Twitter, Facebook, Tumblr,** and your blog or website. We'd also be honored if you told your friends and family about this book. Word of mouth is a book's lifeblood!

For more information on upcoming releases, author interviews, blog tours, contests, giveaways, and more, please sign up for our weekly, spam-free newsletter and visit us around the web:

Newsletter: tinyurl.com/RiptideSignup
Twitter: twitter.com/RiptideBooks
Facebook: facebook.com/RiptidePublishing
Goodreads: tinyurl.com/RiptideOnGoodreads
Tumblr: riptidepublishing.tumblr.com

Thank you so much for Reading the Rainbow!

RiptidePublishing.com

ACKNOWLEDGMENTS

I'm so grateful to everyone who has helped with this book and this series. Thank you once more to my editor, Delphine Dryden, whom I could thank in a gazillion acknowledgments without it being enough. And to every editor who worked on these books, plus Kanaxa for the awesome covers. Thank you to Sarah Lyons, for telling me to do this. To Sam, for beta reading; to Jen, for helping me brainstorm; to Julie, my big boobs consultant; and to AJ, for posing with me in compromising positions to help me choreograph the ménage scenes. A true friend is someone to whom you can say, "Now mount me from behind. Like you mean it," and it's not weird. Many thanks to the readers who have seen this saga through. And, finally, to Shannon, Becky, Brian, and Heather. This series is dedicated to you, for showing me that families don't have to be blood-related.

ALSO BY J.A. ROCK

ABOUT THE AUTHOR

J.A. Rock is the author of queer romance and suspense novels, including *By His Rules*, *Take the Long Way Home*, and, with Lisa Henry, *The Good Boy* and *When All the World Sleeps*. She holds an MFA in creative writing from the University of Alabama and a BA in theater from Case Western Reserve University. J.A. also writes queer fiction and essays under the name Jill Smith. Raised in Ohio and West Virginia, she now lives in Chicago with her dog, Professor Anne Studebaker.

Website: www.jarockauthor.com
Blog: jarockauthor.blogspot.com
Twitter: twitter.com/jarockauthor
Facebook: facebook.com/ja.rock.39

Enjoy more stories like
24/7
at RiptidePublishing.com!

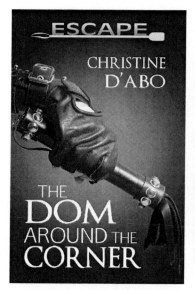

CPSIA information can be obtained
at www.ICGtesting.com
Printed in the USA
LVOW12s1644071216
516244LV00004B/967/P

8